"THERE'S A MONSTER OUT THERE NEEDS SLAYING..."

Kedrigern frowned thoughtfully. "What of Intrepid and Bold, the heroic twins?"

Sariax lowered his gaze. "Some years ago, Intrepid went off to do great deeds. Something ate him. Bold went off to avenge his brother. It ate him, too."

"I'm sorry to hear that, your Majesty."

Sariax shrugged. "If you call your sons Bold and Intrepid, you have to expect things like that. The problem is Formidable. He still looks plenty formidable, and he can cleave through plate armor and chain mail with one mighty blow. His heart just isn't in it. To put it bluntly, I think he's afraid of monsters."

"Most people are," Kedrigern reminded the monarch.

"I want you to work a spell and give him the courage of a lion!"

"Lions are afraid of monsters, too."

A REMEMBRANCE
FOR KEDRIGERN

JOHN MORRESSY

ACE BOOKS, NEW YORK

A REMEMBRANCE FOR KEDRIGERN

An Ace Book / published by arrangement with
the author

PRINTING HISTORY
Ace edition / October 1990

ISBN: 0-441-71244-4

Ace Books are published by The Berkley Publishing Group,
200 Madison Avenue, New York, New York 10016.
The name ''Ace'' and the ''A'' logo
are trademarks belonging to Charter Communications, Inc.

PRINTED IN THE UNITED STATES OF AMERICA

10 9 8 7 6 5 4 3 2 1

I cannot sing the old songs now!
  It is not that I deem them low;
'Tis that I can't remember how
  They go.

—Calverly

···⦗ One ⦘···

a spelling bee

HIS MISSION ACCOMPLISHED, his purse heavier, and his reputation as a master counterspeller intact, Kedrigern bade farewell to his satisfied clients and pointed the silver horn of his black steed toward home. It was a relief to have this commission behind him. Not that it had been a hard one; indeed, the spell he had removed from the son and daughter of Prince Daragil had been a hasty piece of work and easily undone; but it was difficult working with children. Especially when they were stupid, peevish, spoiled, and in all respects obnoxious, as were the offspring of Daragil—"Darry the Dim," to his unhappy subjects.

Odd, thought Kedrigern, how so dull and obtuse a man could foster children of such exuberant nastiness. Apparently they got it from their mother. That would explain why every reference to "our dear departed Princess Mazooba" was accompanied by a happy smile on the face of the speaker.

It was good to be heading for Silent Thunder Mountain, to home and Princess. Homecomings were always nice. Far nicer by a wide margin was never to leave in the first place, but there were always those clients who could not, or would not, travel. Kedrigern sighed and allowed himself a measure of self-pity for having to deal with such selfish clods. He then turned his mind to anticipation of his arrival, and Princess's greeting, and all the domestic pleasures he so hated to leave.

He was especially eager to return home from this particular house call, because throughout his absence he had been greatly concerned for Princess's health. A sudden onset of severe headaches had left her weak and listless. She had expressed no desire to travel with him to the court—"lair" seemed a more apt term—of Daragil, and that was most uncharacteristic. Ordinarily, merely uttering the word "travel" was enough to set her packing, humming merrily as she did so. But not this time. Kedrigern frowned, and wished he were home, where he might comfort her.

If one absolutely had to travel, mid-May was probably the best time to be on the road. The mud of early spring was gone; the insects and heat of summer had not yet arrived. Everything in the wood was a pleasant green, except for the bright scatterings of early wildflowers in the open spaces. It was pretty— if one liked that sort of thing.

Kedrigern made good time, and by nightfall had arrived at a tiny hamlet that boasted a tolerable inn, four houses, and a small shop. He led his horse to the stable himself, generously tipping the hostler beforehand and warning him of the unusual, but tractable, steed he was placing in his care. The man gasped and started in panic at sight of the midnight black, silver-horned, red-eyed horse that towered over every other in the stable.

"He's a unicorn, sir! A real unicorn!" the hostler said in an awed whisper.

"He's nothing of the sort. He's an excellent horse who has undergone a few improvements," Kedrigern said, reaching up to stroke the great beast's muzzle.

"Big, he is, sir. He do look dangerous."

"He's gentle as a baby chick. Just don't get him upset."

"Never, sir! What is it upsets him?"

"Calling him a unicorn, for one thing," the wizard said with a meaningful glance at the hostler.

"He's a fine horse, sir. Good horse. Good boy," said the hostler, ducking respectfully and flashing a nervous grin at the black steed, which snorted thin jets of white smoke.

"He likes you," Kedrigern said, and with an encouraging smile, turned and made his way to the inn.

His entrance attracted only a casual glance from the handful of men in the main room. Kedrigern avoided dramatic entrances, preferring to make a subdued first impression; he took care to dress plainly, in well-worn comfortable garments that offered no clue to his profession. Not for him the steeple-crowned hat, the swirling robe bedecked with arcane symbols, the snow-white beard to the navel, the glittering eye beneath the white-thatched brow. He dressed—as his wife had frequently pointed out—like a merchant or an artisan, or perhaps a cleanly scholar. He had found that it was usually to his advantage to keep his wizardly status to himself, and reveal it only at times and places of his own choosing.

He was thirsty and hungry and tired. Something smelled very good, and he looked forward to a pleasant meal, an undisturbed night's rest, and an early start in the morning. He tossed aside his pack and cloak, and fanning away the resultant dust cloud, he seated himself at an empty table, the surface of which was surprisingly clean. He sniffed the cooking aroma once again, appreciatively. A roast . . . or perhaps a stew. Or meat pies. Whatever was cooking, if it tasted half as good as it smelled, he would have a memorable supper.

He waited a few minutes, and no one came. He waited a few minutes more, and then he began to grow impatient. He was on the verge of bellowing for service when a large man wearing a stained and greasy apron burst from a doorway and hurried to his table. The man gave the tabletop a few energetic swipes with a nearly clean rag, then favored Kedrigern with a gap-toothed smile.

"Welcome, Master," he said, still short of breath from his hurried entrance. "Welcome to Frunsker's Inn. I'm Frunsker. Fine ale, delicious food, and clean beds for the discriminating traveler. Wizards especially welcome, Master."

"How did you know I was a wizard?"

"The hostler told me, Master. Knew it right away when he saw that horse. Wouldn't nobody but a wizard dare to ride such a creature."

Kedrigern slapped the tabletop in frustration. "I keep forgetting about the horse."

"We're always happy to see a wizard here, Master," said Frunsker, nodding eagerly and wiping his hands on his apron.

"I'd be happy to see a tankard of ale and a large helping of whatever it is that smells so good. And I'd like a room for the night."

"Wizards get a complimentary tankard of ale, Master, and best rates on everything. And I can give you a bed all to yourself."

"Good. Excellent, Frunsker," Kedrigern said. "Let's have the food and drink at once."

"Right away, Master," said the innkeeper. He took a hesitant step back, then stopped and stood wiping his hands furiously, looking anxiously at the wizard, the wall, and the floor, in turn. "And then, before you leave, Master—and you're welcome to stay as long as you please—if you could spare a few minutes of your time . . ." he mumbled.

Kedrigern was at once businesslike. "What's the problem?"

"Oh, nothing at all for a wizard, Master, but a great trouble to ordinary folk. Nothing a wizard like yourself couldn't set straight in a minute or two before going on your way—and may your journey be safe and swift and the weather fine. It's only a matter of—"

Kedrigern's raised hand silenced the innkeeper. "Wait. First, food and drink. Then tell me the whole story."

Frunsker got his considerable bulk into swift motion toward the kitchen, and returned shortly with a bowl of savory stew and a small round loaf of bread. Scarcely had Kedrigern cracked the crust before Frunsker returned a second time, bearing a tankard of cool, tasty ale. Kedrigern sipped experimentally, nodded his approval, and drank a great refreshing draft. With a sigh of satisfaction, he waved the innkeeper to a stool.

Arranging himself on the little stool like a man balancing a sack of flour on a fencepost, Frunsker placed his large red hands on his knees, leaned forward, and said, "Well, you see, Master Kedrigern, it's this way. After breakfast this morning, the girl went up to straighten the rooms. A minute after she went, she ran back into the kitchen in a terrible fright, shrieking about—"

Kedrigern gestured sharply to command silence. With a spoonful of stew poised halfway to his mouth, he said, "Just a minute, now. Are you going to tell me something dreadful and spoil my dinner?"

"Oh, no, Master, I wouldn't do that. It's a strange thing I have to tell, but not sickening. Not a bit."

"Very well, then. You may proceed."

"Well, as I say, the girl comes tearing into the kitchen, just as I'm cutting a bit of meat for this very stew, and she falls down screaming about something in the upstairs room. It took me a while to get her settled down, but I finally got it out of her. 'There's a bee up there! A great bee, buzzing around the room where those funny old men were staying!' she wails. 'It scared the life out of me!' she blubbers."

"A bee? Your problem is a bee?"

"A bee, Master. A big one."

"I'm not an exterminator. If you want to get rid of a bee, swat it with a broom. Don't call in a wizard," Kedrigern said, frowning.

"Oh, the girl could have done that easily, Master. She's a strapping big creature, and no ordinary bee would frighten her. But that's no ordinary bee in the upstairs room." Frunsker set his mouth tightly and shook his head slowly from side to side.

"In what way is it not ordinary?"

"This bee talks, Master."

"He talks," Kedrigern repeated after a long pause.

"Aye, he does. We can't make out what he's saying, because his voice is high, and all buzzy, and he talks very fast, and it's hard for us to concentrate with a great blathering bee flying around our heads. But he do talk."

"Perhaps this is wizard's work after all. Go ahead and tell me all you can while I finish eating, and I'll consider how best to handle this loquacious bee."

Frunsker had little to add to the basic fact of a talking bee on the premises. There had been five people staying at the inn the night before. All had settled their accounts and departed early in the morning. Two respectable elderly gentlemen and their servant had spent the night in the room in which the bee appeared, and they had complained of no disturbance by a bee or by anything else. The bee himself seemed friendly—he had attacked no one so far, at least—but since he was an unusually large bee, no one had presumed on his amiability.

Kedrigern listened, interrupting the narrative only once, silently, raising his eyebrows in an interrogative manner and displaying the emptiness of his tankard. Frunsker refilled it at once, and resumed his account. When the innkeeper was done, Kedrigern gazed thoughtfully into the corner of the ceiling and rubbed his chin.

"Were any of last night's guests known to you?" he asked after a long silence.

"Aye, two of them, Master. A merchant and his clerk. They pass through every year about this time."

"So the elderly gentlemen and their servant were strangers."

"Never saw them before, Master. Very respectable they looked to me, though. Long white beards and fine cloaks on the gentlemen, and shiny high boots on their servant, and very dignified the old ones were in their behavior, and their servant as sharp as a pin. Very exacting they were, but a good class of people to have at the inn," Frunsker said.

"And when did they leave?"

"Well, now, I don't exactly know that. The servant took me aside last night, after the two elderly gentlemen went upstairs, and explained that his masters were given to sudden whims, and they might just take a notion to pick up and go in the middle of the night. So he paid me in full, and said I shouldn't be alarmed if I heard them moving about at odd hours. Truth to tell, I didn't hear a sound, but when I got up this morning they were gone. And then the girl went up and found the bee."

Kedrigern nodded weightily and covered a great yawn. "Is the room closed off so the bee can't escape?"

"It is, Master."

"Good. I'll look at him tomorrow."

"Tomorrow?" Frunsker repeated, dismayed.

"Tomorrow," Kedrigern said firmly. "If we're dealing with magic, I want to deal with it when I'm well rested and have my wits about me. And if we're dealing with an ordinary bee that merely sounds as though it's speaking, I want to do so in full daylight, with a broom in my hand. You may show me to my room, Frunsker."

Breakfast was a plain, substantial meal, served in an atmosphere of taut expectancy. Kedrigern ate in as leisurely a manner as he could, but the anxious concern of Frunsker and the frequent appearances in the kitchen doorway of Frunsker's wife and the skivvy, pale and wringing their hands, lent an air of foreboding to an otherwise pleasant refection. The wizard rose at last with a sigh of resignation, brushed the crumbs from his lap, and said, "All right, Frunsker. Show me the bee."

"Right this way, Master," Frunsker said. He snatched up a broom from the hearthside and set off up the creaking stairs, walking with stealthy tread. He halted before a closed door barricaded by a heavy chest, cast a significant dark glance at the wizard, and pointed with the bristly end of the broom.

"In there?" Kedrigern asked.

"Aye, Master."

Kedrigern knelt on the chest and placed an ear to the crack of the door. After listening for a time, he said softly, "I don't hear any buzzing. Are you sure he couldn't escape?"

"Windows are all closed and fastened, and the flue is plugged up. He's in there, Master Kedrigern."

"Let's get this chest out of the way, then."

Frunsker pushed the chest aside and took up position beside the door, broom poised. Kedrigern reached for the door handle, hesitated, pried the broom from Frunsker's grip, and gestured for the innkeeper to open the door. Frunsker did so, slowly and cautiously, and Kedrigern entered, looking all around the room for the bee.

"There he is, Master! There, on the chimney-piece!" Frunsker whispered hoarsely, retreating from the room and closing the door behind him.

And there, emphatically, the bee was, sitting quite still,

making no sound. He was the size of a ripe peach, with huge multifaceted eyes glittering in the morning light. His wings were silvery wafers, his legs solid and bristly as black cockleburrs. Whatever his provenance, this was a formidable bee, thought Kedrigern.

He approached it with slow, cautious steps. With his right hand he gripped the broom. It was lowered now, unthreatening, but ready for instant defensive action. Still the bee did not move, but Kedrigern had the unsettling sensation that it was studying him closely. He came within broom's length of the little creature and there he stopped, unsure what to do next. To approach any closer might be construed as a threat; to step back might be interpreted as flight; either action invited attack. But he could hardly stand here motionless, waiting for the bee to take the initiative. Perhaps it had passed away in the night. Perhaps it was a stuffed bee, or a carved bee, or a mechanical bee, and the voices heard by Frunsker and the skivvy were hallucinations.

In the midst of his speculations, he heard a small voice say, "Brother Kedrigern, is it you? Is it really you, of all people?!"

The voice was high and thin and had a distinct buzzing quality to it, but the words were intelligible. Politeness demanded a reply, so Kedrigern, in his most dignified manner, said, "I am Kedrigern, the wizard of Silent Thunder Mountain. Who speaks?"

"I knew it!" the small voice burred. "It's hard getting used to these eyes, but I was certain I recognized you. I'm Belsheer, Brother Kedrigern. Surely you remember your old colleague."

"Belsheer? Yes, of course I remember. It's been a long time."

"Last time I saw you was on the day you resigned from the guild over the Quintrindus affair. We should have listened to you that day and saved ourselves a lot of embarrassment. That must be five years ago."

"More like six."

"Really? Time does slip by. You haven't changed a bit, though."

"You have. What happened?"

The bee gave an angry buzz, then said, "I was sneak-spelled, that's what happened. After all these years, I was taken in like an apprentice. I'm ashamed of myself, Brother Kedrigern."

Hearing himself so addressed for the third time resolved any traces of doubt in Kedrigern's mind. Of all the members of the Wizards' Guild, Belsheer had been the one most given to punctilio, addressing his fellows as "Brother" and "Sister" and making solemn reference to "The Right Venerable and Puissant Chairman" and "The Illustrious and Unerring Treasurer." Certain now that he was in the presence of his old colleague, Kedrigern requested the details of his transformation.

"It was Grizziscus. Do you remember Grizziscus? Used to do a lot of banishments and spatial dislocations for petty tyrants up in the northeast."

"I never met him, but I recall the name. Wasn't he black-balled for membership in the guild?"

"He certainly was," Belsheer buzzed.

"Yes, yes, I remember now. You made a very forceful speech against admitting him, and persuaded everyone. I don't think he received a single vote."

"That's correct, Brother Kedrigern. But some blabbermouth in our midst must have broken confidentiality. Grizziscus learned about what happened and swore he'd get even with me. And he did, night before last, in this very room."

"How?"

"Trickery and deceit. He cultivated me for years, saying how much he'd always admired me and studied my work, and I was foolish enough to believe him. I started to think that I might be a good influence on him and make him fit for membership in the guild one day. An old man's vanity, that's what undid me, Brother Kedrigern."

"Come, now, Belsheer. You're only a bit over four hundred, aren't you? That's not old, as wizards go."

"I'm over four hundred and eighty, and that's old as *anybody* goes. The fact that Grizziscus took me in so easily proves how much I've slipped. He buttered me up, flattered me shamelessly, even taught me a few of his best spells, and then he suggested that we pay a visit to Brother Tristaver and his wife."

"Tris, married? I hadn't heard," said Kedrigern with interest. "Who is the lady?"

"The way I heard it, he lifted an enchantment from some hideous monster and she turned out to be a beautiful queen who fell madly in love with him on the spot."

"Hard to imagine anyone—especially a beautiful queen—falling for Tris like that. I wonder if he used one of his love potions."

"Wouldn't put it past him."

"Still, it's nice to know that another wizard has settled down. I'll have to get in touch with Tris. Princess will be happy to hear of this."

Belsheer lifted off and flew in a tight circle around Kedrigern's head, then returned to the chimney-piece. "We were talking about me, and how I came to be spelled," he thrummed peevishly.

"Sorry. Do go on."

Belsheer buzzed for a time, then settled down to continue his story. "I was ready for a vacation, and I liked the idea of a chance to chat with an old friend. Tris knows all the gossip, and he's a great talker. It seemed like the very thing I needed. I had been working with the Harkeners to the Unseen Enlightened Ones, studying their adages and wise sayings—do you know anything about the Harkeners, Brother Kedrigern? They're a fairly obscure sect."

"*Obscure* is putting it mildly. I found them all but unintelligible."

"Well, their adages deal with wisdom that's not of this world, you know. I've committed many of them to memory, for contemplation. Mighty interesting stuff. In any event, I welcomed the prospect of a change, and some good clear straightforward conversation, so I accepted Grizziscus's suggestion. He led me out here, far from my study, away from friends and familiar places, and before I knew it I was drinking more ale than I'm accustomed to drinking. Frunsker's ale is very good."

"Excellent."

"Easy to drink more than is good for you. I got quite merry

and let my guard down. Grizziscus started talking about the guild, and how he'd wanted to become a member, and how bitter he was at being blackballed, and just as it began to dawn on me that he knew all about my part in it, he let out a nasty laugh and hit me with a spell. Next thing I knew, I was a bee.''

"Don't lose heart," said Kedrigern stoutly. He reached out to lay a reassuring hand on his old friend's shoulder, but arrested the instinctive gesture midway and turned it into a manly, resolute shake of the fist. "I know a thing or two about counterspells. If you can recall what Grizziscus said, I'll have you back in human form this very morning."

"No need to rush things, Brother Kedrigern. All in good time. I don't want to remain a bee forever, but there's something to be said for it. I haven't had this much energy for over a century. I was at the point where even magic couldn't keep me warm or make me feel good in the morning. Now I'm full of pep. And it's nice to have wings, too."

"My wife says the same thing."

"Is your wife a bee? Someone told me she was a toad."

"Actually, she *was* a toad when we met, but now she's a woman again. She has these wings. . . . It's a long story."

"Tell me about it along the way, Brother Kedrigern."

"Are you coming with me?"

"You don't expect me to stay on this chimney-piece, do you? No point in traveling alone if I don't have to. I'd like to get back to my study one of these days, but I was thinking I could stop off in your garden for a time, if you don't object. I wouldn't be any trouble. I want to take a while to think over what I'm going to do to Grizziscus, and learn something about beehood. A man doesn't get many opportunities like this."

"Hardly any, I'd say."

"The only problem is the eyes. They're good and sharp, but I see so many of everything that it gets confusing."

"You can ride on my shoulder until you're accustomed to your eyes."

"Very kind of you, Brother Kedrigern. Shall we go?"

With the bee on his shoulder, Kedrigern emerged from the room into the empty hallway and descended to the main floor of the inn. Frunsker, his wife, and the skivvy clustered at the foot of the stairs, gaping. Kedrigern grinned and tossed the broom to the innkeeper.

"I didn't need this. He's an old friend," he explained.

"The bee? Friend?"

"Yes. You've had a bit of magic worked in your inn, but there's nothing to worry about. No aftereffects on the room, or anything like that. Anyone who stays there will be perfectly safe."

"Thank you, Master Kedrigern," said Frunsker, and the women curtseyed and joined their thanks to his.

"My pleasure. Tell me, now, do you know where the other two gentlemen were headed?"

"They didn't say, Master Kedrigern. Very close-mouthed, the pair of them."

"That's too bad. It would be helpful to know."

At this, the skivvy began to bob up and down in a frenzy of curtseying. "The Valley of Aniar! I heard him say it, the one with the long beard, that's where they're going!" she blurted. No sooner was the last word out than she clapped her red hands over her mouth and looked about with terrified wild eyes.

"Good girl. Well done," said Kedrigern, setting off another flurry of curtseys.

Close to his ear, Belsheer softly hummed, "Give the child a penny, Brother Kedrigern. She's earned it."

"She has indeed. They all have," said Kedrigern. He reached into his purse and distributed silver pennies all around, and in a short time the two wizards were ready to depart. Kedrigern bore a generous gift of bread and cheese and smoked meat and ale to sustain him on the journey. For Belsheer, there were the wildflowers along the way.

···{ *Two* }···

the horns of elfland

"THE YELLOW ONES are delicious," hummed Belsheer. "The red ones are sweeter, but these yellow ones have a pleasant nutlike flavor."

"This is very good bread," Kedrigern said, chewing on a crust as he reclined by their campfire.

Belsheer, who was perched on his knee, ignored this observation. "Now, the white ones, they were a surprise," he went on. "I expected them to be bland, but they have a nice minty taste. And the pink ones are tangy. A bit like cinnamon."

"It's good cheese, too," Kedrigern said.

Belsheer gave a sharp little burr of distaste. "The very thought of cheese disgusts me. I only wish I knew more about flowers. When I think of all the flowers I've seen in my time, and I don't even know their names . . . shocking ignorance on my part. You really ought to learn your flowers, Brother Kedrigern."

"I have no plans to become a bee."

"Neither did I, and now I have all this catching up to do. If I'd learned about flowers before, I wouldn't have to guess now."

"When you're not a bee, it just doesn't seem so important."

"And when you are, it's too late for anything but trial and error. Does your wife know much about flowers?"

Kedrigern reflected for a time, then said, "I imagine she knows quite a lot about waterlilies. We have a flower garden at home, but Spot does most of the gardening."

"Who is Spot?"

"Our house-troll. It has a real flair for making things grow. Princess does the actual flower-arranging for the house."

"Good. Excellent. Women know more about those things than men."

"I suppose they do. We have a neighbor, Bess, who knows her herbs and simples as well as anyone I've ever met. If I have a question about which herb to use in a potion, and how much of it, and what to mix it with, Bess always knows the answer."

"Bess . . . a good honest name. I can picture her now," Belsheer droned. "A plain countrywoman, close to the soil; sun-bronzed, bright-eyed, apple-cheeked, ankle-deep in muck as she tends her beloved greenlings, a song on her lips."

"Not exactly. Apple-cheeked, I grant you, and she has a song on her lips more often than not. But she spends more time over her cauldron than in the garden. She's a wood-witch."

"Wood-witches are the best kind. I always said so. Once a witch puts on airs and starts calling herself 'The Witch of the Second Bend in the North Road' or something like that, she turns nasty in no time. But a wood-witch doesn't go in for that nonsense."

Kedrigern nodded in agreement. "Bess certainly doesn't. And you're right about the others. My wife had a run-in with a few highly specialized witches a while back . . . but she can tell you all about that once we're home. We should arrive before sundown tomorrow."

"I do look forward to meeting Sister Princess. I only hope she's not put off by my appearance," Belsheer said in a subdued self-conscious hum.

"No need to concern yourself. Princess is acutely aware of how little appearance matters."

Kedrigern took another bite of cheese and munched on it

thoughtfully. After a long pause, Belsheer said, "It must have been hard on her, being a toad."

"It was a difficult time. We don't talk about it much."

"A lot worse than being a bee, I imagine."

"Infinitely worse."

"Considering what a nasty vengeful swine Grizziscus is, I'm amazed he didn't turn me into something loathsome and uncomfortable. If one must be something other than human, I'd have to say that a bee is one of the better options. One can get around."

"I've noticed that you fly quite proficiently."

"It's no trouble at all. Even having six legs seems somehow appropriate. At least I haven't tripped myself up yet. My only difficulty is adjusting to the sight of hundreds of everything, but I'm getting the hang of it."

"I'm happy to see you settling in so nicely. But remember, whenever you feel ready to go back to human form, all you have to do is let me know."

"I appreciate your readiness to help, Brother Kedrigern, believe me. But not just yet. I'm learning too much. And to tell the truth, I'm rather enjoying myself."

Kedrigern heaved a deep nostalgic sigh. "Poor Princess didn't enjoy her metamorphosis a bit. Unrelieved misery, that's what it was. Imagine leading a life that's simultaneously dangerous and boring."

"As I said, a bee is one of the better things to be turned into," Belsheer buzzed.

"It would have been a lot easier on Princess, I'm sure. She could have looked forward to becoming a queen. At the very least, she'd have been busy doing something useful, making honey and wax."

"Sweetness and light," Belsheer pointed out, a trace of smugness in his buzz.

"Exactly. One can take pride. But squatting on a lily pad waiting for the next fly to come by . . . Well, that's all behind us now. I shouldn't dwell on it," said Kedrigern.

"Not much of a life, perhaps, but it does toughen one. Toads are hardy little creatures."

"Oh, yes. Absolutely. I don't know whether it's an after-effect of the spell or not, but Princess has enjoyed excellent health. . . ." Kedrigern paused as something occurred to him, then he asked, "Do you have anything that works for head-aches?"

"Head bothering you, Brother Kedrigern?"

"No, not mine. When I left home, Princess was suffering from severe headaches, and I couldn't come up with a cure."

"There's the old standby in *Spells For Every Occasion*."

"It only provides temporary relief. I was hoping for a cure."

"I'm not certain that there is one, Brother Kedrigern. Surely you know the old saying: *The only infallible cure for a headache is the axe, but it has undesirable side effects*."

"I've heard that. But the one in *Spells For Every Occasion* can be used no more than three times a day—any more than that, and it upsets your stomach. There must be something more effective. I want to provide long-lasting relief."

Belsheer buzzed thoughtfully. "I've got a spell that drives away pain for up to eight days in most cases, and won't upset anyone's stomach. If you like, I'll teach it to you."

"Wonderful! Thank you, Belsheer."

"No trouble at all. Glad to help Sister Princess."

"Would you mind very much if we moved on? We still have a few hours of daylight, and I'd like to make time."

"It's entirely up to you, Brother Kedrigern. I'm only a pas-senger."

Kedrigern was more eager than ever to get home, and so they were soon on the road again. The forest trail was narrow, shadowed by the new foliage, and silent except for an occa-sional birdcall and the steady tattoo of the big horse's hooves on the hard-packed earth. The wizards rode for a long time without uttering either a word or a buzz. Kedrigern was deep in thoughts of home and Princess, and Belsheer, perched on his shoulder, seemed to be asleep.

Faintly, from afar, came a blast on a hunting horn. Neither of them reacted to the sound. Soon after, a second blast fol-lowed the first. It sounded much nearer. A third blast came, louder and prolonged, and the forest all around them came to

life with the noise of frenzied motion. Kedrigern muttered
angrily under his breath and reined in his horse.

"Is something wrong, Brother Kedrigern?" Belsheer asked.

"Bad timing, that's all. I forgot all about the Haunted Huntsman. He passes through these woods every thirteen years and
throws all the wildlife into a turmoil. Blasted nuisance."

"Should we do anything?"

"Just make ourselves unobtrusive and get someplace where
we won't be trampled. Although I doubt that anyone would
try to trample this fellow," Kedrigern said, patting his black
steed's neck. The horse acknowledged the gesture with a snort
of bright flame.

They took shelter under the upturned roots of a fallen tree
that formed a high safe rampart at their backs. The forest was
by this time a great cacophony of sound—plunging hooves,
cracking branches, bleats and squeals and tearing cries of fear,
all coming ever closer and building in volume and intensity.
Even though Kedrigern knew that he had nothing to fear from
the Haunted Huntsman—the fellow was all façade, a fearsome
exterior concealing only bluff and bluster—he drew the horse
deeper into the hollow of the roots, out of the way of traffic.
At his shoulder, he heard Belsheer's uneasy wordless buzzing.

Animals began to rush past them, the rabbits zigzagging in
desperation, squirrels hurling themselves from tree to tree, a
wild boar crashing through a thicket, innumerable smaller creatures perceptible only as ripples in the grass, avoiding the
hooves of deer that moved in great bounds, graceful even in
their terror. They passed, and for a moment the forest was still;
then, suddenly and horribly, a darkness flew over them and
the Haunted Huntsman's great gray mare landed, rearing mag-
nificently as her rider blew a deafening triple blast on his horn,
brandished his glistening spear, and laughed a wild, cruel
laugh.

"Don't mind him," Kedrigern whispered to Belsheer. "He's
never actually harmed anyone."

"It's hard to ignore him," buzzed Belsheer very softly.

And indeed it was. The Haunted Huntsman was a giant of
a man. The hands that gripped spear and horn were the size

of platters, and his weathered arms bulged from his taut green sleeves, thick as an ordinary man's thighs. His shoulders, under their scarlet cloak, were broad as a mantelpiece, and his laughter seemed to shake the very ground. His gray mare reared and plunged and whinnied most dramatically. When the sounds of flight had all died away, and the mare had settled down, the Huntsman blew three long blasts on his horn and shouted after their fading echo, "Fly, fly, ye creatures of field and forest! Fly before the Haunted Huntsman! Fear his arrow, dread his spear, tremble at the note of his horn! He leaves ye now, and goes to take his ease, but be warned! Cower in covert and brake, shiver in dark den and fragile nest as ye wait his return!"

He took several deep breaths, gave one final ringing blast on his horn, and then heaved a great sigh and slumped in the saddle. He slung the horn around his neck by its gold-and-scarlet baldric, wiped his brow, and ran a huge hand through the tangle of red beard and hair that encircled his heavy features. "Well, that's that for this time around," he said in a normal conversational voice, sounding relieved and relaxed. "Back to the cave, old girl, and then you're on your own."

He wheeled the gray mare around, and found himself face to face with Kedrigern. Before either man could speak, events took an unexpected turn. The gray mare neighed softly and rolled her eyes in a fetching *oeillade*. The horned black stallion reared high, nearly throwing Kedrigern, and snorted jets of flame from his nostrils. Then the two horses trotted to one another and began to nuzzle, all the while making low, affectionate noises. Kedrigern looked at the Haunted Huntsman, smiled uncomfortably, and shrugged.

The Huntsman looked him over apprehensively. "Are you an elf? Are you checking on me?"

"No, no, no," Kedrigern said, waving off the question.

"I did my part," the Huntsman went on. "I drove the beasts before me and made my boast. I was all ready to go back to my cave and sleep for another thirteen years. I'm observing the terms of the curse. You have no cause for complaint."

As the Haunted Huntsman spoke, his voice and manner betraying his growing anxiety, the black stallion was nipping fondly at the mare's shoulder while she rubbed her muzzle against his neck. Their mutual interest was obvious.

"My dear Huntsman, I am not an elf," said Kedrigern.

"Why were you spying on me?"

"I was not spying, I was keeping out of the way of all those terrified animals. You make it very unpleasant for travelers, you know."

"Don't blame me. This isn't my idea. I'm operating under an elvish curse. Completely unfair, too, but that's elves for you," said the Huntsman, scowling.

"What did you do to the elves?"

"Nothing, really. Just disturbed a picnic. Rode right into the middle of it and scattered all their ambrosia and nectar and honey-cakes. Didn't hurt anyone. Didn't even break a dish. Apologized as nicely as anyone could wish, offered to help tidy up . . . but the elves were furious."

"Elves are touchy."

"Don't tell me about elves," said the Haunted Huntsman, reddening. "They like to pass themselves off as elegant and fine and dainty and full of fun, but they're as nasty as dungeon rats, the lot of them. Maybe I'm foolish to say these things out loud, but I don't care anymore. I'm fed up, let them do what they please, I'll have my say. Just because I disturbed their stupid picnic, I have to go dashing through these woods every thirteen years, blowing my horn and scaring the daylights out of all the animals. In between, I sleep in a cave under a hill. And all over one miserable elvish picnic."

"It does seem a bit severe," said Kedrigern, tugging fruitlessly on the black steed's reins. "Look, Huntsman, I'm sorry about this. He's an enchanted horse, and I never thought that enchanted horses were still interested in . . . well, in ordinary life."

"No need to apologize, traveler. This isn't my horse. That's another thing about this curse—it's so sloppily managed that I'm ashamed to have any part in it." The Haunted Huntsman's voice was rising again.

"It looked quite proficient to me," Kedrigern said, patting his horse's neck with no perceptible result.

"Well, it's not. I wake up in my cave every thirteen years, and I'm supposed to go off on a haunted hunt. You don't see any dogs, do you?"

"No," said Kedrigern, glancing about. "Where are they?"

"I don't have any! What's a haunted hunt without fiery-eyed slavering hellhounds, I ask you? This is my twenty-eighth time around, and dogs have been provided for exactly three hunts, very early on. Now, I call that a sloppy curse."

"Shocking," said Kedrigern, shaking his head.

"There's usually a horse saddled and waiting by the cave entrance, but once they even overlooked that. And not a word of explanation, nothing like an apology for the inconvenience. I had to fulfill the curse on foot that time, and it was absolutely exhausting. Silly, too. I felt like a complete fool threatening to ride down all those animals, and them running twice as fast as I could."

"That's a very poorly managed curse," Kedrigern said.

"Yes, and I'm stuck with doing it every thirteen years for thirteen times thirteen lifetimes, unless I can—" The Haunted Huntsman stopped in mid-sentence, staring fixedly at the wizard's shoulder. "Don't move. There's a giant bee on your shoulder," he said in a hoarse whisper.

"It's all right. He's a friend of mine."

"Belsheer's the name," the bee buzzed.

"It talks!"

"Of course I talk. I'm a wizard, you ninny."

The Haunted Huntsman gaped at the bee, then turned to Kedrigern. "And you—are you a wizard, too?"

"I am Kedrigern, the wizard of Silent Thunder Mountain. My friend's under an enchantment, you understand."

"You're wizards! You can help me! You can lift this curse!" the Huntsman cried.

Kedrigern raised his hand in a cautionary gesture. "Elvish curses are tricky things. If I tamper with it, we may both be sorry."

"I'm willing to risk it. Otherwise I have to work it out to the end—unless I can find a black doe with a circle of white stars on her left flank, and slay her with a single thrust of my spear in her heart.''

''That's wicked! Monstrous!'' Kedrigern exclaimed with such vehemence that the Huntsman started back and Belsheer took flight, landing on a projecting root overhead. ''The Starry Black Doe of Sallinsell is an enchanted princess of surpassing sweetness and innocence, cursed by a jealous bog-fairy who considered her . . . Wait a minute, now. Wait just a minute. Are you absolutely certain it was elves who put this curse on you?''

''They said they were elves. I never thought to ask for their credentials.''

''This picnic of theirs—did it take place in a bog? Anywhere near a bog? Think carefully, now.''

''It was in the woods . . . but it was a very boggy part of the woods.''

After a profound pause, Kedrigern said, ''My haunted friend, I think you've been victimized by bog-fairies.''

''Why would bog-fairies try to pass themselves off as elves?''

''To give elves a bad name. They enjoy doing things like that.''

''That's vile. It's vicious!'' said the Huntsman.

''Bog-fairies are customarily vile and vicious,'' said Kedrigern.

''That's certainly true. I've never met a decent one in all my years,'' Belsheer buzzed from his perch on the root.

They were all silent for a time, pondering Kedrigern's revelation. The horses continued to rub cheeks, making soft breathy noises to accompany their gestures. Belsheer, sensing calm restored, flew back to Kedrigern's shoulder.

''I'd like to help you, Huntsman,'' said Kedrigern. ''I can't promise anything, but it would please me greatly to confound the machinations of bog-fairies and help someone out at the same time. I'll do what I can.''

''That's good enough for me,'' the Haunted Huntsman replied.

''Fine. As long as we understand each other. My home is a

day's ride from here. Can you spare a day or two?''

"Is it absolutely necessary? Can't you work a quick counterspell right here?''

"I must consult my library. A hasty counterspell is usually worse than the spell it counters,'' said Kedrigern, and Belsheer buzzed sharply. "My friend agrees,'' Kedrigern added.

"If I must, I must. The curse allows for travel time back to my cave.''

"Then you have nothing to worry about. If I can't resolve the problem in a day or two, we'll get you to your cave. That will leave me thirteen years to work something out. There's just one thing more we ought to discuss.''

"I'm not a wealthy man, Master Kedrigern. In fact, I haven't earned a penny for . . . oh, about three hundred and fifty years now,'' said the Haunted Huntsman.

A small sigh at his shoulder caught Kedrigern's attention momentarily. "Those were the days. I was a green lad then, scarcely a century old,'' Belsheer fondly droned.

"I don't want money. I want your horse. As you can see, my own horse has taken a certain interest in her, which she seems to reciprocate.''

"That's a unicorn you're riding,'' the Huntsman said.

"He is not a unicorn, he is a horse altered by enchantment,'' Kedrigern said.

"I'm a huntsman, and I know horses when I see them, Master Kedrigern. He looks like a unicorn to me.''

"Don't judge things by appearances. Observe his behavior.''

The Haunted Huntsman did as Kedrigern bade him, and after a time he said reluctantly, "He behaves like a horse. I'll grant you that. And there's a lot of horse in him. He's *mainly* horse, I'll admit. But that silver horn. And the silver hooves. And breathing fire, as he does. That's unicorn, Master Kedrigern.''

"It's horse, enhanced. And before he and your mare start acting even more like horses, I suggest we start for my house— at a gallop.''

····❦ Three ❧····

home is the wizard

EXPERIENCE AS WIFE of a practicing wizard makes a woman difficult to surprise. When Kedrigern turned up in mid-afternoon two full days before his anticipated date of return, with a giant red-bearded huntsman in tow, and his horned stallion prancing like a trained pony and nuzzling an oversized gray mare that nuzzled him enthusiastically in return, Princess did not cry out in astonishment. She did not raise an eyebrow. She merely waved a welcome and took to the air to greet him at the foot of the path.

"A fairy godmother! It's your fairy godmother, Master Kedrigern!" the Haunted Huntsman exclaimed as she rose smoothly from the ground with rapid strokes of her opalescent little wings.

"Must you always judge by appearances?" said Kedrigern with a frown of annoyance. "My wife is no more a fairy godmother than my horse is a unicorn."

"Your wife? But she flies!"

"Of course she flies. She has wings, doesn't she? What do you expect her to do, swim?"

"I never saw a flying woman before."

"Well, now you have. I do wish people—" Kedrigern began, but another shout interrupted him.

"What's *that*?!" the Huntsman cried in alarm as a knee-high grotesque burst from the cottage and made for them, ecstatically shrieking "Yah! Yah!" as it came on in great bounds, ears flapping, huge hands and feet flailing.

"That's our house-troll. I suppose you've never seen one of *them*, either."

Kedrigern urged the black stallion forward with a twitch of his heels. It neighed once, and the gray mare broke into an eager trot at its side. The Haunted Huntsman slackened the reins and abandoned himself to whatever might befall.

The next few minutes were hectic. Kedrigern sprang from his mount, Princess swooped down to land in his open arms, and Spot cartwheeled around them repeating its "Yah! Yah!" of welcome as they embraced. The black stallion, delivered of his rider, turned his full attention at once to the gray mare, who responded with such wholehearted exuberance that the Haunted Huntsman found it prudent to dismount and stand with eyes averted from the surrounding scenes of tenderness.

"It's so good to be home. My dear, you're lovelier than ever," Kedrigern said, cradling Princess's face in his hands.

"It's wonderful to have you back—and earlier than you had expected," she said, laying her hands over his.

"Those awful headaches—are they gone?" he asked, kissing her gently on the forehead.

"Almost entirely."

"Well, I'll soon have a spell that will give you relief for days at a time. I met an old acquaintance—"

"It doesn't matter!" she broke in joyously. "The headaches brought back my memory!"

"Marvelous, my dear! What do you remember? Tell me everything!"

"Well, I don't remember all that much just yet, but it's coming back. A piece here, a piece there. A face, a name, a scene. All very fragmentary at this point, but it's a beginning."

"Indeed it is. I always said you'd start remembering eventually. I'm only sorry you had to endure those awful headaches."

"I'd willingly put up with any amount of discomfort to have my memories back." Princess gestured toward their giant vis-

itor, who stood with his hands clasped behind his back, studying
the clouds, the vegetable garden, the toes of his boots, the tops
of the trees, and other impersonal phenomena, obviously feeling superfluous and rather awkward. "Is that your old acquaintance? Should I remember him?" she asked.

"No, my dear, this is someone else I met along the way,"
said Kedrigern, turning and putting his arm around her slender
waist. "He's under a curse, and I said I'd try to help him."

"Oh, that's nice."

Clearing his throat to attract the giant's attention, Kedrigern
said, "Haunted Huntsman, allow me to present my wife, Princess."

The Huntsman turned to them, bowed, and said, "I am
honored to meet you, my lady."

"Princess, the Haunted Huntsman," Kedrigern said, com-
pleting the introductions.

"Call me Tergus, if it please you, my lady. Tergus is my
real name, and I look forward to using it again."

"How reassuring it must be to know one's own name! Welcome, Tergus," said Princess, with a smile that dazzled him.
She was looking her most beautiful this day. A surcoat of pale
rose-colored silk, trimmed with gray fur, heightened the gleaming midnight of her hair. A silver circlet set with tiny diamonds
ringed her brow.

"I brought an old friend, too. He's somewhere out in the
garden now," Kedrigern said.

Princess shaded her eyes with one delicate hand and peered
in the direction suggested. She looked for a time, glancing to
all corners of the garden, then said, "I don't see anyone."

"He's a bee. Been spelled."

"Oh . . . Oh, yes, there's a very large bee around the daf-
fodils."

"That's Belsheer."

"Are you going to help him, too?"

"Whenever he's ready. Right now, he seems quite comfortable just being a bee."

"I'm sure it's much nicer than being a toad," said Princess.
"So much drier. So many more things to do."

"We were discussing that very question along the way, my dear. I'm sure you and Belsheer will have lots to talk about. He's full of news. Do you know what he told me? Tristaver's married! You remember Tris, don't you?"

"Yes. He didn't strike me as the marrying kind. Too much in love with himself, I thought."

"Well, apparently he met this monster that turned out to be an enchanted queen. He disenchanted her, one thing led to another, and now they're married. She fell madly in love with him at first sight."

Princess gave a doubtful little sniff and looked at him with a critical eye. "It wouldn't surprise me to learn that he spelled her into it."

"Belsheer and I speculated on that very possibility. Well, what does it matter, as long as they're happy?" said Kedrigern. "It's nice to see that the example of our domestic happiness is changing the attitudes of my bachelor colleagues. Even old Belsheer may decide to settle down once he's properly despelled. Do you mind if he stays on for a few days? He'll be in the garden most of the time. No trouble for us at all."

"He's quite welcome. Perhaps he'll attract others, and we can have our own honey. But we're neglecting our other guest. You must stay for dinner, Tergus. Spot will care for your horse. You can freshen up at the house."

"Thank you, my lady," said the bearded giant.

He handed the reins to Spot, bending double to do so. The little house-troll accepted them with a polite "Yah" and led both horses to the stable. They rubbed necks and whinnied softly all the way.

Taking Princess's hand, Kedrigern said, "The gray mare and my black stallion have formed a warm relationship. The mare is my fee for lifting the curse on Tergus."

Princess sighed. "Do we really need another horse?"

"There's plenty of room in the stable. Living out here, one can never have too many horses."

"What about Tergus? Where will he go on foot?"

"Anywhere he likes, my dear. What interests me is the

opportunity to learn whether enchanted characteristics can be passed on to offspring.''

"That might be useful to know,'' Princess conceded, without much discernible enthusiasm. "But about helping Tergus—what, exactly, is his problem?''

"A bog-fairy's curse. I'm almost certain of it.''

"Really?'' Princess exclaimed, her interest awakening.

Kedrigern sketched out the tale of the Haunted Huntsman, and at Princess's urging, Tergus added the details. By the time they crossed the threshold of the cottage, Princess had heard all she needed to know. She clapped her hands excitedly, gave a little flirt of her wings, and said, "My wand—this is the perfect test for my wand!''

"My dear, of course!''

"Wand?'' Tergus asked dubiously.

"It's a bog-fairy's wand—a bog-fairy's wand for a bog-fairy's curse,'' Princess explained. "It can't possibly fail.''

Shaking his head, Tergus backed out of the doorway. He held his hands raised before his chest in a protective gesture.

"What's wrong, Tergus?'' Kedrigern asked.

"My lady is not a fairy godmother—is that true?''

"It is.''

"And she is not a bog-fairy, either.''

"Certainly not,'' Princess snapped.

Tergus took another step backward, still shaking his head. "But you have those little wings, and a bog-fairy's wand. I don't want to seem ungrateful or suspicious, but I don't understand what's going on. I don't want to get mixed up in something I don't understand.''

"You've been mixed up in something you don't understand for several centuries, Tergus. This is your chance to get out of it. Trust us,'' Kedrigern said, reaching up to lay a reassuring hand on the huntsman's brawny shoulder.

Tergus flinched and drew away. "I don't want to have anything to do with bog-fairies. Nothing at all. Not with them, not with their wands. I thought you were just going to say a few magic words, Master Kedrigern, or make passes in the air, or throw some magic dust at me, but now you're talking about using a fairy wand, and I don't like it one bit."

"If you want the help of wizards, you must trust them completely," said Kedrigern.

"I do, Master Kedrigern. Believe me, I do. I trust you and I trust my lady. But I don't trust bog-fairies or their wands."

"Let me assure you, Tergus, that aside from her extraordinary beauty and uncommon sweetness of disposition"—and here the wizard interrupted his discourse to take Princess's hand and raise it to his lips—"my wife is a perfectly normal woman. She is neither fairy nor witch. The wings are a useful and decorative acquisition, and nothing more. Thanks to native intelligence, diligent study, and superior instruction, she has learned much about the proper use of magic, and thanks to a fortunate coincidence, she possesses a wand long wielded by an exceptionally active bog-fairy."

"That was no coincidence, it was poetic justice," Princess said.

"Perhaps something of both. In any event, Tergus, you are fortunate to have here two wizards, one of whom can employ in your behalf an instrument snatched from the very creatures who cursed you, and the other a master of counterspells and disenchantments. So stop flinching, banish your doubts, get inside, and do as you're told," Kedrigern concluded sharply, emphasizing his command with a dramatic sweep of his arm and a digital indication of direction.

Tergus wilted. Meekly he stooped and followed the pointing finger, passing through the doorway without a word. Princess and Kedrigern followed.

Spot prepared, and served, an exquisite dinner, enhanced by liberal goblets of the finest wines from the vineyards of Vosconu the Openhanded, a satisfied client who had on more than one occasion demonstrated his satisfaction by living up to his name. As the evening wore on, the glances that Princess and Kedrigern exchanged in the flickering candlelight grew ever tenderer and more lingering, and conversation ceased for long periods. Tergus cleared his throat several times and looked from one to the other. They were both oblivious to his large presence.

"About my curse, Master Kedrigern," he said at last.

With a mild start, Kedrigern said, "Your curse? Oh, yes. Terrible things, curses."

"Dreadful," Princess murmured.

"Yes. That's why I want it lifted. You said you'd help me."

"Oh, *your* curse. The hunting. Sleeping in a cave. Yes, we'll help you. Trust us."

"I'm willing to trust you both. When do we start?"

"Tomorrow. It's always best to work by daylight. You come here tomorrow and we'll get right to work."

Tergus looked at him blankly. "I *am* here. Where would I come from?"

"From the stable. Spot has prepared a place for you in the loft. It's nice and roomy, and you'll be undisturbed. You can sleep as late as you like," Princess said.

Smiling pleasantly, Kedrigern observed, "That should be no problem for you, after sleeping for thirteen years at a stretch."

After a pause, Tergus asked, "What time is breakfast?"

"Late," they replied in unison.

When the door closed behind their guest, Princess rose from her place with a soft hum of wings and landed gently in Kedrigern's lap. She put her arms around his neck and laid her head against his shoulder as he embraced her.

"Alone at last," she said.

"Sorry I turned up with a client, my dear. That sort of thing does blunt the delights of homecoming, I know, but the poor chap needs help."

"Say no more. We'll fix him up tomorrow, and then we won't have anyone to disturb us."

Kedrigern sighed in pleasant anticipation. "Were there no messages while I was gone? No urgent summonses?"

"Not one," said Princess.

Once again he sighed with contentment. Peace, quiet, and solitude cast the rosy glow of a summer sunrise on the horizon. No more intrusions, no demands on his time, no heart-rending pleas to set him packing and traveling long distances in the heat and dust of midsummer, only to find himself dealing with a half-baked enchantment that could have been undone by any reasonably astute apprentice or fledgling wizard. Only solitude, quiet, and peace. It was wonderful to contemplate; all the more wonderful because it was so rare.

Clients were necessary, and could be very generous, but they made the most painful demands on one's time. Clients had absolutely no regard for a wizard's privacy or convenience. Take the kindest of men, the most considerate of women, place a spell on that individual, and at a single stroke you created a monster of selfishness prepared to burst into the privacy of a wizard's home and disrupt his domestic life, or to wrench the wizard from his wife's side at a moment's notice, or to drag both wizard and wife halfway across the known world to get the client out of a mess that no sensible man or woman would have gotten into in the first place. Clients could be very exasperating, especially the ones who lived in remote and all but inaccessible places and got themselves into difficulty during the rainy season, or in the dead of winter, or in the hottest days of summer, or whenever traveling was most awkward, perilous, and uncomfortable. It was bad enough having to deal with clients; having to travel long distances to do so was compounding the outrage.

Wizardry was a good life, bar the traveling. The trouble was that there was no way to bar the traveling. One simply had to grit one's teeth, get it over with as quickly as possible, and make the most of homecoming.

Princess broke the silence by asking very softly, "Don't you want to know what I remember?"

"Of course I do, every bit of it, my dear!"

Bounding to her feet, she said, "Well, there isn't very much so far, but I'm getting more every day. At least I was, until a few days ago. But I have a very clear picture of my father and mother now. He was very tall, with black hair just like mine, and a black beard streaked with white on either side of his mouth. I can't recall the color of his eyes, but I know they were dark. He had a long scar on his left arm, and an arrow-wound in his foot that caused him to limp in damp weather."

"Your memories have returned in remarkable detail."

"My mother is almost as clear. She was small, with auburn

hair that reached her ankles when she let it down. She had blue eyes.''

''Just like yours.''

''Slightly darker, I think. And I recall both of them as being sad much of the time.''

''It's not easy running a kingdom, not even a small hereditary kingdom. Kings and queens have their problems, my dear.''

''So do princesses. And I remember a sister, too—an older sister!''

''You spoke of a sister once before, I believe, but you weren't certain.''

''I am now. She came back to me in a flash. She had my mother's hair and my father's eyes, and everyone said she was very clever and quite beautiful,'' said Princess with a slight chill in her voice.

''A lovely child,'' Kedrigern murmured.

''Not to me, she wasn't. I still don't remember the details, but I have a strong feeling that we didn't get along.''

''There's bound to be a certain rivalry between two beautiful young ladies, my dear, even if they're sisters. Were there any other sisters that you recall? Any brothers?''

''I'm almost positive there weren't. And I think there was more than just a normal rivalry between my sister and me.''

''Don't draw hasty conclusions. When you can remember more of the details, I'm sure the picture will be different. What else do you recall?''

''I clearly remember falling down the grand staircase of the castle. I scraped my knees and elbows, and got a big bump on my head. And once I slipped into the moat and nearly drowned. Then there was the time the elk's head fell off the wall and nearly impaled me.''

''A childhood rich in thrilling incident.''

''Yes. I had quite a few close calls.''

''Well, you're safe now, my dear. And I'm home. And it's just about time for bed,'' Kedrigern said, rising and stretching. ''Have you any more memories?''

''Nothing very exciting. But they're coming back.''

He took her hand and squeezed it affectionately. Hand in

hand they made their way through the silent cottage to their bedroom.

Tergus gave a tentative rap at the front door as Kedrigern and Princess were finishing a shamelessly late breakfast. Spot admitted him, and Tergus stopped in the entrance to the breakfast nook, cap in hand, looking uncomfortable. Considering his bulk, and the size of the breakfast nook, his discomfort was understandable.

"Good morning, Tergus. Lovely morning. Have a muffin and some strawberry jam," said Kedrigern in welcome.

"And some nice hot porridge," Princess added.

"Thank you for your kindness, but Spot brought me a tray."

"Wouldn't you like a little more? Surely a big fellow like you . . ." Kedrigern extended the muffin dish.

"No, thank you, Master Kedrigern. Spot brought me two dozen muffins and a loaf of bread, and a big bowl of porridge, and a pitcher of milk, and some boiled eggs."

"Spot loves to see people enjoy its cooking."

"It watched me until I finished every bit." Tergus rubbed his stomach and looked queasy. "I had to force myself to finish the last half-dozen eggs. Being spelled takes away the appetite, you know."

"Ah, yes. Your spell." Kedrigern nodded, and preparing to rise, said, "Well, come along, and we'll see what—"

"No need to leave the breakfast nook," Princess broke in. She reached behind her and produced the wand she had acquired from Bertha the Bog-fairy. The star at its top flashed in the morning sunlight.

Tergus gave a start. "That's very kind of you, my lady, but if it's all the same, I'd—"

"Just leave everything to me," she said, turning back the sleeves of her robe in so businesslike a gesture that Kedrigern would not have been surprised to see her spit on her palms and rub them together before settling down to the task at hand. Rising, she said, "There's just one thing I have to know: Did anyone tap you on the forehead with a wand when you were spelled?"

Tergus furrowed his brow, rolled his eyes, tugged at his bright thicket of beard, and then blurted, "Yes! Yes, there was a very pretty lady—pretty in a hard kind of way, if you know what I mean—and she said something, and tapped me with a wand just like the one you're holding. Next thing I knew, I was waking up in a cave, all stiff, with a tremendous urge to hunt.''

"What did she say?'' Princess asked.

"Something about a curse . . . and how it could be worse. That's all I can remember.''

"Listen to what I'm going to say, Tergus, and tell me if it's what the lady said. Listen very carefully. This is important.

> 'Here's a blow to seal the curse;
>   Be glad it isn't ten times worse.'

Is that what she said?''

"It is, my lady! Her very words!'' he cried, looking from Princess to Kedrigern in amazement. "That's what she said, and then she tapped me with her wand!''

"I thought as much,'' said Princess. Turning to Kedrigern, she explained, "A typical bog-fairy curse. You noticed the vagueness of the wording, of course. Even the pronoun reference is ambiguous.''

He nodded. "Just something to have ready to hand in case you want to curse anyone in a hurry.''

"Exactly. It has 'bog-fairy' written all over it. That lot would rather curse than eat.''

"Nicely done, my dear. I suspected bog-fairies the moment I heard Tergus's story, but I think you've proven their involvement beyond a doubt.''

"I did a lot of studying while you were away, and remained in constant practice with my wand. Watch this.'' Stepping forward, raising her wand, Princess said, "Stoop over a bit, Tergus. I have to tap you on the forehead.''

Tergus did not move. Uneasily, he said, "My lady, are you sure—''

"I'm positive, Tergus. Come on, stoop.''

The giant sighed and inclined his body forward, lowering his head to within easy range of Princess's wand. She cleared her throat, made a graceful pass in the air, and touched him lightly on the brow, between the eyes, just below the hairline, saying:

> "A second blow undoes the first;
> Rejoice! You are no longer curs't."

Tergus blinked and gave a little twitch of his shoulders. He straightened to his full height, leaving scarcely the thickness of a blade of grass between himself and the ceiling. He blinked again, then slowly broke into a broad boyish grin.

"I feel lighter!"

"And no wonder. You've just had a curse lifted," Kedrigern pointed out.

Tergus dropped to one knee, with a thump that set every movable in the breakfast nook to dancing. "Thank you, my lady. And you, Master Kedrigern."

"Well done! A masterful piece of work, my child!" buzzed a small but spirited voice from the direction of the table. They all turned and saw a very large bumblebee seated on the lip of the jam pot. The bee's two front legs were working furiously in a gesture that resembled applause. "Brother Kedrigern, your wife is not only lovely, but talented. That was as neat a disenchantment as I've ever seen. *Brava! Bravissima,* my dear child!"

"Allow me to present Belsheer, my dear," said Kedrigern, gesturing toward the jam pot.

Princess, slightly flushed but smiling, curtseyed and said, "I'm delighted to meet you, Master Belsheer."

"Please, dear Sister Princess, let us not be formal," the bee buzzed genially. "Call me Brother Belsheer."

"I will. And you must call me Princess. I've been looking forward to a good long chat with you. Kedrigern told me about your change."

"Best thing that ever happened to me. I feel better every day," he hummed, strutting about on the rim of the jam pot.

"You're looking very fit."

"Thank you. I'm bursting with energy. Can't stay still. If you'll excuse me, I'm simply aching to get back outside and bumble around a few flowers. We'll get together soon, dear girl, I promise. Compare notes, as it were." Belsheer rose, circled the kitchen with a soft droning hum, then darted out the window.

"Nice of him to drop in," Princess said.

"I think we'd better keep an eye on Belsheer. He's becoming more beeish every day. If he doesn't change back soon, he may never do it," Kedrigern said.

"Do you really think so? I'd say he's just enjoying the novelty. It's nice to be able to fly and have lots of new energy."

"You may be right," Kedrigern said thoughtfully. He did not sound convinced.

"My lady Princess, what do I do now?" came the deep bewildered voice of Tergus.

"I don't know anything about huntsmen. Ask my husband."

"Master Kedrigern, what now?"

"The world is your oyster, Tergus. You may go where you like and do as you please. The curse is lifted, and you are your own man."

"My own man?" Tergus repeated in a chastened voice. He was silent for a moment, then went on. "I don't know as I like that. I've never been my own man before."

"Whose were you?"

"I was a huntsman for Jottron of the Hidden Wood. He's a great lord in these parts."

"Not anymore, he isn't. I never heard the name before. You must remember, Tergus, you've been under that curse for over three hundred years. Things change in that time."

"Yes, they do. I've lost track of a lot of things, only waking up once every thirteen years, and then being kept so busy I had no time to catch up on the news. So that must mean . . ." Tergus looked up in sudden dismay. "There is no hope of getting my old place back!"

"Not with Jottron. But there's always work for a good huntsman. You're big and strong, you have lots of experience, you're well rested—any number of great lords would be pleased to add such a man to their household.''

"Could you recommend me to one of them?"

"Well, I can't think of anyone who is in *immediate* need of a huntsman, but I'll write you a nice letter.''

"I'll write one, too," Princess volunteered.

"There you are, Tergus. With two good letters of recommendation, you'll have no trouble getting an excellent place. We'll write them today, and you can take them with you in the morning.''

"In the morning?"

"Or you can leave this afternoon, if you prefer. I don't want to keep you hanging about. I'm sure you have all sorts of things to catch up on after being cursed for so long.''

Tergus licked his lips and ran a hand nervously through his beard. "To tell the truth, Master Kedrigern, I was thinking that it might be good for me to stay on here for a time. Just until I get used to going around without a curse on me.''

"Oh, dear, no. That would be the worst thing in the world for you, Tergus. You have to plunge back into life right away,'' said Kedrigern.

"I wouldn't be any trouble. I'd stay up over the stable. I could help Spot with the horses.''

"Spot doesn't need help. We'd only hurt its feelings if we brought someone in to help.''

"But the little fellow and I get on something splendid, Master Kedrigern, really we do. Spot's strong and willing, but awfully short. You've got some fine big horses in your stable, and it's hard for Spot to groom them properly. Now, me, I can do that sort of thing easily.''

"Oh, no, Tergus. I couldn't think of imposing on you,'' said Kedrigern, guiding the giant out of the breakfast nook in the direction of the front door. "The world awaits you. Opportunity. Adventure. It would be terribly selfish of us to keep you here for our own benefit.''

"I'd be happy to stay," Tergus protested. "I could help with the fruit trees, too. They need a good pruning. And I could patch the roof. And repair the chimney. And those—''

"Nice of you to offer, but we—"

"—Two lovely big oak trees out behind the house need looking after, what with those broken limbs way up—"

"—Would never dream of . . . Trees? Oak trees?"

"—Where Spot could never reach," the huntsman concluded.

"Gylorel and his wife," Princess said. Her voice revealed her concern.

"It does a lot of harm to a tree, my lady, having those split branches and broken limbs way up at the top."

"Keddie, we can't ignore Gylorel."

"No, no, I'm not saying we should," said Kedrigern, feeling cornered.

"I could probably take care of both trees in no more than four or five days, my lady," said Tergus, unerringly sensing where his best hopes lay. "Then I could get to work on the fruit trees. You'd be surprised at the yield you'll get once they're properly pruned."

"Can you start work on the big oaks today?" she asked.

"Right away, my lady. There's a rope in the stable. I'll get it, and go right to work."

"Good. I'll speak to Gylorel first, to let him know what you're doing. We don't want him shaking you loose."

As Tergus dashed off to the stable, Kedrigern sighed and said, "Well, there goes our privacy."

"We can't be selfish. We must think of Gylorel and his wife."

"Spot could have done whatever was necessary. Why do we suddenly need an overgrown disenchanted huntsman bustling about the grounds?"

"Tergus will get the job done much faster. And he really will be a help in the stable. We owe the lad something. You've often told me that a good wizard accepts professional responsibilities. One does not disenchant someone and simply walk away."

"That's not what I had in mind. I was hoping *Tergus* would walk away, and allow us some privacy."

"We'll have our privacy," Princess said. She put her arms

around his neck and kissed him long and sweetly. "There, now. No one came bursting—"

A golden missile hummed through the open doorway, circled them once, and lit on Kedrigern's shoulder. Breathless from fear and exertion, it bombinated, "Brother Kedrigern, it's a jungle out there!"

"Well, it could use a bit of trimming and pruning, but I—"

"I was nearly killed! A huge bird came swooping down like a bolt of lightning. If it hadn't been for these eyes, I would have been gobbled up. I'll never complain about bee vision again, believe me."

"You're safe now, Belsheer."

"Not with that bird around. Do you have house plants, Brother Kedrigern?"

"Well, yes. We have . . . one or two."

"That's a relief," buzzed Belsheer, vigorously combing himself with his front legs. "You don't mind if I stay indoors for a few days, do you? You won't even know I'm in the house."

Kedrigern thought of those multiple eyes following his every move, and Princess's. Tergus, at least, had only two normal eyes, and he was so big he could not go about unnoticed. But a bee, even an oversized bee, might be anywhere, and at the least opportune moments. Still, Tergus was doing his best to be helpful; and one could not expose an old colleague to mortal danger simply in order to enjoy the privacy of one's own home in the sole company of one's spouse. One might be sorely tempted to do so, but one could not give in.

"I'm sure we won't, Belsheer," he said with a sigh, hoping that bees had the decency to buzz before entering a room.

"There are fresh flowers on the table in the other room," Princess said.

"Thank you, Sister Princess," Belsheer buzzed, and was off.

When he was gone, Kedrigern and Princess exchanged a long, significant glance. Kedrigern smiled ruefully and drew her close. "A pretty lively homecoming, my dear. Now we have a giant and an enchanted bee sharing our dwelling."

"Tergus will be working outside, and we can keep all our house plants in the breakfast nook. It could be worse," Princess said.

With a brief, humorless laugh, Kedrigern said, "Worse? The only thing that could possibly make it worse is—"

His hypothetical apocalypse was never articulated. The sound of trumpets, excited bursts of "Yah, yah!" and the deep voice of Tergus shouting, "Heralds and messengers, Master Kedrigern! Pennant bearers and men-at-arms! Horsemen by the dozen!" caused the wizard to close his eyes, grit his teeth, and groan in pain.

Princess gave his cheek a consoling pat, took him by the hand like a mother drawing a recalcitrant child to some nasty but inescapable encounter, and said, "Let's see who's calling."

···❦ *Four* ❧···

the king's pleasure

TERGUS, IN HIS excitement, had exaggerated the number of visitors. There were not even two dozen of them. But the appearance of those assembled in orderly array along the road was so impressive as to make his exaggeration pardonable. They were nineteen in all, wearing unfamiliar but splendid livery of green, gold, and blue, and riding identical magnificent white horses. Two heralds with silver trumpets had drawn up outside the waist-high wall facing the cottage, one on either side of the garden gate. At their sides were pennant bearers, and as Kedrigern and Princess watched from the doorway, a dozen knights, bearing lances, joined the heralds and pennant bearers, six knights on either side of the gate; they dipped their lances in salute, then raised them smartly erect. Behind them, on the road, two men sat stiffly on a flat wagon.

The nineteenth man, a silver-haired knight of dignified mien, dismounted and stepped through the gate. Removing his crested helmet, he bowed low to Princess, pointedly ignoring everyone else of the household. Rising to his full height, he said in a deep clear voice, "Greetings, fair lady. I seek the abode of Kedrigern, the wizard of Silent Thunder Mountain, and his wife, Princess, a woman as far-famed for her beauty as for her powers of enchantment. Have I far to go?"

"Not a step farther, my good man. I am she whom you seek."

"And I'm Kedrigern," said the wizard.

"Indeed? Forgive my obtuseness, gentles both," said the knight, bowing again. "I did not recognize you as wizards from your attire."

"I know, I know," Kedrigern said, raising his hand and nodding in a gesture of patient resignation. "You expected someone with a long silver beard and a glittering eye, and wearing a steeple-crowned hat and flowing robe covered with cabalistic symbols."

"Something like that," the knight confessed.

"I keep telling you to dress properly, but you won't listen," Princess said *sotto voce*.

"Everyone judges by appearances these days," said Kedrigern.

"It's your own fault."

"My dear, this is all beside the point. I'm sure this gentleman . . . What is your name, sir knight?"

"I am Orbolon of Trimigen-on-the-Cliff, called Orbolon the Unafraid. I serve Sariax the Incomparable, King of Kallopane, who sends his greetings and his thanks to you both."

"Handsome's father," Princess whispered. "Remember the Handsome Prince of Kallopane?"

"Yes, of course. He kept saying that his father would be grateful, but I never believed . . . oh, this is very nice," Kedrigern said, all annoyance banished by the thought of a chest of gold and precious gems, or some equally extravagant remembrance. Opening his arms, he said, "You and your men are welcome, sir knight. If you'll give us a few minutes, we'll have refreshments for everyone. Meanwhile, if there's anything you'd like to give us . . . anything you were sent to deliver . . ."

Orbolon stepped forward. Drawing a small chamois pouch from his tunic, he took out two rings. "From my master, Sariax the Incomparable, as token of his gratitude."

Princess appeared pleased, but Kedrigern was a bit disappointed. They were very nice rings, exquisitely crafted, with fine stones in each, but they seemed rather a scanty reward from a king whose son they had helped so generously. That's kings for you, Kedrigern thought, priming himself for a bitter inward tirade; but then Orbolon went on, "These rings, you must understand, are but an earnest of the reward that awaits you at the court of Kallopane. Will it please you to return with us?"

"With you? Now?"

"His Majesty Sariax the Incomparable is most anxious to pay this debt of honor so long neglected. It sorrows him to acknowledge that years have passed since your kindness to his son, and he would delay showing his gratitude no longer."

"How are the prince and his wife?" Princess asked.

"Deliriously happy and passionately devoted to one another, my lady," said Orbolon with evident satisfaction. "They are never apart. Their marriage is the delight and envy of all who know them, the joy of Kallopane, and the wonder of the world."

"I'm so glad to hear it. They were a lovely couple. It will be nice to see them again."

"It will indeed, someday," Kedrigern said, "but surely Sariax is a busy man. Couldn't he just send us a suitable expression of his gratitude? We'd understand. After all, a mighty king—"

"Don't be obtuse," Princess broke in. "We must go to Kallopane."

"But my dear, I just returned from a long trip. I'm exhausted."

"You can relax once we reach Kallopane."

"You will relax in sybaritic comfort," Orbolon said. "You will have a suite all to yourselves, and a score of servants."

"See? It will be delightful," Princess said.

"But I haven't been home even one full day. Would you have me rush off on another journey without a good long rest and some time for the two of us to be together?" Kedrigern appealed to her.

With a sweet smile and a firm voice she replied, "While you were on your journey, I was here with only Spot for company. Spot is loyal and hard-working, but as a companion it has its shortcomings. I would be very happy, Keddie, to speak with human beings and converse in complete sentences. Kallopane is a king's residence, and I sorely miss the refined atmosphere of such places.''

"But Kallopane is so far away." Kedrigern felt trapped for the second time that morning, and this was a much worse trap than the earlier one.

"I would not care if Kallopane were on the moon. In Kallopane we will be guests of a puissant king, surrounded by the splendors of a royal court, fêted, celebrated, honored, and waited on hand and foot. You forget that I am a princess—"

"I do not!"

"Then you ignore the fact, which is even worse. I am a princess, and require occasional visits to court in order to remain *au courant*. It will give troubadours a chance to compose ballads in my honor, bards to recite a new romance to me, young knights to enter the lists wearing a sign of my favor. People need these things. So do I."

A wizard most emphatically does not, thought Kedrigern. A wizard needs peace and quiet and lots of rest, and no crowds milling about singing, chanting, reciting, gossiping, fawning and flattering, chattering and nattering, and making concentration impossible; and certainly no hewing and hacking and thumping and bashing and whomping and all the other forms of mayhem that well-born males practice in the name of chivalry, honor, courage, and the love of a fair maid. But he wisely kept his feelings to himself, saying instead, "I understand perfectly, my dear, but must we rush off at such short notice? Surely Sariax would understand if we . . ."

He fell silent as the implications of delay became clear to him and he realized that the belated generosity of Sariax had placed him in a bind. He could have the escort on its way back to Kallopane within the hour if he committed himself to following them in the very near future. That would be postponing the undesirable, not avoiding it, and a long journey in the heat and dust of summer, on crowded roads, from one squalid inn to the next, was a prospect distressing to contemplate. Merely to protect against spoiled food, fleas, and robbers would be a costly drain on his magic. And if he prudently chose to economize on magic by keeping the escort on hand until he was refreshed and ready for travel, then he would find himself, just when he most desired a quiet withdrawal from worldly cares, playing host not only to a disenchanted giant and an enchanted bee, but a small army, as well. He was trapped. There was nothing left for him but to put a good face on it and salvage what he could from the wreckage of his hopes.

"My dear, I've been shamefully selfish," he said, taking Princess's hand in his and giving it an affectionate squeeze. "If it's your wish to go to Kallopane, we will do so. We will depart at sunrise." Turning to Orbolon, he said, "I trust you and your men will be ready."

"At your command, Master Kedrigern," said the knight with a bow and a flourish.

"Very well. We leave at sunrise."

"At sunrise," Orbolon repeated. "I will give the order."

"Do so."

"I shall."

They stood looking expectantly at one another, and at last Kedrigern took a step back and said, "Until sunrise, then."

"Until sunrise, Master Kedrigern." Orbolon, too, took a single backward step, then halted.

"Do join us for dinner," Princess said. "We will have something prepared for your men."

"No need to worry about us, my lady. We've had good hunting along the way. If you will permit us to make camp in the clearing, we will find for ourselves."

"Whatever you prefer."

"I am grateful for my lady's kind invitation, but I think it best to remain with my men. We have much to do if we are to leave at sunrise."

"As you wish, Sir Orbolon. Until sunrise, then."

"Until sunrise, my lady," said Orbolon, bowing once again.

"Yes, all right—until sunrise. That doesn't leave much time, so if you'll excuse us . . ." Kedrigern said, tugging at his wife's hand.

* * *

Inside the cottage, Kedrigern let out a great relieved whoosh of breath and said, "I thought we'd be saying 'until sunrise' until sunrise. That man doesn't know how to end a conversation."

Princess responded with a preoccupied, barely audible, "Hmmm." She said nothing more, but looked searchingly at Kedrigern. He bustled about, displaying unusual energy and high spirits, keeping up a flow of cheerful small talk to which she listened in silence. At last she said, "You're being very good about this." Her tone was guarded.

"Anything to make you happy, my dear," he said with a sweeping gesture signifying unbounded natural generosity.

"But you hate to travel."

"When it's a question of your happiness . . ." He lifted his hands and shrugged, smiling beatifically.

She studied his features for a long time. His expression remained as innocent as a child's. Shaking her head slowly and uneasily, she said, "You're up to something."

He placed a hand on his heart. His expression turned to one of wounded innocence. "You do me an injustice. You pain me deeply."

"I do not. You've just come back from a trip, you've complained since you walked through the gate about how we have no privacy and you get no rest, and now you're willing to travel all the way to Kallopane with a company of soldiers and spend weeks amid the stir and bustle of a royal court. I find it hard to believe."

"Believe it. I'm being kind and considerate."

"I know, I know. And I appreciate it. I just find the sudden change hard to believe, that's all."

"I don't think it's such a sudden change. It's not a change at all," said Kedrigern, looking hurt.

"When I think of the fuss and uproar you've made over a simple little jaunt to the top of the mountain . . . Well, enough about this. We'd better start packing."

"I haven't even unpacked," Kedrigern grumped, quickly adding, "but I'm not complaining. It will save time."

"Bring something nice to wear. We're going to be meeting people, and I want you to look your best."

"I'll pack my other brown tunic and an extra pair of trousers."

"I said 'something *nice.*' Dress like a wizard, please. Nobody ever looks at you and knows at once that you're a wizard."

"Good."

"It's not good at all. It's embarrassing."

"Not for me."

"Think of others, then. Orbolon had no idea. And there was that young knight who thought you were a cottager."

"Turll of the Bronze Shield," said Kedrigern, nodding. "Not exactly a paragon of quick perception, that lad."

"That's irrelevant. You're a wizard, and when you're in polite company you should dress the part. I don't mind your wearing nasty old clothes and scuffed boots when we're on the road, but in a royal court you really ought to look your best."

"Why? I don't have to impress anyone. I'm a wizard."

"It's not a matter of impressing anyone, it's a matter of protocol. It's nice to look your best. You might even work better if you dressed more suitably."

"I work better when I'm comfortable."

"You have that nice black outfit, and the good black boots. You'll look very wizardly in that, and it's comfortable. You said so. And wear your medallion so it can be seen. Don't keep it tucked inside your shirt."

"You want me to show off."

"I want you to look distinguished."

"Next thing I know, you'll want me to grow a long white beard."

"Well, that would make you look distinguished."

"It would make me look ancient, that's what it would do. People would think you were traveling around with your great-grandfather. Time enough to think of a beard when I'm getting up near three hundred. Besides, beards are itchy."

"Only when they're first growing."

"Well, you don't expect me to grow one overnight, do you?" Kedrigern frowned, thought for a moment, and added,

"I could if I had to, but I can think of a lot better things to do with my magic. And even when they're fully grown, beards are a nuisance. Things get stuck in them."

"You could wash it."

"Then it gets all fluffy and flies up in your face when you're trying to concentrate."

"Oh, all right, don't grow a beard. But make sure you pack that nice black outfit. And don't forget the black surcoat with the scarlet trim."

"I'll pack it right away, my dear." Kedrigern started from the room, pausing in the doorway to ask, "And what will you take?"

"I'll just have them load the chest of things that Ulurel gave you. Did you know that it's inexhaustible? I keep finding new things in it every time I look. Lovely things, too. And every garment is a perfect fit."

"Ulurel was a sorceress of excellent taste."

"I'd love to have the chance to thank her properly."

"No need for that. Ulurel could read the future. She knows you're grateful."

"All the same, I'd feel better. Oh, Keddie, before you pack, would you speak to Gylorel and let him know that someone will be pruning his upper branches? And tell Tergus that he'll have to finish the job today. And have Orbolon send some men to carry out the chest."

"I will. And I'll tell Belsheer what's happened," said the wizard, turning and heading for the door.

Before leaving, he checked the house plants, but Belsheer was not among them. He went out the front door, and looking toward the meadow he saw Orbolon's men rushing about in what looked, from this distance, to be purposeful and efficient activity: Some tended the horses; others gathered firewood; two were erecting a small tent. As Kedrigern observed their labors, Tergus came into sight, a heavy coil of rope slung over one shoulder like a baldric.

"Ah, there you are, Tergus. Well met," Kedrigern greeted him. "I'd like you to go down to the encampment and ask

Orbolon to send up the wagon and a few men. Princess has a chest of clothing to be loaded.''

"I'll be happy to move anything my lady wants moved, Master Kedrigern.''

"I don't doubt that, Tergus, but you have a full day ahead. You'll have to finish pruning those big oaks today. We leave at sunrise for Kallopane.''

Tergus's eyes rounded in wonder. "Kallopane, Master Kedrigern?''

"That's right.''

"What's Kallopane?''

"It's a kingdom. The king is much indebted to me. Perhaps I'll be able to get you a place in his service.''

"Oh, thank you, Master Kedrigern! Will he want a good huntsman?''

"I'll ask him, Tergus. Now you'd better deliver that message, and then get to your pruning.''

Tergus posted off to the clearing, and Kedrigern proceeded to the two mighty oaks that overspread the arbor to the west of the cottage. Belsheer's sudden appearance gave him something of a start: The transmogrified wizard burst out of the clover, circled Kedrigern's head three times with a very loud drone, then landed precisely on his shoulder. "Lovely clover you have out here,'' Belsheer hummed. He sounded quite content.

"You're rather exposed, aren't you? I thought you'd be keeping close to the house.''

"I'm being very watchful. I've got the hang of these eyes, I think. Anyway, it's worth the risk. The smells, and the flavors . . . I never imagined it would be this much fun.''

"Do you really like being a bee?''

"I love it!''

"Can I take it that you're in no hurry to be despelled?''

"No hurry at all, Brother Kedrigern. I haven't felt so good or enjoyed myself so much for over a century.'' Belsheer gave a little burr of sheer exuberance and went on, "Wicked his intentions may have been, but Grizziscus did me a great service. Next time I see him, I'll give him my heartfelt thanks.''

"Better let me change you back first, or he may wallop you with a broom before you can get a word out."

"That's true. Didn't think of that."

"I'd think about it if I were you, Belsheer. However much fun it is to be a bee, it's a lot more dangerous than being a wizard."

Belsheer buzzed thoughtfully, but said nothing. Kedrigern walked on in silence for a dozen paces, then said, "Princess and I have been invited to the court of Kallopane. We leave at sunrise."

"Decent little kingdom, Kallopane. As I recall, it's to the south. They must have lovely flowers this time of year."

"You're welcome to the house while we're gone. The gardens, too, of course."

"Why, thank you, Brother Kedrigern. But if you have no objection, I'd prefer to go with you to Kallopane."

"You're quite welcome."

"As a bee, of course."

"That's entirely up to you. I felt obliged to point out the hazards of the apian mode, but I would not attempt to force a choice on a colleague."

"I'm sure if you permit me to ride on you, there will be no trouble along the way. Perhaps when we've been in Kallopane for a while, I'll be ready for a change. Would that be an imposition?"

"Not at all. I'll probably be aching for an opportunity to work some good useful magic."

Belsheer gave a soft hum of curiosity and asked, "Aren't you going to Kallopane on business?"

"We've been summoned to receive a reward from Sariax the Incomparable. I helped his son out of some difficulties a few years back, and now he wants to repay me."

"Generously, I hope."

"He seems a generous sort. His messenger gave us each a nice ring as a sample of what to expect once we're in Kallopane. But I do wish he'd sent the whole reward and gotten it over with. I don't much fancy weeks of feasting, and celebration,

and being presented to everyone, and hearing—and telling—
the same stories over and over."

"That can be very boring."

"Very," said Kedrigern with a sigh.

"Still, you never know what may turn up on the way to
Kallopane, or during your stay, or on the way home."

"No. You never know." Kedrigern sighed in a way that
suggested very dim expectations about his forthcoming journey.
Belsheer maintained a sympathetic silence until they were almost within shadow of the two oaks that dominated the arbor
to the west of the cottage. As Kedrigern halted and looked up,
Belsheer lifted off, buzzed, "Until sunrise," and darted arrow-
swift to a patch of wildflowers.

Cupping his hands around his mouth, the wizard called
loudly, "Anlorel! Gylorel! It's Kedrigern. I'd like to speak
with you."

High in the upper branches, lights twinkled sporadically;
they came together, slowly at first, but with increasing speed,
until there was a cluster of lights bright against the dark leaves;
then the cluster drew out into a ribbon of sparkling points of
brilliance that spiraled downward, encircling both trees, and
coalesced before Kedrigern's eyes to become a tiny, beautiful
dryad, who greeted him with a voice as sweet as distant crystal
chimes. As the wizard returned her salute, a deep rumbling
voice filled the air and the upper branches of the larger oak
swayed toward him, while the lower ones dipped in dignified
welcome.

"Is all well with you, wizard?" Gylorel's voice boomed.

"Very well indeed. And you?"

"The winter was hard, but it has been a good spring," the
tree said, and Anlorel added, with a burst of tiny motes of the
palest green light, "We lost a few branches. Nothing serious,
but it's uncomfortable."

"Exactly why I'm here. I've got a man who's going to trim
them, if you have no objections."

"That would be a great kindness," said Gylorel with a cheerful rustle. "I could do with a nice trim."

"I thought I'd best ask you first, so you wouldn't be suspicious and fling him out when he got near the top.''

"Will he care for my wife, too?" Gylorel asked, his deep rolling voice gentled with concern.

"Of course. He'll have to work quickly, though. Princess and I are leaving on a journey at sunrise, and he's coming with us.''

"Another journey? So soon?" Anlorel chimed.

Kedrigern sighed and nodded his head. "Can't be helped, I'm afraid. Would you keep an eye on the place while we're gone? And on Spot?''

"Delighted to," said Anlorel.

"Thank you. And once I'm home again, I'll be staying put for a time. We'll be able to have a nice long chat.''

"We look forward to that. Good traveling, wizard," they said, their voices joined in a melodious harmony, like small bells stirring to the roll of distant thunder.

Kedrigern waved farewell, then turned to trudge back to the cottage. Nothing remained but to pack. He would have Spot prepare one of its specialties for dinner—the little troll was a superb chef when given precise, painstaking instructions—and open a bottle of Vosconu's best wine to accompany it. Tonight would be a feast.

And tomorrow, at sunrise, it was off to Kallopane.

···❧ *Five* ❧···

the king's hospitality

THE JOURNEY TO Kallopane was a pleasant one, all things considered. Except for two mornings of soft intermittent rain, the skies were clear and the days sunny. The little band stopped at no inn, but rested each night at a campsite carefully preselected by Orbolon, at which the wizards' tent was pitched in the choicest spot. Insects were few, and even at midday the heat was not excessive.

Princess greeted each day with delight: Rainy intervals aside, the weather was perfect for flying. Tergus got on famously with Orbolon and his men, and saw to it that the party had fresh game for dinner every evening. After dinner, the travelers gathered for songs and stories around the fire. Kedrigern did not sing, ever; but one evening he unbent and told the tale of Flaine of the Four Fates, one of his personal favorites. Princess yawned frequently during the narrative, but otherwise the story was well received. The next day, several of Orbolon's men told Kedrigern that they had never heard a better yarn in their lives.

All of this bothered Kedrigern and made him feel uneasy. He was traveling, and travel was intrinsically nasty, unpleasant, and uncomfortable; yet everyone was behaving so nicely, and everything was going so smoothly, that he found himself almost enjoying the journey. In fact, if he had not applied himself conscientiously, he might well have been quite merry, and that simply would not do. He made it a point to complain about something every day: either the roads, the weather, the dust, the occasional insect, the campsite, the food, or the pace of their progress—one could always find something—but his heart was not in it. His complaining was not from the heart, as good complaining should be; it was purely ceremonial, something done to keep his hand in. He simply was not as miserable as he usually felt when heading away from his cottage on Silent Thunder Mountain. Several nights he awoke and lay staring into the darkness, wondering if he was going soft.

Of course, Princess was with him, and that made a major difference in his attitude. And they were on their way not to some perilous and unsightly wasteland bristling with macabre enchantments, but to a royal court where they were to be honored, praised, and generously rewarded. That helped. And during their stay in Kallopane they would surely be able to find some happy solution to the problems of Belsheer and Tergus, and thus return home unaccompanied, to peace and solitude. All in all, things could be a lot worse. When one traveled, they usually were.

Even transportation was working out satisfactorily. Princess was on the transparent mare she customarily rode, and Tergus was on a mount provided by Orbolon. Since his enchanted stallion was preoccupied with affairs of the heart, Kedrigern had chosen to ride the shaggy black war horse that once had belonged to the barbarian swordsman Buroc the Depraved. He had always felt misgivings about the horse, which he had named Dudgeon, but the shaggy black was behaving like a model of equine deportment: responsive, tractable, and while not affable, at least nonbelligerent. That was good enough for Kedrigern, and had the pleasant side effect of winning him added respect from Orbolon's men. Horsemen all, they bestowed their admiration as professionals on any man who could handle a barbarian war horse with just the proper mix of mastery and comradeship.

Day followed uneventful day until one morning, as Kedrigern stood by the fire, warming himself against the early chill.

Orbolon approached, and even in the faint light and mist, Kedrigern could see the broad smile on the knight's face.

"A good day to you, Master Kedrigern. I trust you and my lady Princess slept soundly," Orbolon saluted him.

"Pretty well. A bit on the chilly side, isn't it?"

"Most unusual for this time of year. As a rule, we enjoy summer weather by now," said Orbolon in apparent perplexity, extending his hands to the fire.

Kedrigern nodded, chafing his own hands briskly. He would have been surprised by any other response. In a long life filled with travel, he had yet to hear anyone say, "Sorry about this lovely weather. It's usually cold and wet here in May," or "I can't understand why the days are so pleasant. Our spring is always terrible." Bad weather seemed always to be the exception in conversation, even though it was the rule in experience.

After a pause, Orbolon turned to the wizard and said with a smile, "Tonight, though, you will sleep in comfort and luxury."

"We will?"

"You will indeed. We are but a day's ride from the royal palace of Kallopane. We will cross the frontier this morning and be at the palace before sunset."

Kedrigern gave a great sigh of relief. "Wonderful news, Orbolon. Marvelous news."

Beaming at the wizard's words, Orbolon said, "Two men have already been sent ahead with word of our arrival. All of Kallopane will be waiting to greet you."

"That's as may be. I'm more interested in the part about sleeping in comfort and luxury."

"Sheets of purest silk. Pillows of the softest down. Blankets of airy lightness, yet warm as sunbeams."

"Blankets?"

"The evenings are cool in Kallopane, even in summer—a condition that promotes sound and healthful rest."

"I'd better tell Princess. She'll be delighted to hear," Kedrigern said, turning to re-enter his tent. Before he had taken two steps, the flap opened and Princess emerged. She was cloaked for warmth, and her hood was pulled forward, but her smile glowed out of the obscuring garments, piercing the pale mist. "I overheard," she said. "Kallopane by sunset!"

"By sunset," Orbolon repeated.

"Let's not get into that," said Kedrigern. "What's our itinerary?"

"We will pause this morning at the king's hunting lodge. It is a modest place—only a score of servants to attend you—but you will have time to refresh yourselves before the royal carriage conducts you to the palace," Orbolon said.

"And the sooner we leave here, the sooner we arrive there, eh, Orbolon?"

"Exactly so, Master Kedrigern. We depart forthwith."

When he had left, Kedrigern said to Princess, "That's your warmest cloak, my dear. Are you cold?"

"I'm thinking of my wings. I want to keep them limber."

"No need for you to fly, is there? The king's own carriage will be taking us to the palace."

"I know that. I might want to fly from the carriage when we arrive. It makes an impression."

"True," said Kedrigern, nodding. "Pity you never let me get you the knitted wing covers. They're just the thing for weather like this."

"I don't *want* knitted wing covers. They'd make me look like a moth."

"They're very practical."

"No. Maybe *you* don't care if I look like a moth—"

"I care very much!"

"Then stop trying to get me to wear knitted wing covers." Kedrigern shrugged. "I won't mention them again, my dear."

By mid-morning, Princess and Kedrigern were comfortably established in the king's lodge. Early in the afternoon, having bathed and changed and enjoyed a simple but elegant lunch, they settled into the royal carriage and set out for the palace, arriving just as the sun sank behind the tallest tower.

Their reception was all that had been promised. The long

avenue leading from the gates of Kallopane to the palace was lined with cheering, waving crowds who called out their names, shouted words of gratitude, praise, and benediction, tossed flowers into the carriage, and blew kisses at the pair. Well-wishers and the curious lined the rooftops and leaned from upstairs windows. Twin ranks of guardsmen in glittering breast-plates and plumed helmets stood facing one another on the palace steps, and splendidly attired courtiers filled the great hall. Seeing no sign of the royal personage, Princess decided to leave the carriage on foot. Flying could await the proper moment.

As they entered the palace, servants clustered to attend them. When Princess unfurled her wings with a swift flutter that set them flashing under the brilliant light of torches and candelabra, the company gasped and murmured in wonderment. She smiled serenely on the assemblage, took Kedrigern's arm, and fell in behind Orbolon for the procession to the throne.

Kedrigern felt awkward and out of place. He did not like attention, and he was getting more of it right now than he considered healthy or desirable spread out over twenty years' time. True, the cynosure of all eyes was Princess; but those looking at her could not help seeing him, albeit fleetingly and peripherally, and the thought displeased him, believing as he did that a wizard should be a force and not a spectacle. The black outfit he had worn at Princess's urging fit him comfortably enough, but made him feel foppish and affected. He fingered his medallion—worn outside, where it could be seen and com-mented upon—and glanced about furtively.

"Relax," Princess whispered.

"How can I relax with a crowd of people staring at me?"

"They're not staring, they're gazing in awe."

"I consider it staring, and I don't like it."

Three young men in resplendent costume bowed deeply as Princess passed. She smiled upon them. Kedrigern made a little snorting sound of disapproval.

"Don't be rude," Princess said.

"Why not? It seems to be the local custom. It's rude to gawk at strangers, isn't it?"

"We're not strangers, we're guests."

"That only makes it worse. People shouldn't stare at their guests."

"You have no social graces. It's easy to tell you were raised by peasants and a hermit."

"We never gawked at people."

"You never had anyone to gawk at."

Kedrigern drew himself up, looked straight ahead, and said, "I am what I am: a plain blunt wizard."

"That's very obvious."

Two white-haired dignitaries bowed to her, and three very elegantly dressed and attractive young ladies curtseyed to Kedrigern. He nodded and made an awkward gesture of salutation.

"That's better. Try to look as though you do this sort of thing all the time," Princess said, smiling and waving with indiscriminate benevolence.

"What an appalling thought," he said in a pained voice.

"If we got out more, you'd know how to behave."

"I know how to behave. It's these people who don't, with their gaping and gawking. Why couldn't Sariax just send us a wagon piled with treasure? Why did he have to work up all this?"

"Don't be peevish. Kings like to do things on a grand scale."

"Kings like to make everyone line up and mill around and waste a lot of time and energy on silly ceremonies. *That's* what kings like to do."

Princess gave a long-suffering sigh and waved to a group of courtiers. "You'll never learn," she said.

"And they like to see people dress up like coxcombs and jackanapeses. Look at me!"

"For the first time in memory, you look respectable."

"I look like Grodz. Greasy Grodz of Grodzik. Or the Black Jester. All I need is—"

"Oh, look! Handsome and Lazica! Aren't they sweet, Keddie?"

On a dais ahead stood the Handsome Prince of Kallopane and his wife, each with an arm tightly around the other's waist. With their free hand, each of them waved to the crowd, to which they were otherwise oblivious. They whispered together like conspirators. Handsome nibbled at Lazica's ear. She turned to kiss him enthusiastically. The sight of them softened Kedrigern's feelings, and he smiled.

"The love potion is still working, I see," Princess whispered.

"Like magic," he said, winking at her.

A throne was now visible on the dais, above Handsome and Lazica. Orbolon halted and dropped to one knee in obeisance. Upon rising, he stepped aside and with a sweep of his arm, announced, "Great Sariax, Incomparable King of Kallopane and all adjacent lands, regions, precincts and territories high and low, sun-baked and snow-mantled, populous and barren, I have accomplished the mission with which my king has done me the honor of entrusting me. I present to Your Incomparable Majesty Kedrigern and Princess of Silent Thunder Mountain." With that, he backed off, bowing at every backward step.

"Bow nicely," Princess said, curtseying.

The king of Kallopane rose. The assembled court fell silent. Sariax was a man of no more than average height, a bit thick about the middle and generously jowled, and while the resemblance could be seen between him and his son Handsome, his own version of the family features was no more than plain. But Sariax had a voice like ringing iron and an air of command that more than overcame his unprepossessing appearance.

"Goodly wizards, we bid you welcome," he said. "You have done great service to Kallopane, and your deed shall be rewarded in such manner as befits a king."

"Your Majesty is most kind," said Princess.

"And generous," Kedrigern added.

"All Kallopane is in your debt. We have proclaimed seven days of festivity in your honor. We begin with a great feast this very night. In days to come there will be dancing, feats of arms, magical illusions, buffoons, minstrels, jesters, recitations, masquerades, banquets, and—" Sariax stopped abruptly when Princess gave her wings an excited little flap and rose a handbreadth off the ground, but he recovered at once and concluded, "other delights too numerous to mention.

But now, kindly wizards, approach the throne that we may greet you properly.''

Arm in arm, Kedrigern and Princess ascended the dais. Sariax took their hands and smiled warmly, but his eyes betrayed uneasiness. ''My lady Princess has little gauzy wings,'' he said.

''I do indeed, Your Majesty.''

''Such wings are customarily found on fairies, are they not?''

''I believe they are, Your Majesty,'' said Princess, and Kedrigern nodded to indicate his concurrence in this opinion.

''But you yourself are not a fairy,'' said Sariax.

''Oh, no, Your Majesty, not at all. I'm just an ordinary princess.''

''Hardly ordinary, my dear—but definitely a princess,'' Kedrigern added.

''Thank you. Thank you both for clarifying the matter,'' Sariax said, his relief evident in his voice and expression. ''The sight of those wings gave me a turn. The last woman I saw with wings like that was a bog-fairy, and she turned my youngest boy into a toad. I was doing my best to be gracious, but she took offense at something I said, and before I knew what was happening Handsome was a toad and then he and the bog-fairy had vanished. Since then, I've been uneasy at the prospect of dealing with a woman who has wings.''

''Understandably,'' Kedrigern murmured.

''I assure Your Majesty that I am not a fairy, bog or otherwise. In fact, I suffered a misfortune similar to your son's at the hands of a bog-fairy,'' said Princess.

Enlightenment and relief shone on Sariax's features. ''Then you were the princess who became a toad.''

''I was one of them.''

Befuddlement returned to the king's visage. ''One of them? How many toads were there?''

''Four, counting your son.''

''But not all at the same time,'' Kedrigern added.

''And not all because of bog-fairies, either.''

Sariax looked from one to the other several times, then said, ''Perhaps you will tell me the whole story before you depart.

Handsome has given me an account, but I confess I am still confused. All those toads . . . and all of them princes or princesses.''

"One was only a knight," Princess said.

"Ah. I see. Yes, I do hope you'll tell me all about it. But now the feast awaits. Let us to the banquet hall. The queen will join us there."

The hall was splendid. The feast was magnificent. Dish after dish of superbly prepared food came from the royal kitchen until the table sagged under the weight, and the tabletop could not be seen beneath the abundance of gold and silver vessels and the lavish decorations. A forest of greenery, rivers of sparkling wine, confectionery castles, and tiny figures of pastry dough formed a miniature world among the platters, salvers, bowls, tureens, and dishes of various sizes that covered the board.

Kedrigern and Princess sat at the high table, on either side of Sariax. An empty place, the queen's, was between Kedrigern and the king. On the wizard's other side was a large overdressed woman who regaled him in a confidential manner with exceptionally dull stories of cures for warts, wens, and corns worked by a second cousin of her husband who practised wizardry in his spare time. Kedrigern nodded frequently, said, "Ah!" or "Indeed?" at regular intervals, and concentrated on the food, which was delicious beyond all expectation. It matched Spot's cooking at its best.

The queen did not appear, and next day Sariax said something about Incorruptible's youngest coming down with toothache, which appeared to be the explanation of the queen's absence. At the even more elaborate banquet given on their second night, they were informed that Methodical's oldest daughter's second son had caught a chill, and the queen could not leave him. She also missed the tumblers on the third night, the trained animals on the fourth, and the jugglers on the fifth. Princess was growing concerned about her when, on the sixth night of their visit, she slipped into her place at Sariax's side just as the servants were removing the pastilles, sugared almonds, preserves, jellies, glazed fruits, and sugared fennel of the final course. Giving Sariax a peck on the cheek, she squeezed Princess's hand warmly and then turned to Kedrigern.

"Can't stay long. Just wanted to thank you," she said breathlessly.

"We are honored to meet Your Majesty, however briefly," said the wizard.

"You've done wonders for my Handsome. Had to tell you that. Wonders. And that's a lovely girl you found for him. She's devoted to the dear boy."

"He's quite likeable."

"Oh, adorable, absolutely adorable. But you know what people are like. Always finding fault. Jealousy, that's what it is. But he showed them all, thanks to you," said the queen, rising.

"Must Your Majesty leave us so soon?"

"It's Circumspect's boy. Colic. Must see him before he starts screaming for me and upsets the whole palace. Oh, I almost forgot." She handed Kedrigern a soft leather pouch that clinked delightfully in his hand. "Well done, wizard." And off she went.

As Kedrigern mused over the sudden appearance and equally sudden disappearance of the queen, whose name was still unknown to him, Sariax leaned across the empty place and said, "I'm glad you had a chance to meet Jussibee. She doesn't get to many state functions. Very involved with the children. And the grandchildren. Fond of the youngsters, she is."

"I gathered that."

"How she can still be fond of children after having twelve of them, I don't know. But there you are."

"She seems very kind. And generous."

"Too generous, if you ask me. She'd give away her crown if I didn't keep my eye on her."

Kedrigern squeezed the pouch. He felt through the thin supple leather the outline of large coins, and smiled. He had a fondness for bounteous royalty, the more unstinting the better. In his view, "too generous" was a term inapplicable to a ruler.

"Oh, by the way, wizard—" Sariax glanced about, then beckoned Kedrigern closer. Lowering his voice, he went on,

"I'd like to speak with you in private. I've been meaning to, but the time slips by. Tomorrow's the last day of the festivities, and then I'll be off to tour the western defenses with Indomitable's oldest boy. Come to the state chamber at noon tomorrow."

"At noon, Your Majesty."

Sariax gave a single curt nod of acknowledgment and turned his attention elsewhere. Kedrigern popped a sugared almond into his mouth and glanced at Princess. He could not catch her eye. She was chatting with three bedazzled young men, and he did not wish to interrupt. She enjoyed court gossip, the bustle and crowd at feasts, the moonstruck attention of handsome young courtiers, and all the routine of palace life. It was, after all, a part of her childhood and youth.

He realized that she had said nothing about her returning memories since their departure for Kallopane, and wondered at her silence on the topic. It seemed unlikely that memories would begin to return and then abruptly stop; yet he was sure that if some significant fact of her past had suddenly come into her head, he would be the first to hear of it. She was not in the habit of keeping secrets from him.

Perhaps, he speculated, there had been a slow, steady trickle of minutiae that she had not thought worth mentioning—a cherished toy, a bedtime song, a summer outing, a favorite pet—that sort of thing. Perhaps she was quietly and privately assembling a mosaic of her early days, intending to reveal it only when complete. The present surroundings might be just the thing to provoke remembrance of things past, being of a nature similar to the world of her upbringing. A king, a queen, a palace, courtiers and court protocol, ritual and ceremony, lavish feasts and elaborate entertainment had once been part of her daily life; present events might echo past experience and stir up memories long dormant under the shock of repeated enchantment and disenchantment. Perhaps she was so involved in the present that she had forgotten that she had forgotten all that she had forgotten, and it would come back in a rush once they returned to the peace and solitude of Silent Thunder Mountain. These were deep and complex matters, beyond the scope of wizardry. One could do little but wait and see.

Meanwhile, the food was superb, the accommodations luxurious, the living comfortable, the queen generous, and the king promising to be so. Princess was enjoying herself, Belsheer was reveling in the royal gardens, Tergus was making friends everywhere, and no one was bothering Kedrigern for free magical advice. His worst moments so far had been spent in the company of a windy old minister of works who had gone on interminably through one long dinner about fen drainage and moat sanitation; otherwise, the stay in Kallopane had been pleasant and relaxing. Annoying as it was to admit it, even to himself, he was having a good time. On the morrow, in his conference with Sariax, he expected to reap the reward of his service to the prince. And once tomorrow was over, they would be preparing to return to Silent Thunder Mountain.

This night's entertainment was minstrels and an illusionist. The musicians were already gathering in the center of the room, tuning up, taking position, waving and bowing to admirers. Kedrigern sat back, stretched out his legs, and sighed with contentment. This journey was turning out remarkably well. Tomorrow could only make it better.

·⋅⊰ Six ⊱⋅·

the king's dilemma

"I DO WISH you could come with me," Princess said as she fastened her cloak. "It's a lovely day for a picnic."

"A glorious day, my dear. But when monarchs summon—" Kedrigern shrugged, extending his palms in a gesture signifying the futility of questioning one's duty to the crown.

"This may be your only chance to meet the royal grandchildren. Queen Jussibee will be so disappointed."

"I'm bitterly disappointed myself."

"It's hard to tell from that big grin on your face."

"I'm thinking of the reward, my dear. I always grin when I think of lavish rewards."

"Don't get your hopes up. Jussibee has already rewarded us."

"A mere purse of gold. A trifle, considering what we did for her youngest son, the apple of her eye. I expect Sariax to outdo himself."

"Seven days of festivity, two lovely rings, and forty gold pieces is hardly stingy," said Princess. "Sariax may have other reasons for wanting to see you."

"Other topics of conversation may well arise, but I'm certain the main reason for this conference is to recognize and reward our benefaction to Handsome."

"Then why doesn't Sariax want to see both of us?" Princess asked, pausing at the door.

He hesitated before replying, "He knows of the queen's plans, and would not deprive his grandchildren or his wife of the pleasure of your company. Surely that's obvious."

"I wouldn't call it obvious. It's possible, I suppose. But I should think the little princelings have seen their fill of princesses and would like to meet a wizard."

"You're a wizard, my dear."

She shook her head. "To them, I'll be just another princess."

"You have wings," he reminded her.

"I'll be a princess with wings. They won't be impressed. They want to see a wizard. All children do."

"Well, it can't be helped," said Kedrigern, kissing her and then opening the door. "Give the little cherubs a hug for me," he said in farewell.

No sooner had she disappeared round the far corner of the corridor than he remembered that he had intended to ask about her memory. Too late now. He would ask her tonight, before the grand culminating feast. Or perhaps after. Yes, after. The entertainment on this last night was to be the recitation of a heroic poem based on the deeds of Tasarando the Orphan, a legendary figure in Kallopane and the surrounding lands. A good rousing tale of chivalry and derring-do might give Princess's memory just the jog it needed.

Kedrigern was admitted to the state chamber precisely at noon. It was a long narrow room, with most of the space at one end taken up by a large round table and several chairs. A sideboard stood against the far wall, with a servant at either side. Sariax sat alone at the table, which was bare except for a single silver goblet.

Waving Kedrigern to a chair, the king gestured to a servant, who brought a second goblet. He placed it before the wizard and filled it with deep ruby wine. When the servant had returned to his post, Sariax raised his own goblet.

"The king drinks to Kedrigern—his health, prosperity, and continued success," he said.

Kedrigern smiled and nodded to show his appreciation, and sipped the wine. It was very good. He leaned back in his chair, eager to hear how Sariax planned to implement his toast to prosperity. Land and castles? A bother. Titles and decorations? Empty show. A place in the royal household? Unthinkable. A cask of this excellent wine? Good. A great big sack of gold coins, a chest of emeralds, a bag of pearls the size of plums? Better. Much better. Just the thing. Having roughed out his parameters of remuneration, he awaited the king's words.

Setting down the goblet, Sariax leaned forward and in a frank down-to-earth manner said, "I've seen the results of your work, and I don't mind admitting that I'm impressed."

"Your Majesty is most generous."

"I speak the plain truth. I had my doubts about that boy all along. His nurses spoiled him, his mother spoiled him, his brothers spoiled him, the people of Kallopane spoiled him— even I spoiled him. We couldn't help ourselves. He was a beautiful baby, a charming child, and he grew up to be a splendid-looking young man. Of all my sons, he was the handsome one. But it was all skin deep. Underneath his magnificent facade was the shallowest, silliest, most egocentric, empty-headed, vain, worthless twit I've ever met. It was almost a relief when that bog-fairy turned him into a toad and whisked him away. But now—why, he's a changed man."

"Enchantment will do that."

Sariax shook his head. "Don't be self-effacing. Enchantment can change a man into a toad and a toad back into a man, but I never before encountered magic that could turn an obnoxious popinjay into a devoted son, a loving husband and father, a loyal brother, the soul of courtesy, the paragon of princely deportment, and the model of courtliness and chivalry. You've done an outstanding job."

With lowered eyes, Kedrigern said, "Your Majesty is most kind. Surely the lovely Lazica deserves some credit."

"She sings your praises as loudly as he does. Oh, Lazica's a lovely girl, and she's been a good influence on the lad, but she gives you and your wife all the credit for making him what he is today and bringing them together."

Kedrigern made a small, self-deprecating gesture and sipped his wine. This was going better than he had hoped. At a signal from Sariax, the servant refilled both goblets and whisked off to his place by the sideboard. Wizard and king raised their goblets and drank.

"You've done wonders for Handsome, Master Kedrigern, and I will see to it that you're suitably rewarded."

"I thank Your Majesty."

"And I'm wondering—seeing that you're here in Kallopane, and may find the time passing rather more slowly than you like—I'm wondering if you could do as much for Formidable as you did for Handsome."

"Formidable, Your Majesty?"

"My tenth son. He's Formidable. Only he hasn't been, lately."

"Hasn't been what?"

"Formidable. And right now, the kingdom needs someone formidable. Bold and Intrepid would have taken care of this matter without hesitation, but . . . well, no point in talking about them. So we need Formidable, and I'm hoping that you can help him live up to his name and do his duty for Kallopane."

Kedrigern scratched his chin, pondered the king's words for a moment, then said, "Am I correct in assuming that your son is Formidable by name but not by nature, and you wish me to bring his name and nature into agreement?"

"Formidable isn't his name, it's his label. That's the custom here in Kallopane. Perhaps I'd better explain," said the king.

"I think that would help."

"Very well, then. More wine?"

"No, thank you."

Sariax pushed his own goblet to one side, but still within reach, and then leaned back and stretched out his legs, crossing them at the ankles in the manner of a man preparing to deliver a long, leisurely tale. Kedrigern adopted a similar posture and settled down to listen. He would have preferred to hear elaborate descriptions of the treasures to be lavished upon him in gratitude, but he knew that that would come in time, and if he could work a bit of beneficial magic for Sariax in the interim, so much the better.

"My father, king of Kallopane before me, was a very wise man, wizard. He traveled widely, observed closely, and thought long and hard on the principles of good governance. One precept he learned was that people generally live up to what's expected of them. He found that if you tell a person, from his earliest days, that he's brave, or clever, or trustworthy, the person will grow up certain that he's brave, or clever, or trustworthy—as the case may be—and so will everyone around him, and as a result, the person will actually *be* brave, clever, or trustworthy," Sariax began.

"A unique and fascinating theory," Kedrigern said.

"No mere theory. He put it into practice. As his firstborn son, I was prince royal, heir to the throne of Kallopane. He intended me to be a first-rate ruler, so from the cradle I was known as the Incomparable Prince. When my brother was born, my father determined to make him my Lord High Chancellor; consequently, he was called the Wise Prince. My youngest brother was to be Grand Marshal of the Forces. He became the Invincible Prince. As things turned out, I have been an ideal monarch, my Lord High Chancellor's decrees have been the model in all the neighboring kingdoms, and the Grand Marshal has fought sixty-one battles and never known defeat."

"A striking vindication of your father's views," said the wizard.

"So striking was it that I resolved to follow the same method with my own children. My firstborn son was called the Magnificent Prince of Kallopane. Next came twins. Perceiving that the duties of the Lord High Chancellor's office had become burdensome and unwieldy, I decided to divide the position when the time came, separating administrative and legal duties. The administrative duties were to go to the Methodical Prince, legal to the Circumspect. My fourth son was called the Indomitable Prince, and given to my brother the Grand Marshal to raise and educate. My fifth son I called the Amiable Prince, and destined for ambassadorial duties. The sixth I called the Incorruptible Prince."

"To become Lord Treasurer."

"Of course."

"A brilliant stroke, Your Majesty."

Sariax acknowledged the compliment with a faint smile and a light wave of the hand. He cleared his throat and took a sip of wine before proceeding. "By this time, with the key positions accounted for, I saw the need for long-range planning. Accordingly, I called my seventh son the Philosophical Prince and set him to the study of philosophy. My eighth and ninth sons were another set of twins. Sensible of the people's craving for adventure and romance, I called them the Bold Prince and the Intrepid Prince, and filled them from childhood with tales of the exploits of heroes. They would devote themselves to knight-errantry, roaming the world in search of opportunities for heroism and spreading the glory of Kallopane. My tenth son, the Formidable Prince, was intended for heroic feats closer to home, such as the slaying of local dragons and the subduing of ogres. Worldly matters I now felt were adequately covered. My eleventh son I called the Pious Prince and sent to a monastery, where he now prays unceasingly for his family and the kingdom. And when the twelfth son was born, my wife and I felt that it was time to spruce up a bit, so our twelfth, and as it turned out, our last son, was called the Handsome Prince of Kallopane."

"Do your sons have names, Your Majesty?"

"Of course they do. My boys want for nothing. But we use their names so seldom that scarcely anyone remembers them— even the princes themselves. It's much easier to refer to them as Handsome, Pious, Formidable, and so forth."

"I'm sure it is. And it would appear that this theory of cognominal influence has proven effective."

"With everyone but Formidable, and his problem is of recent origin. That's why I want you to do something for him. And quickly. There's a need for his services out beyond our eastern territories," said the king, drawing in his legs, leaning forward, and gazing intently at the wizard. "A monster out there wants slaying. It's not in our kingdom yet, but I see no sense in waiting. I want Formidable to handle the matter."

Kedrigern placed his elbows on the table and pressed his fingertips together. He frowned thoughtfully and said, "If the matter is truly pressing, it would seem that Your Majesty has other resources."

"No, I don't. Indomitable is on a punitive expedition against the hill people. He could be gone for years."

"What of Intrepid and Bold, the heroic twins?"

Sariax lowered his gaze. "Some years ago, Intrepid went off to do great deeds in the Desert of Horrors. Something ate him. Bold rode off to avenge his brother. It ate him, too."

"I'm sorry to hear that, Your Majesty."

Sariax shrugged. "If you call your sons Bold and Intrepid, you have to expect things like that." He sighed, rose from his chair, and paced the room. He returned to the table, but did not seat himself. "There's no one for this job but Formidable. Magnificent, Methodical, Circumspect, Amiable, and Incorruptible are all settled down; they have their duties to the kingdom, and their estates and families to worry about. Besides, they're all too fat to get into their armor. Philosophical is up north at school, getting another degree. He's not a fighter, anyway. More like an old Roman than one of us. Pious is out of the question. Handsome won't leave his wife's side for a minute. I've never seen such devotion. So it has to be Formidable."

"It would appear so. And if I understand Your Majesty correctly, there is some impediment to Formidable's acting."

"That's right, wizard. He still looks plenty formidable, and he can cleave through plate armor and chain mail with one mighty blow of his great sword Embrenor, but he's lost the will to be formidable. His heart just isn't in it. To put it bluntly, I think he's afraid of monsters."

"Most people are," Kedrigern reminded the monarch.

"My son is a strong and stalwart prince, a superb horseman, master of every weapon, inured to hardship, scornful of pain, contemptuous of weakness, eager for glory. He's not supposed to fear monsters, he's supposed to slay them. I want you to work a spell and give him the courage of a lion."

"Lions are afraid of monsters, too."

"You know what I mean, wizard."

"Yes, I think I do. But this isn't really my line of magic. I specialize in disenchantment and counterspelling. Now, if your son is under some kind of enchantment . . . Has he been behaving in an odd manner?"

"Aside from not going off to kill the monster, he's been perfectly normal."

"I see. Has he refused to confront the creature?"

The king's eyes narrowed. His face went crimson and his jaw thrust forward. "Refuse? *Refuse?!*" He brought his fist down hard, making the goblets jump. "I am his king and his father! He dare not refuse!"

"Of course not. Sorry, Your Majesty."

"But he shilly-shallies. He dawdles. He temporizes. First he needs more practice with the lance, then he wants a special shield that has to be forged by a very slow process, then his war horse goes lame, then he can't find his sword, and when he does find it it's all blunted and rusted, and then he sprains his wrist—and all the while, the monster is out there destroying villages and eating people." Again, Sariax paced the room, head lowered, muttering to himself. After three circuits, he stopped before the table and said soberly, "He's not a bad boy, wizard, and he's certainly no coward. At heart he's still formidable. He just needs a push in the right direction."

"I will provide whatever pushing is necessary."

"Do it immediately. I leave on my tour of the western outposts in two days, and I want this matter settled before I go."

"It shall be so," said Kedrigern. He did not stir.

"You will find me most grateful," said Sariax.

Kedrigern rose, his expression earnest. "Where will I find the Formidable Prince?"

"In the armory, most likely. If not there, he'll be in the tiltyard. Help him, wizard."

"Consider him helped, Your Majesty."

The way to the armory took Kedrigern past the royal stables, where his attention was caught by the sight of an unusual creature frisking about in the interior shadows. He entered the

stable for a closer look, and exclaimed with delight at the sight
of a parti-colored foal with a slender trunk. Its head and legs
were a pale sky blue; its body was irregularly striped in red,
yellow, and green; its trunk was violet, with slender bands of
creamy white. The moment it saw him, the foal hurried to
thrust its trunk into his tunic in search of dainties. Laughing,
Kedrigern stroked the appendage gently.

A stablehand entered, looked on for a moment, and then
said, "Quite a little filly, isn't she, Master?"

"Indeed she is. Do you still have her sire?"

"Oh, aye, we do. He's the magic stallion as brought our
Prince Handsome and his bride home from the enchanted
places. We wouldn't let him go for the world."

"Has he sired any others?"

"Oh, aye, he has. The twin colts in the end stall," said the
stablehand, pointing to the rear.

"Are they as colorful as this one?"

"Well, one's blue and green with orange stripes and red
dots, and a long purple trunk. The other is black."

"Ah. So the magical characteristics don't always breed
true."

The stablehand stared at him blankly for a moment, then
said, "If you say so, Master."

"What I mean is, the foals don't always resemble their
father."

"That's right, Master. Not all of them. Some of them look
like their dam."

With a final pat on the filly's trunk and a wave to the stablehand, Kedrigern took his leave and proceeded to the armory.
His step was light. Things were going well, and he was in a
good mood.

An emboldening spell was a fast, straightforward piece of
work, and Sariax had been very clear about showing his gratitude. A bit more specificity regarding the amounts involved
would have been to Kedrigern's liking, but kings were noto-
riously hard to pin down; almost as bad as prophets in that
respect. No need for concern, though, he told himself. Once
Formidable went galloping out the gate, lance at the ready,

eyes blazing, battle cry echoing off the walls, Sariax would be scattering gold around like confetti. Best to trust to paternal pride and impulsive generosity. And in another day—two at most—he would be returning to Silent Thunder Mountain for a leisurely summer. And there was every possibility that in a few years he would have a stable of silver-horned, fire-eyed black steeds, and a few fine grays, as well.

He walked on, dreamily smiling at thoughts of home, and when he was about fifty paces from the armory he saw the doors opening wide. He halted, and as he stood watching, a pair of husky men emerged, staggering under the weight of a thick iron bar. Behind them came two more, straining to carry a shield of immense size, and then two more bearing a sword almost as tall as a man. In their wake a towering figure followed with long strides.

The first pair of armorers affixed the iron bar horizontally between two posts set in the ground close to where the wizard stood. The second pair mounted the shield on a heavy tripod nearby. The third pair stopped and held out the sword. The big man stripped off his shirt, tossed it to a servant, and drew the sword from its plain iron scabbard.

For the next two minutes he put on a display of swordsmanship whose like the wizard had never seen. He whirled the great blade overhead, under his legs, around his back, switching smoothly from hand to hand, slashing sometimes one-handed and sometimes two-handed, to the side, overhead, underhand, backhand; at last, with a lunge and a great cry, he hewed the iron bar in two with an upward stroke and the shield in half with the downstroke before the pieces of the bar had touched the ground. He sighted carefully down the blade, turning it slowly to inspect the edge for nicks. With a curt, "Sharp as ever," he slammed the blade home in the scabbard and held out a hand for his shirt.

"Formidable!" Kedrigern cried.

"Yes. And you?" replied the swordsman.

"I am Kedrigern of Silent Thunder Mountain."

The swordsman's hard features softened into a smile of pleasure. "The wizard who aided my brother Handsome! Welcome to Kallopane. And my thanks for your aid to our family.''

"I'm always glad to be of assistance.''

Formidable gave him an appraising look. "Is this mere politeness you speak, or are you truly willing to help?''

"You need only ask,'' said the wizard. He had to struggle to contain his delight. The lad was not merely approachable, he was as cooperative as one could wish. He *wanted* to be helped. An already promising situation was improving by the minute.

"You have been sent by my father, the king, have you not?'' asked the prince.

"I have. He is convinced—''

Formidable raised a hand to silence him. "Best we converse in private. There is a shady spot behind the armory. Join me in a light repast.''

At the prince's behest, a servant dashed to the kitchen. Formidable pulled his shirt over his muscular shoulders and chest, and saying only, "Come,'' set out with long, even strides for the far side of the armory.

There, under a spreading chestnut tree, stood a rude table and two benches. Wizard and prince seated themselves, and Formidable laid one corded forearm on the table, cupped his chin in the other hand, and sighed.

"My father, the king, wishes me to slay The Great Crawling Loathliness of Moodymount. He has sent you to urge me on, using magic if necessary. Is that not so?'' he said.

"Your father mentioned a monster he wants you to slay, but he didn't tell me the creature's name. I assume it's the one you mentioned.''

"It is. It comes down from Moodymount every few years, ravages for a time, then goes back up the mountain. It is said to be indestructible.''

"If that's your problem, I can help.''

"I need no help of that kind. The great sword Embrenor is enchanted.''

"I see.'' There was a long silence, then Kedrigern said, as tactfully as possible, "I've had to face several dreadful creatures in my time, and I know that feeling in the pit of the stomach when you're just sitting and waiting. But I can help with that, too.''

''Do you think I fear this creature?'' the prince asked in a low, even voice.

''It's nothing to be ashamed of. Fear is the only sensible reaction to the prospect of facing an indestructible monster.''

Formidable laughed loudly. It was a reassuringly good-natured laugh. ''Then I am not sensible, wizard. I do not fear monsters. I fear nothing,'' he said.

''In that case, go kill this thing and make your father happy.''

''It is not that simple. I lack motivation.''

''That's nothing to worry about. Once you see the thing face to face, you'll be motivated.''

''But why face it at all? This particular monster is not even one of ours. It ravages a kingdom of which little is known. Why should I seek out monsters to slay? I have slain four so far, and I am no happier or better for it. If I slay the Great Crawling Loathliness of Moodymount, what difference will it make? I ask you, wizard—what is the point?''

''Survival?'' Kedrigern suggested.

''What about the monster's survival? At the rate things are going, monsters will soon be extinct. Have they no right to live?''

Formidable's impassioned question touched Kedrigern on a tender spot. Some of his best and oldest friends were what narrow-minded folk would certainly classify as monsters. He was on good terms with several dragons; his loyal and useful household servant was a troll; he had been generous to giant, demon, and afreet in situations in which others would have been severe. Perceiving the wizard's hesitation, the prince pressed his argument.

''Monsters are being slain at a cruel rate. Soon the last monster will vanish from our midst. Think of it, Master Kedrigern—a world without monsters!''

''Some people would consider that an improvement. Monsters do a lot of harm, you know.''

Formidable dismissed that observation with a gesture. ''They are misunderstood.''

"That may be, but they still do damage. This one of yours is destroying villages and eating people. There's no excuse for that kind of behavior."

"A village or two, a few dozen peasants—they can be replaced. A monster is unique."

"What's made you so sensitive about monster rights, Formidable? Have you been talking to someone?"

The prince nodded. "My brother Philosophical. He came home from school at Christmas time and spoke to me of his studies. In one moment of enlightenment, I perceived the absurdity of a life spent in meaningless monster-slaying, and determined to abandon it forthwith."

"Why don't you just tell this to your father?"

"He would be enraged. I am not the Philosophical Prince. I am the Formidable Prince, and I am expected to remain formidable."

His few conversations with Sariax inclined Kedrigern to agree with the prince: his father, like most kings, was not a man to be sweetly reasonable. They were both silent for a time, then Kedrigern said, "Look at it this way. This thing may soon be eating your father's subjects. It's a threat to his kingdom."

"The threat is insignificant. If we ignore the creature, it will soon go away for another ten or twenty years. Perhaps longer."

"How can you be sure?"

"It has always done so."

"But how do you know it will do so this time? Have you spoken to it?" retorted the wizard. No sooner were those words out than he knew he had found the solution to the king's problem and the prince's dilemma. He clapped a hand on Formidable's forearm. It was like slapping an oaken beam. "That's what you must do, my boy! Go out there and speak to this creature—if you're going to stand up for monsters, you have to start talking to them."

"That never occurred to me," said Formidable, bemused.

"Surely you can see that it's essential. You have to move quickly, too, or the thing will go away. If it stays away too many years, it may have a whole new generation of heroic monster-slayers to deal with when it returns."

"Yes. That is true," the prince said. His interest seemed to be growing.

"And as you yourself pointed out, there aren't that many others around. This may be your last chance for a conversation with a monster."

"Very likely. All too likely," said Formidable, rising. "I must leave at once."

"Tomorrow morning is soon enough."

Formidable sat down again. "Yes, of course. I will need time to gather my thoughts. And I must go unarmed."

"Oh, dear me, no. Not unarmed."

"But I go in friendship."

Kedrigern shook his head emphatically. "You must not give the monster a false sense of security. Your goal is to save it from extinction, is it not?"

"Indeed it is."

"Then you must acquaint it with the danger it faces. Show it your enchanted sword and your lance, and your mace, and bow, and battle-axe. Hack up a few trees, smash a few boulders. Then it will take you seriously, and you'll be able to communicate your views more effectively."

"Do you think, then, that I should travel with an armed band?"

"Well, you don't want to overdo it, either. There's such a thing as making a point too strongly."

"True, true. I must go alone."

"That's overdoing it in the opposite direction."

Formidable was silent for a moment, thinking, and then he reached out and clasped the wizard's forearm in an iron grip. "Come with me. You can help me to communicate with the Great Crawling Loathliness in the proper way."

"I'd love to, but I can't make it."

Formidable withdrew his hand. His face fell. Despite his great size and bulging muscles, he looked like a woebegone little boy.

Kedrigern relented slightly. He still had no intention of setting off on a monster quest when he was only a day or two from returning home, but there were other ways to help. "If

I may make a suggestion . . ." he said. Formidable at once beamed and nodded to affirm his willingness to hear. "Take one strong trustworthy man who knows the ways of trail and forest. My own man Tergus—a huntsman of long experience— has expressed a wish to enter the service of a prince. I'll send him to you this very day."

"You would give up your own servant?"

"Your need is greater."

For nearly a full minute, Formidable said nothing; he merely stared at Kedrigern with an expression of great solemnity on his strong features. When he spoke, his voice was subdued. "You are generous as well as wise, Master Kedrigern. I am very much in your debt," he said.

"Happy to be of service."

"How can I hope to repay you?"

Kedrigern caught sight of three servants heading their way, bearing trays and tankards. "Let's discuss it over lunch," he said.

⚜ *Seven* ⚜

memories, memories

LATER THAT AFTERNOON, following a leisurely postprandial stroll around the walls of Kallopane to assist his digestion, Kedrigern returned to his chamber. He was quite pleased with his handling of the day's affairs.

Formidable was now eager to seek the Great Crawling Loathliness of Moodymount. If he could persuade the thing to reform, it would be a great feat. If he could not, he had his enchanted sword and his impressive martial skills to protect him. Whichever way the meeting went, the outcome was sure to please Sariax; and Sariax, pleased, was sure to be generous.

Tergus now had a place in the service of a prince, just the sort of position he had hoped for. He, too, would be grateful, once he was informed. Best of all, he would not now be spending the next few months hanging about the cottage on Silent Thunder Mountain, getting in Spot's way.

The only remaining problem was the beehood of Belsheer; and that was properly a matter for Belsheer himself to decide. The old wizard had not been much in evidence since their arrival in Kallopane. Perhaps he was still browsing the royal gardens, which were in full bloom; perhaps he had met a queen, and was making plans to settle in a hive of his own, and raise a swarm of little workers. It would be a loss to wizardry if he did so, but the choice was his. If a man could not choose for himself after nearly five centuries, there was little justice in the world, thought Kedrigern.

He tugged off his boots and flopped heavily on the bed. The day was at the sleepy mid-afternoon hour and a long night lay before him. The feast was sure to go on well into morning, and the tale of Tasarando the Orphan might last until dawn. Once those trouvères got started, they were all but impossible to shut up. Kedrigern enjoyed a good lyric poem or ballad, and appreciated clever rhyming and wordplay; he was not fond of epics, chivalric romances, or *chansons de geste*, all of which struck him as much too long to be pleasurable. And sloppy, as well. The authors of those interminable works always threw in a lot of magic and never got it quite right. One would think that a poet who took the time to write fifty thousand lines of elegant verse would take the additional time to check the facts; but one would be wrong, because poets never did. They had Merlin doing and saying things no wizard would dream of doing or saying. They made sorceresses and enchanters work astonishing feats and then had them commit silly errors simply to make blustering heroes look good. Trouvères were a nuisance. Give me a plain old minstrel anytime, thought Kedrigern.

The prospect of a long evening filled with inaccurate verses made him yawn. Clearly, it was time for a nap. He settled down comfortably, and was fast asleep almost at once.

Restful dreams of vague but pleasurable import were disturbed by a hum that grew to a drone that became a bombinating intrusion that finally brought him awake. He opened his eyes to the spectacle of a large bee bobbing spiritedly above his face.

"I was beginning to wonder if everything was all right," he said, raising himself on his elbows. The bee responded with inarticulate buzzing and spasmodic darting about. "Is anything wrong? You are Belsheer, aren't you?"

Amid bursts of bee noise came the words, "Villains! Assassins! I barely escaped alive!"

"Who tried to murder you?"

"Nasty little brutes—violent—Sister Princess saw it all!"

"I don't understand. What has Princess to do with it?"

Belsheer was in a state that made meaningful verbal communication impossible. His movements became ever more agitated, and Kedrigern began to fear that in his excitement, he would do himself harm.

"Belsheer, old friend, you must compose yourself. Why don't you relax in that bowl of flowers? Princess can tell me the whole story when she returns," said Kedrigern.

The angry bee sounds settled to a steady thrum. Belsheer hovered steadily before Kedrigern's face for a moment, then darted to the bowl, where he vanished into the bright blooms. With a relieved exhalation of breath, Kedrigern fell back on the bed. Here was a puzzle. Who would want to murder Belsheer? And why would Princess stand idly by if an attempt were made? He stared at the ceiling, pondering. He closed his eyes to assist concentration. In a very short time, he was again asleep.

This time it was Princess who woke him. She looked down with an expression that suggested a much less than perfect picnic.

"How was your day, my dear?" Kedrigern asked, following the question with a great yawn.

"It was terrible! The royal grandchildren are the worst pack of brats I've ever seen in my life!" She flung aside her cloak and folded her arms tightly. Her eyes flashed. "I was trying to be nice. Auntie Princess, all smiles and hugs. The youngest one fell and scraped his knee. I took him for a little jaunt, just to treetop height, to take his mind off the scrape. As soon as I touched ground, the other princelings insisted that I take them up, too. All of them, one by one, in order of precedence. Magnificent's youngest son—a fat obnoxious thing of twelve— demanded that I carry him three times around the walls, because *his* father outranked all *their* fathers. Oh, I was furious with them!" she said, stamping her foot.

"What did Jussibee say?"

"She was no help at all! She expected me to do it! And when I refused, she promised those little monsters that she'd summon their favorite acrobats and have them perform every night for a week."

"Sariax mentioned that she's very fond of the grandchildren."

"Fond? She dotes on them. She's spoiled them rotten, every one."

"Grandparents tend to do that," Kedrigern said in his most soothing voice. "Would you like me to give your wings a little massage?"

"What I'd like most is to turn that whole lot into worms, and then take them fishing. After that, I'd shake some sense into Jussibee," said Princess in a cold fury. She fumed in silence for a time, then turned and said, "Maybe Belsheer can do something about the brats. They tried to squash him, you know."

"Why would they do that?"

"Sheer nastiness. Belsheer flew by, and I introduced him to the children. Methodical's daughter said, 'That's no wizard. It's nothing but an overgrown bee,' and they all went for him with sticks. He barely escaped. I kept hoping he'd come back with a swarm of friends and sting the daylights out of them."

"He came here. He was very upset. I told him to rest in that bowl of flowers."

"He's had a hard time, the poor old thing." Princess's voice was a bit softened. She sat on the bed, sighed, and said, "Frankly, this whole trip has turned out to be a disappointment. Sariax is a pompous bully, Jussibee is practically invisible, the grandchildren are little beasts, the entertainment at the feasts is second-rate, the conversation among the courtiers is insipid, and none of them dances well. Even the food isn't up to Spot's best. And you don't look as good as I thought you would in black. I like you better in your ordinary working clothes. I never thought I'd say this, but I can't wait to get home."

His face lit up. "Really?"

"If Kallopane is a true picture of what royal households are coming to, we're better off on Silent Thunder Mountain with Spot and a couple of well-behaved trees. My father's palace was never like this."

"Have you remembered anything more?"

"Only fragments, but they're very nice fragments. I can

remember a lullaby my mother sang . . . the pony I received
for my twelfth birthday . . . things like that.''

"That's a very good sign," Kedrigern said, taking her hands.
"You're starting to get clear, precise memories.''

She frowned and looked mildly distressed. "Yes, but they're
all scattered. I can't fit them together into a coherent past. And
sometimes . . . sometimes I have a vague feeling of something
very unpleasant . . . some family tragedy buried deep in my
memory, mercifully forgotten. . . . That frightens me, Keddie."

"All families have their dark secrets, my dear.''

"I was hoping mine wouldn't. But I suppose I'll just have
to face it if I want my memory back.''

"Bravely spoken.''

"And how was your day?" Princess asked. Kedrigern gave
a brief account, and his news seemed to cheer her. When he
had finished, she kissed him sweetly. In a sudden burst of
inspiration, she cried, "Why don't you try getting Belsheer
back in human form? After what happened today, I'm sure
he's ready, and it would be the perfect way to end our visit.''

He bounced up from the bed and dashed to the bowl of
flowers. It took him a moment to locate Belsheer, who had
concealed·himself deep in the blossoms. In a soft voice, he
called, "Belsheer, are you awake?" The bee stirred, but did
not speak. Kedrigern went on, "Do you think it might be time
to go back to your old shape? If you repeat Grizziscus's spell,
I'll get right to work, and you can join us at tonight's feast.''

Belsheer rose from the bowl and circled Kedrigern's head
several times. He flew over to Princess, who greeted him cheer-
fully, and then he returned to hover above the flowers. He still
did not speak.

"Think it over. There's no rush. All I need is the words
Grizziscus spoke, and you'll be human again," Kedrigern said.

Belsheer seemed to go into a fit. He arrowed across the
chamber, zipped from wall to wall, darted up and down and
sideways in fitful jerks, and finally hung before Kedrigern,
bobbing erratically, and buzzed, "Can't rememmmm . . . ber
. . . Grizzzz . . . wordzzzz!''

"Oh, dear me. If I don't know the spell, despelling can be a long and uncertain process."

"I know, I know! Memmmmoriezzzz . . . gone all fuzzzz . . . zzzz . . . zzzzy!"

"Don't panic. That's the important thing. Get back in the bowl and stay there. Relax. Get your rest. Don't force your memory."

Princess, now at his side, added, "He's right, Belsheer. You've had a very stressful day."

"Those rotten kidzzzz!"

"Never mind them," she said. "Try to get some sleep. Your memory will come back on its own."

Belsheer returned to the bowl and disappeared into the petals. Kedrigern and Princess withdrew to the far side of the room, he shaking his head, she staring disconsolately at the floor.

"This could be serious. The spell is starting to take hold, and the bee part of him is getting stronger. I didn't expect it to happen so quickly," said Kedrigern.

"How long will it be before he forgets everything?"

"That depends on how powerful a spell Grizziscus cast. I'm sure he used the strongest one he knew." Kedrigern sighed. "I should have gotten the wording from Belsheer as soon as I found him."

"Don't blame yourself. If anyone is to blame, I am. I never should have introduced him to those nasty children."

"We shouldn't have brought him along to begin with."

"I should never have insisted on coming to Kallopane immediately. I should have listened to you and waited," Princess said. They stood for a time in melancholy silence, heads bowed, eyes downcast, and then Princess looked up and said, "On the other hand, we didn't force Belsheer to come along."

"No, we didn't. He asked to come."

"Well then . . . I mean, after all . . ."

"Yes. Belsheer's nearly five hundred. He's responsible for his own choices," Kedrigern said.

"He wouldn't want it any other way."

"Certainly not. It wouldn't be fair."

"The experience will make him more alert."

"Give him a new perspective."

They smiled at each other happily. Princess took a deep, relieved breath and said, "I feel much better."

"So do I, my dear. It's good to talk these things over. Shall we dress for dinner?"

Jussibee attended the dinner on the final evening of official festivities, though her attendance was fitful. She was out of her chair at least a dozen times during the first five courses, returning breathless to gasp of teething problems, a headache in this grandchild, a bad dream in that one, mysterious blotches on another, and gas pains in still another. When she was at her place, a procession of scurrying servants with updated health bulletins kept her from downing more than a mouthful from each dish. Not until the vegetables and puddings of the sixth course did the queen enjoy a reprieve from the exactions of her valetudinarian grandchildren. She took several spoonfuls of blancmange and a small helping of squash pudding, and then turned to Kedrigern with a weary smile.

"Wonderful stuff, blancmange. It keeps me going."

"Your Majesty is extraordinarily active," the wizard said. Blancmange was not his idea of a lively conversation opener, but it was preferable to a discussion of nursery ailments.

"I couldn't have raised the boys without it."

"Fine young men, your sons. You're the envy of all the surrounding kingdoms. A family of strapping boys is something every royal couple hopes for."

"Yes," said the queen with a sigh. "Sariax is very happy with the boys. He had everything all nicely planned for them." She sighed once again, a deeper, more wistful sigh. "Pity they aren't girls, though, isn't it?"

Taken aback by this unexpected question, Kedrigern could only manage, "Is it? I mean, don't royal families always hope to have lots of sons? For succession, and all that?"

"The kings do. The people do, too, I suppose. But the queens want girls."

"I never realized."

"Girls are so much nicer than boys. All sweet and delicate, like little flower-fairies, and with such musical voices, too. They always look so pretty, and smell so nice. They dance, and skip, and sing like little angels, and their laughter is like tiny chimes. Boys are all elbows and sweat and shouting and bloody noses. There's no comparison, really."

"Your Majesty has given me a new insight."

"I would have been perfectly happy with the twelve princes if I could have had twelve sweet little princesses, too," Jussibee went on dreamily, staring into her blancmange. "Heaven knows we have the room. I had my titles picked out, too, just like Sariax. First would have been the Especially Beautiful Princess of Kallopane. They all would have been beautiful, you see, but she would just be that tiny bit more beautiful than all the rest. Then the Sensitive, the Nurturing . . . if we'd had twins, they'd have been the Merry and the Melancholy Princesses. And Creative, and Graceful, and Considerate . . ."

A servant appeared at the queen's side and dropped to one knee to deliver a breathless account of wind and shrieking and appeals for Grandmama's healing ministrations. Jussibee sprang up and dashed off without a word of parting. Kedrigern wondered which of the nasty princelings it was this time. With grim amusement, he speculated on the naming practice of Kallopane as it might be applied, in strict justice, to the rising generation. Was there an Obnoxious Princeling of Kallopane? Or a Repulsive Princeling, or an Odious? Certainly there were, but they had not been officially recognized as such, and the titles formally conferred. It would be fair warning to the neighboring royal families, whose children might one day be approached for marriage into the house of Kallopane.

As he sat smiling to himself, Kedrigern became aware of the droning voice of the trouvère. The fellow had recited a canto, or fytte, or strophe, or whatever he called it, of the tale of Tasarando the Orphan between courses throughout the feast, and the wizard had given up listening after hearing the third.

For a legendary hero, Tasarando seemed to have had a singularly monotonous career. Every adventure so far had consisted of a bold vow, an encounter with a villain in an enchanted wood, a dreary dialogue in which the villain boasted of his villainy and Tasarando exhorted him to reform, a battle in which the villain was cleft from crown to navel, and the appearance of a spirit who helped Tasarando fulfill his vow.

It was much nicer being a wizard than a legendary hero, Kedrigern thought. Wizards lived a life of thought rather than violent action; they used their minds, not their muscles. Wizards were not always rashly vowing to slay something or liberate someone; more often than not, they were called in to rescue those who had.

"Sst! Wizard!" came a sharp summons.

Kedrigern turned and saw Sariax beckoning him nearer. The king had resolutely looked the other way all through the meal, but now he seemed intent on conversing. Kedrigern drew closer.

"Have you spoken to Formidable?" the king asked.

"Directly after seeing you, Your Majesty."

"Well? Did you set him straight?"

"He leaves in the morning to seek the Great Crawling Loathliness of Moodymount," Kedrigern said with studied nonchalance.

The king's eyebrows shot up. "He does?"

"He wished to go alone. I persuaded him to take my servant with him."

"This is wonderful news, wizard!"

Kedrigern smiled and made a little gesture of self-effacing modesty, his eyes lowered all the while. Sariax pulled a ring from his finger and held it out to the wizard. Even for a king, Sariax seemed unusually prone to the giving of rings.

"Take this, and the thanks of Kallopane," said the king.

"Your Majesty is generous. Very generous," Kedrigern said when he saw the stones clearly and felt the weight of the ring. This was no bauble. It was of an opulence to dazzle the eye, and a size and mass to weary the hand that bore it.

"You have earned our gratitude. Wear it in good health, happiness, and prosperity," said the king.

"I hope I shall."

Sariax gave him a hard impatient look. "Well, aren't you going to put it on?"

"I am indeed, Your Majesty." Kedrigern slipped the ring on his finger and held his hand out to the light of torch and candelabra. The ring gleamed warm and bright. It was a thing of great beauty: a flower of precious stones, with an emerald as big as an almond at its center, surrounded by seven rubies the size of wild strawberries, all set in finely worked gold. "And again I thank you," he said, but Sariax had turned his attention elsewhere.

Kedrigern appreciated the king's impulsive generosity and was impressed by the immense value of the ring, but he felt at the same time uncomfortable, for he was not given to the wearing of jewelry. The practice struck him as ostentatious. He was willing to concede that it might be different for a king: If one was in the habit of dispensing rings as tokens of recognition and gratitude, it made sense to keep a few handy at all times, and there was no handier place for a ring than on one's finger.

But it was unsuitable for a wizard to go about bejeweled and bedecked, even if he planned to divest himself of his finery in favor of deserving acquaintances, thought Kedrigern. The only object he possessed that might be classified as an adornment was the medallion of the Wizards' Guild, which he wore around his neck at all times—but that was no trinket. It was at once a badge, a tool, a shield, and a weapon. It had saved him from severe, perhaps terminal, nastiness on at least one occasion, and been helpful on scores of others.

Rings were different. He rested his hand on the tabletop and watched the play of light on the faceted gems. Lovely, to be sure, but essentially frivolous. Now, if a ring conferred invisibility or immunity to poisons, or granted wishes, or enabled one to travel great distances in an instant, then there would be some point in wearing it. Some rings were known to possess these powers, and Kedrigern would have been happy to see any one of them on his finger. Otherwise, rings were mere show, and not for wizards. He liked to think of himself as a man as appreciative of beauty as anyone, but more sensible than most. Practical. Levelheaded.

In the midst of his musings, he noticed that a hush had fallen upon the banqueting hall. The lively conversations had given way to brief whispers; laughter was subdued; the sounds of eating and drinking were stilled. The voice of the trouvère could be clearly heard, and all present were now attentive. Apparently he had come to the good part of Tasarando's story. Kedrigern leaned forward to listen.

The trouvère struck a chord on his lyre, cast an intense glance around him, and took up a declamatory stance. He continued his recitative:

> "Then Tasarando brave
>   Forthwith did him bespeak:
> 'O wretched caitiff knave!
>   O man of courage weak!
>   O low and skulking slave!
>   O false betraying sneak!
> My taming blade shall make thee mild and meek!'

> "Before reply he could
>   That sly and perjured knight,
> A roar came from the wood.
>   Anon, before their sight,
> A horrid creature stood,
>   Beslimed, and black as night:
> A thing to fill all mortal hearts with fright.

> "They heard with great distress
>   The grisly creature's cry:
> 'Great Crawling Loathliness
>   Of Moodymount am I!
> Upon ye now I press,
>   And ye shall surely die,
> And here your corpses rot and putrefy!'

"But Tasarando bold
Cried out, all undismayed—"

As if to make manifest the poet's words, a soft cry came
from near at hand. Kedrigern turned in time to see Princess
rise unsteadily from her place. She was pale, her eyes wide in
horror and astonishment. She reached out one hand as if to
steady herself, laid the other on her breast, and then fell to the
floor in a swoon.

·····⁙ *Eight* ⁙·····
a change of plan

PRINCESS GROANED AND stirred, and then she lay still for a time. She called out an indistinct phrase, shook her head from side to side, and gestured fitfully, like one deep in a frightening dream.

Kedrigern, kneeling at her side, looked up at Sariax. "I must get her to our room at once."

"I will summon servants," said the king.

"I'd prefer to carry her myself. Must be careful of the wings, you know."

Sariax studied Kedrigern's wiry frame and said, "It is some distance to your chambers. There are many steps to climb."

"I'm stronger than I look," said the wizard, rising. "And she's light as a feather."

"As you wish, wizard." Sariax signaled for torchbearers to precede and follow, and servants to attend the couple. Kedrigern took Princess up in his arms and left the banqueting hall, oblivious to the curiosity of the guests and the pique of the trouvère interrupted at the height of his performance.

Their chamber was indeed some distance away, and the number of steps to be climbed was astounding. In his comings and goings about the palace during the past few days, Kedrigern had always been accompanied by someone, or preoccupied with some matter, and paid little attention to distances. Now he was painfully aware of every step. By the time he reached the top of the final staircase, he was puffing like a blacksmith's bellows and a long corridor still lay before him. He conceded. He worked a small, simple spell to reduce Princess's weight to about one-fifth normal for the next few minutes. When he entered the chamber, Kedrigern was breathing easily, carrying his burden with no sign of strain. He directed the servants to place the bowl of rose water and the clean cloths by the bedside, had them light the candles, and then dismissed them all.

He placed Princess on the bed with extreme care, smoothing out each drooping wing carefully before letting her rest on it. Wings, especially those as delicate of texture as Princess's, could easily be bent or rumpled during sleep, and take the better part of a day to restore themselves. When she was properly settled, he dipped a cloth in the rose water, wrung out the excess moisture, and began gently to pat her brow.

She opened her eyes and looked about, momentarily disoriented, then she sighed with relief and closed her eyes again. She took Kedrigern's hand tightly in both of hers.

"It's all right, my dear. We're in our chamber," he said.

"I . . . I fainted. Didn't I?"

"You did. The banqueting hall was rather overheated."

"It wasn't the heat."

"The gravy, then? Very heavy gravy, I thought."

"No, it was something . . . The poem!"

"Of course. I didn't like it much myself, but then, you're more sensitive than—"

"No, no, no, it was something *in* the poem!" she said, squeezing his hand tightly. "It was . . . oh, I can't remember!"

Kedrigern put down the damp cloth and scratched his chin. "I wasn't really paying close attention. It was not a very interesting poem."

"It was dreadful. But there was something . . ." She frowned in her effort to recall.

"I remember a lot of ranting. Tasarando had just finished insulting one character, and was about to start on another. He seemed to do a lot of that. Very unpleasant fellow."

"If only I could concentrate. I'm still lightheaded."

"That's probably the spell. It will wear off in a few more minutes."

"Spell?"

"I lightened you a bit, so I could carry you safely."

"Oh? Was that really necessary?"

"My dear, you know about my back," Kedrigern said, rubbing the region of his kidneys gingerly.

"There's nothing wrong with your back."

"There would be if I had tried to carry you down corridors and up long staircases. Let's concentrate on the poem, and see if we can't recall what was happening. Tasarando was about to talk when someone interrupted—"

"A monster!"

"That's right. Yes, of course. How could I forget? I noticed the coincidence at once."

"What coincidence?"

"The monster in the poem is the one that Formidable is going off to seek tomorrow: The Great Crawling Loathliness of Moodymount."

Princess moaned and sank back on the pillow, eyelids fluttering. Kedrigern called her name and patted her cheek to no avail. He was steeping the cloth in rose water when she came around.

"The monster," she said in a weak uncertain voice. "It was the monster."

"Just something in a poem, my dear. Nothing to fear. We've faced worse creatures than that thing."

"This monster has something to do with my past, when I was a very little girl. The instant I heard the name, I had a clear picture of my parents seated close together, talking in low voices. I came in, but they didn't notice me right away. And one of them—I think it was my mother—said that I must never be told of The Great Crawling Loathliness of Moodymount."

"Maybe she didn't want you to have bad dreams."

"No, it wasn't that. I'm certain, because my father said that I couldn't be prevented from learning about the family's tragedy. I remember that clearly. He used those very words: 'the family's tragedy.' It all came back in a flash when I heard that name.'' She sighed and covered her eyes with her forearm. For a moment she lay still, then she sat bolt upright and cried, ''But Formidable's going after The Great Crawling Loathliness tomorrow! We must find it first, Keddie—that monster is a link to my past!''

''Relax, my dear. Formidable's only going to talk with it. Perhaps he'd carry a message.''

''What if he kills it?''

''He's determined not to. He wants to preserve monsters, not slay them. He's come to believe that monsters are in danger of extinction.''

''He ought to know. From what I hear, he's slain quite a few.''

''His views have changed.''

''However peaceful his views may be at present, Formidable is an experienced heroic monster-slayer going out fully armed to meet a legendary monster. Habit may prevail over good intentions. He may even be forced to slay the thing in self-defense.''

''That occurred to me, too,'' Kedrigern confessed. ''It would make Sariax very happy if he did.''

''We can't permit it! Not until we've had a chance to speak with that creature, anyway.''

''No. My dear, why didn't your memories come back this afternoon, when I mentioned the monster?''

''This afternoon you told me that Formidable was going out to meet a monster. You didn't give the monster's name.''

''I didn't?''

''You're never specific when you tell me about your work. I've mentioned it to you I don't know how many times,'' she said.

''I don't want to bore you with details.''

''Some details are highly significant.''

''Yes, but most are boring.''

They looked at one another peevishly for a moment, then Princess said in her most reasonable manner, ''We have to go with Formidable. You see that, don't you?''

Kedrigern gave a grunt of uncertain intent. He looked very unhappy.

"I know you want to go home," she continued. "So do I. But this monster is the first tangible link to my past. If Formidable kills it, I may never have another opportunity to find out who I really am, and who my parents are."

Kedrigern gave a glum, reluctant nod. "He said he wouldn't kill it. He did say that."

"Suppose he only chats with it and then it goes back to its lair, or den, or wherever it stays when it's not out marauding. It won't emerge for years. We could do nothing but wait."

Kedrigern sighed deeply. "I suppose you're right."

"We'll just go and speak to this Great Crawling Loathliness, and then turn around and go right back to Silent Thunder Mountain. I'm sure the whole trip won't take more than a few days," said Princess.

"Unless the thing gives us directions to your parents' kingdom."

"Well . . . if it's not too much out of our way . . ." she said, looking off to one side and plucking at the coverlet.

"All right. All right, we'll go. I'll send a servant to Formidable with word, and then I'll have Tergus . . . Oh, dear me, Tergus! I promised him to Formidable. I thought that would be just the kind of position Tergus wanted."

"He wanted to be huntsman to a great lord," Princess reminded him.

"He'll work for a prince. That's nothing to complain about. I suppose Formidable will let him help us out, too."

"I'm sure he will. He wanted you to come with him, didn't he? He'll be glad to have us along."

"Yes, I suppose he will. This is a stroke of luck for Formidable."

"And Belsheer—we must take Belsheer."

Kedrigern glanced uneasily at the bowl of flowers. "That's going to be tricky. Once he's outdoors, with flowers blooming everywhere, he may go completely bee."

"He'll just have to fight the spell."

"That's not easy, even for a wizard."

"I did it," said Princess, setting her jaw.

"You were not approaching the end of your fifth century, my dear. One tires easily at that age."

Princess looked thoughtful. She nodded and then said, "Isn't there a spell he could use?"

Kedrigern looked at her in alarm. "One does not spell one-self—particularly when one is already spelled. The effects could be calamitous."

"Couldn't you . . . ?"

He shook his head. "One does not request, or permit, friends to do so, either. Spells on top of spells are an unhealthy mix. Despelling is an entirely different matter, of course."

After an uneasy silence, she asked, "What are we to do about poor Belsheer, then?"

"As you said, he'll just have to fight it. We'll give him all the moral support we can, but it's up to Belsheer to hold out until we can get him to my workroom."

"Or until he remembers the wording of the spell."

"That's unlikely. He'll have a struggle to keep himself from forgetting more."

"Poor old Belsheer. I feel terrible causing a delay, but unless I speak with The Great Crawling Loathliness, I may never learn the truth about my past. You do understand, don't you?"

"I do. I only hope . . ." Kedrigern sighed, then shook his head and said no more.

After a moment of expectant silence, Princess said, "What do you hope?"

"I hope you're not pursuing unhappiness. There may be things that you're better off not knowing. Remember your father's words: 'the family's tragedy.' "

"If my family has suffered, I want to know."

"There are many kinds of tragedy, my dear, and some of them are very unpleasant. Digging up the past is like turning over a rock: one never knows what—"

"I will thank you not to compare my family history to something one finds under a rock," she broke in coldly.

"I was merely employing a figure of speech."

"Please don't."

"Very well, then, I will illustrate my point with an anecdote. It concerns Parmangard of the Dark Secret, a warlord of considerable—"

"Oh, bother Parmangard, and all warlords, and all anecdotes!" Princess snapped. "I want to know who I really am, and where I came from. I want to know my name! I'm a grown woman, a married woman with a home, a career . . . a troll . . . wings . . . I *deserve* a name!"

"What's wrong with 'Princess'?"

"That's not a name, that's a title. Calling people by titles may be just the thing in Kallopane, but I personally consider it dumb. The *Handsome* Prince and the *Formidable* Prince . . . What nonsense! How would you like it if you had nothing but 'Wizard' to go by?" she demanded.

After a moment's reflection, he said, "Not very much."

"Well, then, try to be supportive."

"I will, my dear, I promise you. I just don't want you to learn anything that will make you unhappy."

"I'll be a lot unhappier if we miss speaking with that monster."

"Then we shall speak with this creature and go wherever it leads us," Kedrigern said. Rising from her side, he went on, "I'll send word to Formidable at once, and start packing my things."

"You're being very good about this, Keddie. I know you want to help Belsheer, and I know how you hate to travel. There just isn't any other way."

"Say no more, my dear. Do you want to pack, or would you prefer to rest for a while?"

"I think I'll rest. Why don't you . . . ?" She inclined her head and directed a meaningful glance at the bowl of flowers. Kedrigern nodded.

Within minutes he had dispatched a servant with a message to Formidable, rolled up his traveling kit, and divested himself of the black tunic, which he had come to loathe. It was almost bearable to be traveling again, if he could wear his comfortable old outfit. Almost. But not quite.

Travel was never bearable, and a quest was the worst kind

of travel, and the search for a monster was the worst kind of quest. A quest was literally looking for trouble. Some people— mostly those who remained safely at home, composing epics and romances—called this sort of thing high adventure, derring-do, or chivalry. Kedrigern employed other, less flattering terms, the kindest of which was 'idiocy.' He had never seen any reason to look for trouble. The need had never arisen. He had only to tug off his boots, settle into a comfortable chair by the fire, and open a good chronicle, and troubles queued up to pound on his door. With no effort at all, he found himself knee-deep in the troubles of friends, acquaintances, total strangers, and, on occasion, enemies; of the highborn, rich, and powerful, and of the lowly and impoverished; of the spelled, ensorcelled, bewitched, enchanted, and accursed, and of the merely unfortunate. He was begged, besought, implored, entreated, supplicated, adjured, and sometimes (without success) commanded to leave the comfort, peace, and safety of his cottage, the companionship of his wife, the ministrations of his house-troll, the repose of his garden, the fascination of his workroom, the solace of his books, and the cheer of his wine cellar in order to travel through ugliness, peril, and desolation amid ogres, monsters, and evildoers of every variety to some remote and unattractive destination where, more often than not, his assistance turned out to be unnecessary, his journey a waste of time and effort, and his summoning the impulse of a desperate moment. And when a genuine victim of hurtful magic awaited him, the poor soul's difficulty was usually of a kind that any apprentice could remedy with a minimum of application.

This quest would probably turn out to be typical. Rain, mud, flies, ogres, brigands, spells, giants, obscure curses, unanticipated monsters, inconvenient enchantments, and nowhere to get a decent meal. And at the end, they might well find that The Great Crawling Loathliness had crawled back to its unknown den for another fifty years. Or, if they managed to confront it, the thing might answer Princess's anguished question with a perfunctory, ''I know your family well. I ate your grandparents,'' and then vanish in a puff of fetid smoke, leaving the poor woman worse off than before.

Should have known something like this was coming, he told himself bitterly. Everything had gone so smoothly on the road to Kallopane; Formidable's problem had been so easily resolved; both Sariax and Jussibee had expressed, in tangible form as well as verbal, their gratitude for his efforts; Princess had for the first time in memory expressed her preference for the cottage on Silent Thunder Mountain over a royal palace complete with courtiers and festivities. Any sensible wizard would be on his guard when all was going so well on the surface. But not this one, he thought. Not Kedrigern. He was content to gloat, count his gold, admire his ring, pat himself on the back. And now he found himself booked for a quest on something like eight hours' notice.

And with an enchanted bee on his hands, who was slowly losing his memory. And a wife who was slowly regaining hers. And a monster-slayer turned philosopher.

This quest was not going to be fun.

···⚜ *Nine* ⚜···

the speckled hag's bridge

THE FIRST LIGHT had just begun to suffuse the misty morning air when Kedrigern and Princess, puffy of eye and yawning helplessly, joined Formidable and Tergus at the royal mews. Formidable was already mounted; Kedrigern's shaggy black war horse, Princess's transparent mare, and a handsome chestnut stood saddled and waiting.

Formidable greeted the wizards with a word, and they responded in an equally taciturn manner. Tergus was more talkative. Indeed, he was ebullient as he bustled helpfully about.

"Thank you, Master Kedrigern, and you, too, my lady Princess—here, let me take that—for placing me in the service—I'll tie that for you, my lady—of the formidable Prince Formidable," he burbled. "I promise you, I will serve him faithfully and well—I'll swing that right up here, Master Kedrigern—and you will never have cause to regret your kindness."

"Good," Kedrigern muttered.

"He's given me this fine horse, and when we return from our quest he will have me fitted out in handsome livery, and arm me as befits the servant of—allow me, my lady—a prince, and every year, at Christmas time, he will give me twelve silver pieces," Tergus went on.

"How nice," Princess said, covering a great yawn.

"And not only that, but he will teach me the—" Tergus fell silent in mid-burble, peered into the gray mist, and said, "But soft—someone approaches. The king! It is the king!" he cried, dropping to one knee.

And indeed it was. Sariax came on with an energetic stride and hailed them in a strong clear voice. Close up, his red-rimmed eyes suggested weariness, but the knowledge that Formidable was departing on a quest for The Great Crawling Loathliness of Moodymount had obviously lent him new vigor. It occurred to Kedrigern that he had not made clear to Sariax the non-violent aim of his son's mission, and he felt a moment of apprehension. But the press of time kept the departure brief and free of embarrassing revelations.

"Go, my son, and my blessing with you. May you succeed in this brave quest," Sariax said.

"I thank you, my father," said Formidable, clasping the royal hand.

Sariax turned to Kedrigern and Princess. "And my thanks to you for rising at this early hour to wish the lad well. Are you recovered, my lady?"

"Oh, quite."

"As a matter of fact, we're going along," Kedrigern said.

"Going with Formidable? Both of you?" Sariax cried in happy surprise.

"We thought we might be of some use. One is liable to run across all sorts of things on a quest, and the company of wizards can be helpful."

Sariax took each of them by the hand and said in a voice thick with emotion, "Kallopane is much indebted to you both. When you return, you will find me generous." He released their hands, took a step back, and waved farewell. "Go now, and all good fortune go with you!"

Formidable led the way, with Tergus close behind. Princess followed after an interval, and Kedrigern brought up the rear. The gates of Kallopane rumbled shut behind them. They rode down the hillside and entered the dripping, mist-shrouded forest, and suddenly Princess turned and cried, "Belsheer! We forgot Belsheer!"

"No, we didn't, my dear." Kedrigern pointed to Dudgeon's poll. There, deep in the thick black mane, a rounded black-and-yellow form could be distinguished by a close observer. "He didn't want to ride in my hood. He was afraid I'd lean back against something and squash him. So we settled on this."

"I see. Are you comfortable, Belsheer?"

"Yezzzz," the bee droned sleepily.

They both yawned. Without further discussion, they rode on. Not another word was uttered or another buzz buzzed until they stopped to rest. Even then, conversation was subdued.

That day passed without incident, as did the next, until early in the afternoon, when they had their first encounter with the unusual. They came to a narrow stone bridge which was flanked on either side of the entrance by a mound of bones, skulls, bits of armor and mail, rusting weapons, and rotting banners. The mounds appeared to be of some age, for thin grass, moss, and unpleasant-looking fungoid growths had softened the outline of the lower portions; but the debris, human and otherwise, of the topmost layers looked to be recent. Access to the bridge was barred by a slender chain that stretched from side to side. It was made of links of clear glass that glittered attractively in the afternoon sunlight.

They drew up four abreast to study the scene. Formidable's features were impassive; Tergus looked uncomfortable; Kedrigern was fascinated; Princess made a *moue* of distaste. Formidable broke the silence.

"What do you make of this, wizards? Is there magic in it?"

"It looks to me like the typical showing off of some recreant knight," said Princess.

"What say you, Master Kedrigern?"

"I think there's more to it than that. I sense the presence of magic," said Kedrigern. He dismounted, took up a handful of dirt, crumbled it in his fingers, and then touched a fingertip to his tongue. He sniffed at the air, and reached into his tunic for the medallion of the Wizards' Guild.

Formidable looked on for a time, frowning, and then grew impatient. He reached for his broadax. "Let us leave this place.

I will shatter this chain that we may pass.'' He urged his horse toward the bridge. Kedrigern raised the medallion to his eye, peered through the Aperture of True Vision at its center, and cried, ''No! Don't touch it!''

Formidable stayed his upraised arm, and Kedrigern ran to inspect the barrier more closely. He studied the sockets, then reached out a cautious hand to the fragile-seeming links but drew it back quickly without making contact. ''Enchantment. No doubt about it,'' he said. ''And of a very nasty kind.''

''What would happen if I severed the chain?''

''Those heaps of bones would come to life and you'd find yourself fighting a deathless army of skeletons.''

''Then I would overcome. I wield an enchanted blade.''

''They're enchanted, too. You'd have a fight on your hands.''

''Fighting is what I do best,'' said Formidable, laying a hand on his sword hilt.

''If you want to mix with them, please wait until we're on our way back. Now, let's lead the horses down to the bank, and get across this stream.''

''That chain is not even waist-high. Our horses can jump it easily,'' Formidable said.

''The bridge is enchanted, too.''

''This is dreadful,'' said Princess, who had come to Kedrigern's side at the mention of magic. ''Who would lay such a cruel snare for innocent travelers?''

''It looks to me like the work of the Speckled Hag of Grotcliff.''

''Grotcliff, say you?'' Formidable pointed to a craggy mountain rising in the distance. ''That is Grotcliff.''

''Then this is the Speckled Hag's doing. She hated everything and everybody. We may find more of this sort of thing ahead.''

''What are we going to do about the bridge?'' Princess asked.

Kedrigern scratched his chin and thought for a time. ''We can post a sign warning people off, and then Formidable can come back and break the chain whenever he has a mind to.''

"That won't do. Unsuspecting travelers may pass this way before we return."

"They can read the sign. We'll write big."

"Not everyone can read."

Kedrigern sighed. Reluctantly, he said, "All right, I'll do something. I'd rather save my magic for emergencies, but if you really want me to break this spell . . ."

"I do," said Princess. "It's your duty."

"Then I will. But if we come up against something ten times worse than this, and I'm low on magic, I want you to remember—"

"I'll remember that you did your public duty."

"That's a wonderful epitaph."

"And you must remember that I have power, too. If you're low, I can protect us."

"We may need everything you've got." Turning to Tergus, Kedrigern said, "How good an archer are you?"

"If I can see it, Master Kedrigern, I can hit it."

"Good. Let's get across the stream, and then I'll tell you what to do."

When they were safely on the opposite bank, Kedrigern had the huntsman select an arrow. He took it, suggested to the others that they rest, and went apart to work his disenchantment. When he rejoined them, he handed Tergus the arrow and said, "Aim for the chain."

Tergus tested the wind, knelt at the edge of the bridge, and took careful aim. His shot cleanly shattered the middle link. A low, moaning, mumbling drone at once arose from the mounds, and they began to stir, with a rattle of bone and clatter of metal. Before the travelers' eyes, the bleached and rusted fragments came together, and in a very short time a force of perhaps threescore skeletons stood in loose formation at the far side of the bridge.

"Hardly a mighty army," Formidable said, drawing his enchanted blade with a soft whisper of steel.

"Don't be so eager," Kedrigern said, reaching out a hand to restrain him. "I thought you were getting philosophical about fighting."

"Do not confuse philosophy with cowardice. I am philosophical only about destroying monsters. Those skeletons look like good exercise."

"You can't interfere now. It would mess up my disenchantment."

The skeletons began to mill about, their movements slow and jerky. They acted like very stupid men looking for something and not sure where, or what, it was. One of them bashed another with a mace, knocking his skull loose. That served as the signal to action. Swords swung, maces and war hammers rose and fell, daggers slashed and thrust, and a great din of steel on ivory filled the air as the charnel force engaged in a clumsy but extremely thorough mêlée. Bones, and bits of bone, went flying in all directions as the skeletons, though dismembered piecemeal by the blows of their fellows, hacked and hewed and smote with insanely methodical wildness, quite oblivious to their own steady dilapidation.

When this had gone on for ten minutes or so, and half the skeletons were reduced to flailing arms, kicking legs, and gnashing skulls skittering about among the smaller fragments, doing what damage their diminished capabilities permitted, Kedrigern stepped forward and whistled. Dry skulls turned empty sockets in his direction. He waved his arms vigorously, jumped up and down, and shouted, "This way! We're over here!"

"Battle at last," said Formidable, unsheathing his blade.

"If any of them get this far, you're welcome to them," said the wizard.

The skeletons ceased their intramural battling. In a slow, dragging, shuffling mass they started across the bridge, their progress impeded by the angry bits and pieces squirming across underfoot and causing frequent stumbles and consequent pile-ups. When the last of them set his bony foot on the bridge, and the first was still a dozen paces from the travelers, the bridge gave a twitch, like a sleeping dog's paws as he dreams of a hunt; and then, with a horrible half-human growl, the sides of the bridge rose up and closed like stone jaws on the grisly band. They ground, and crunched, and crackled; then, with a roar that faded to a breath, the bridge shuddered, cracked, and tumbled into the stream, amid fragments of bone and crumpled metal.

"That's that," said Kedrigern. "Nice bit of bowmanship, Tergus. Better luck next time, Formidable. Did you follow it, my dear?"

"I think so," said Princess. "It was a two-part spell, and you turned the two parts against each other, so it canceled itself."

"Exactly. There's nothing here now but stone and bone and metal. The magic's gone."

"Then it's all over?" said Tergus.

"Completely."

Formidable sheathed his sword, muttering, "And I struck no blow. Not one blow."

"No, and a good thing for us you didn't."

"But this is *my* quest! *I'm* supposed to do the heroic deeds!"

"Formidable, my boy, let us settle one thing right here and now. In matters of physical danger, when the sword or broadax can decide the issue, I will defer to you. In matters of sorcery, magic, or enchantment, I am in charge. If that is not acceptable to you, we will part company here and now," said the wizard.

Formidable frowned gravely as he pondered the ultimatum. "What about dragons and such things? Do you classify them as physical or magical?"

It was Kedrigern's turn to pause and think. After a time he said, "It all depends. They might be either one, or both."

"But they're mostly physical. They should be mine."

"All right, as long as they don't use magic. If they start using magic, they're my responsibility."

"Agreed," said Formidable. He extended his big calloused hand. Kedrigern took it with misgivings, but Formidable was not a bully. His handshake was firm, not pulverizing. The bargain was sealed.

As they rode on, Princess sought further information on the Speckled Hag of Grotcliff. Kedrigern could add very little, for scarcely anything was known of her origins or the reason for her all-encompassing malevolence, or why she had settled on Grotcliff.

"She simply hated everything and everybody, and taught her children to do the same. A creature of consummate nastiness," he said.

"Is there any chance of encountering her?"

"Oh, no, she's long gone. She ran into someone even nastier than she."

"Who?"

"The Devil. The way I heard it, she summoned him up and tried to make a bargain, but she was so very wicked he wanted nothing to do with her. She threatened him, and he had her whisked off to one of the isolated regions of Hell."

This information disturbed Princess, and it was a while before she asked about the children left behind by the Speckled Hag. Kedrigern smiled to reassure her.

"She went quickly, so she had no chance to pass her magic on," he said.

"Did she leave them nothing?"

"She conferred certain gifts and powers on her children during her lifetime, but only because they kept pestering her. To one son she granted the power to give himself a splitting headache whenever he wished. To another, she gave the Cloak of Insignificance; he had only to throw it over his shoulders, and no one listened to a word he said. A daughter could make herself invisible, but the spell worked only when she was alone in a dark room. Her youngest son received the gift of losing essential items when he most needed them."

"Those are not very useful gifts and powers."

"The Speckled Hag didn't like her children any more than she did the rest of the human race. She was a very bad mother."

About the middle of the afternoon, they came to an attractive campsite and decided to stop for the night. Several hours of light remained, but thick upland forest lay ahead, and another spot like this one was unlikely to be found. A shaded knoll, open to the east and the morning sun, a fast-running stream nearby, and open meadows allowing clear sightlines in all directions made this place ideal. Tergus unpacked, watered and tethered their horses, and erected the tents, and then set out to hunt for dinner. Formidable and Kedrigern rested under the trees, while Princess went to the stream to bathe.

Conversation between the two men had subsided to drowsy monosyllables when Princess, barefoot, wet, and *en déshabillé*, flew to the campsite with cries of alarm: "Armed men! Four of them! They're coming this way!"

She plunged into her tent as Kedrigern and Formidable sprang to their feet, alert on the instant. They looked about, and Kedrigern saw figures emerging from the trees at the far end of the meadow. "There!" he cried, pointing to them.

Formidable raised a hand to shade his eyes and studied the intruders. There were four horsemen, as Princess had warned them, but men on foot soon joined them, to bring their total to sixteen. Kedrigern observed them through the Aperture of True Vision, and described them aloud.

"The horsemen are wearing full armor, and their horses are armored, too. They're looking for a fight, no doubt about it. The men on foot aren't as well-protected—a few mail shirts, a couple of breastplates, seven helmets—and only five have swords. The rest have cudgels. Looks to me like a pack of robbers led by recreant knights," said the wizard, lowering the medallion and rubbing his eye.

"It is Sproggart the Ravager and his band. I have long sought them." Formidable smiled and took up his sword belt.

"Now that you've found them, we'd better work out how—"

"*We*? They are mine. We agreed."

"Yes, but there are sixteen of them. Don't you think—"

Formidable raised a hand for silence. In the manner of a schoolman setting forth an elementary syllogism, he said, "The horsemen are weighed down by armor, and their horses will be slowed. The men on foot are disorganized rabble. With my enchanted blade Embrenor and my brave and agile steed Kariakol, I will fall upon them like a wolf in a hen-house."

"Do you mind if I ride along to watch?"

"Not at all. But please stay well back. I'll want room to maneuver."

"Let's saddle up, then. We'd better—just a minute, For-midable. They're sending a messenger."

One of the unmounted men was crossing the meadow at a lope. He stopped at the foot of the knoll, raised a hand to salute them, and when he had regained his breath, said, "My master, Sproggart the Ravager, sends his greetings and bids you wel-come to his lands. Deliver up everything you have here, in-cluding the lady who was bathing in the stream, and you may proceed in peace. Otherwise you die."

Formidable listened with folded arms, looking coldly on the brigand. He spat on the ground, then announced in the voice of a hangman reading the death sentence, "Your master is a false and recreant traitor, a caitiff and coward whose days are at an end. I am the Formidable Prince of Kallopane. These lands are my father's, and my mission is to rid them of such putrescent carrion as Sproggart the Ravager. Go, bid him pre-pare to die."

The messenger stood in stunned silence for a moment, then turned and ran at top speed to where his comrades waited. When Kedrigern and Formidable were saddled and ready, they observed the robbers in what appeared to be lively de-bate.

"I think you may have frightened them off," Kedrigern said.

"I hope not. It would be time-consuming to have to hunt them down one by one."

"Would you?"

"I have my duty. Ah, but fortunately, it will not be nec-essary. They choose to fight. Come along, but stay well in back of me," said Formidable, guiding his horse forward at a walk.

The mounted robbers had already started toward them, work-ing up to a slow trot as they gathered momentum. Formidable studied their loose formation, horsemen in front, the rest jogging behind and to their left. He kept straight on, then angled slightly to his own left. The horsemen turned in a wide sweep to meet him, their speed increasing as they rode. Suddenly Formidable spurred his horse to an all-out gallop, cutting across the path of the robbers, and then wheeled around behind them. Their frantic efforts to turn their own horses led them to near collision and great confusion, and made Formidable's work easy. The clang of steel on steel rang across the meadow, and in scarcely any time at all, four riderless war horses were slowing to a halt at the edge of the trees.

Formidable now turned his attention to the men on foot, who had already begun to scatter. As he rode down one after another, Kedrigern saw two of those farthest from him unaccountably fling up their arms and tumble headlong; then he spied Tergus at the forest edge, taking careful aim with his bow at a third fleeing robber.

By the time Kedrigern joined him, Formidable had dismounted to dispatch the wounded. Tergus had re-entered the forest.

"Very thorough work," said the wizard.

"Thank you. Nothing as sophisticated as what you did at the bridge, but it gets the job done." Formidable wiped his dagger on a fallen man's jerkin, sheathed it, then surveyed the meadow with obvious satisfaction. "This presents a small problem, though."

"Of what nature?"

"I ought to get Sproggart's head back to Kallopane as quickly as possible. It won't last long in this weather. But that will mean a loss of three or four days, and we can't spare the time."

"Is it absolutely essential to bring the head back?"

"It would please my father greatly. And it would reassure the people. Sproggart had built quite a reputation in these parts over the past few years. I was off slaying monsters, and Indomitable was campaigning against the hill people, so Sproggart had a free hand."

"You could send Tergus back with the head."

"I suppose I'll have to do that. I'd prefer keeping him with

me, though, to train him properly," said Formidable, looking
unhappy with the situation.

Kedrigern dismounted and inspected the fallen figures.
"Have you already removed Sproggart's head?" he asked.

"No, but it won't take long. I caught him a good slash across
the neck, so the hard part is done. Let's go find him."

They crossed the meadow to where the four armored figures
lay sprawled in grotesque contortions on the blood-spattered
green. Their horses had gathered nearby, and were grazing
serenely. Aside from the corpses and the blood, the scene was
quite peaceful.

Formidable stooped to take up a shield. He brushed the dirt
from its surface and turned it for the wizard's inspection. On
a black ground were two mailed fists, crossed, above a
mound of plunder. One fist held a dagger dripping blood, the
other a flaming torch. Beneath the design was inscribed
Sproggart's motto: *Semper laetitia mons spoliorum est.*

" 'A heap of booty is a joy forever,' " Kedrigern translated.

"He had a different motto in the old days. Something about
honor, faith, and a pure heart, as I recall. When he went
recreant, he changed it," Formidable said.

"At least he showed a certain sense of propriety. Which one
of these is Sproggart?"

"This one in the black armor." Formidable rolled aside the
body with his foot. The head remained where it lay, and he
smiled. "Oh, good. I got in a cleaner stroke than I thought."
He undid the helmet, removed the head, and held it up. It was
quite ugly, and menacing even in death.

"That won't add to the beauty of Kallopane," Kedrigern
said.

"No. But my father has wanted it for a long time." Formidable set the head aside, surveyed the carnage, and said, "It
would be good to get the armor and horses back to Kallopane,
too. Now I wish I'd brought more men along."

As they stood among the fallen brigands, a distant cry came
to them. They looked and saw Tergus at the edge of the wood,
waving. He started toward them at a run, and as he emerged

from the shadows, they could see a small figure seated on his shoulders.

"A child?" Kedrigern asked.

Formidable shaded his eyes and peered closely at the approaching figures. "A dwarf," he said.

···❧ Ten ❧···

words to the wise

THE DWARF WAS bursting to tell his story, as was Tergus, but Formidable insisted that there be no narration from either of them until the work at hand was done. Only when the armor had been stripped from brigands and horses and tidily packed, the horses walked and tethered, Sproggart's head carefully wrapped, and a hearty supper consumed did the travelers settle down by the fire to listen. Tergus spoke first.

"After I downed the third brigand, I saw that my master needed no further support, so I slipped into the wood to hunt down any who might be skulking behind," he said, looking about fiercely. "I found none. But I came upon a sack hanging from a tree." Here the dwarf nodded enthusiastically, and pointed to himself. "A very strange sack it was, too, swaying slowly in a most mysterious and unnatural manner, and not a breeze blowing to give it motion. I was about to put an arrow through it, had the arrow nocked and my bow raised—but just as I drew back my arm, the sack gave a groan. Astonished, I lowered my bow and approached more closely. A strained voice whispered, 'Save me! Help me!' I cut down the sack and freed the occupant, who proved to be this small man."

The dwarf rose, bowed to the company, and mounting a rock where the firelight shone full on his compact, sturdy form, struck an orator's posture. His garments were rather the worse for recent rough usage, and he sported an impressive black eye, but his manner commanded attention and his words held it, when he announced, "I am Bledge, servant of the Fair Glynfynnyn. Forty perilous days and nights have I wandered these woodlands in search of a bold champion who will rescue my lady from the threat of The Great Crawling Loathliness of Moodymount, and now my search is at an end." Hopping nimbly from his perch, he dropped to one knee before Formidable, and flinging wide his arms, said, "Brave warrior, battler against odds, slayer of brigands, come with me to the castle where Glynfynnyn huddles in terror while the monster rages and threatens, lays waste the countryside, devours peasants and livestock, crushes picturesque groves, and fills the air with stench and execrations! Slay The Great Crawling Loathliness and set us free!"

Formidable rose to his feet, took up his sword, and brandished it overhead. In a mighty voice, he declaimed, "The Formidable Prince of Kallopane will rescue the Fair Glynfynnyn and her household from The Great Crawling Loathliness! This I, by the strength of my arm and my sword's edge, pledge, Bledge!"

Tergus and Bledge cheered loudly, and Princess and Kedrigern applauded the bold words. Kedrigern was reassured. Formidable's true nature was asserting itself; there would be no détente between warrior and monster; Kallopane would be rid of a potential danger and Glynfynnyn of a real and present one; Sariax would have new cause to be proud of his son, and would consequently be pleased and generous. This journey would be an all-round success.

But now there was another problem: Bledge had spoken of wandering forty days in his search. That could mean a round trip of eighty days, plus fighting time, and then another few days in Kallopane being fêted and rewarded, and finally the trip home. Summer would be over before he and Princess were back on Silent Thunder Mountain. They would, in fact, be lucky to escape the first snowfall. He groaned and covered his eyes with his hand.

"What ails thee, Master Kedrigern?" the dwarf asked, coming to his side.

"Forty days going to Glynfynnyn's castle and forty coming back, that's what ails me. I didn't pack for a long trip."

"Then be at peace. The castle of the Fair Glynfynnyn is but three days' ride from here."

"But you said you were forty days and nights in these woods."

"And so I am. But I set out in the opposite direction. I also lost my way from time to time. My plan was to carry my search to Kallopane, and I was finally on the right road when Sproggart seized me this very morning, as I left the stable."

"What stable?" Formidable asked.

"The stable at the old couple's farm, my Formidable Prince. Sproggart has spared their lives, but they must feed him and his men and horses whenever he arrives. The farm lies on our way. We will be there by midday tomorrow, if we get an early start," Bledge explained.

"Then we will leave horses and trophies there while we proceed."

"Old Clurt would gladly pickle Sproggart's head for you. Only last evening he expressed his heartfelt wish to do so."

"Then that's settled. Let us rest. We leave at dawn," said Formidable, rising and stretching.

Princess yawned. "Are you coming, Keddie?"

"I think I'd better check Belsheer before I turn in. He went out in the meadow after the battle, and I haven't spoken to him since he came back."

"You sound concerned."

"I am," Kedrigern said, gazing into the fire. "The spell is tightening its hold. He has to fight hard against it or his memory will be wiped clean."

"But you can despell him even if that happens."

"Probably. But if he goes completely bee, I may not get him home to work on him. If he decides to fly off one day . . ."

"Bees don't live long, do they?"

"He won't last till winter," Kedrigern said, rising and taking her hand.

"Can't we do something to help him fight the spell?"

"We must make sure that his mind is occupied. As long as he's thinking, he's human. If his memory goes, so does he. I'll talk to him for a while, try to get him interested in some kind of intellectual activity."

"Good luck," said Princess, kissing him and slipping off to their tent.

Belsheer was resting in Dudgeon's poll, snug in the mane, but he was not asleep. He responded at once to Kedrigern's greeting with an abstracted buzz.

"Did you have a good day?" Kedrigern asked.

"Yezzzz. Found lovely flowerzzzz."

"Don't think about flowers, old friend, think about your magic. Think of enchantment. Wizardry. Spells."

"Spellzzzz . . . ? Yezzzz! I remember . . . spellzzzz."

"You must remember, if you want to go back to being a wizard."

"I want . . . to be a wizzzz," Belsheer buzzed forlornly.

"Then keep your mind active. Exercise your memory. Think. Reason. Work out puzzles and riddles. Sing songs. Recite poetry."

"Only know one song. Can't remember the wordzzzz."

"All right, no songs. It doesn't have to be songs. Surely you know some rhymes."

Belsheer thought for a time before responding, "All the rhymezzzz I know . . . involve spellzzzz. Don't think it's prudent to repeat them . . . under the circumstancezzzz."

"Very sensible. Good thinking. See, it's beginning to work!"

"What will I think about?"

"How about wise sayings, and maxims?"

"Do you mean adagezzzz, and aphorismzzzz? I learned hundredzzzz of them from the Harkenerzzzz."

"Well, there you are. That's a good starting place. Just keep repeating them. I'd do so on a regular basis, to keep ahead of the spell."

"I will. Here'zzzz one: *The cooked bird does not fly, except under very unusual circumstancezzzz.*"

"Very good. You scarcely buzzed."

"I'll try another: *Dead men tell no tales, but they make very poor blacksmiths,*" Belsheer enunciated carefully.

"Excellent!"

"*No man limps because another hurts his foot, but a good lawyer will yell very loudly.* It works, Brother Kedrigern—it really works!"

"Now you have to keep it up. First thing in the morning, several times during the day—especially when you find yourself getting involved with flowers and clover—and last thing at night, recite a dozen or so of your wise sayings. And don't spend too much time by yourself. Talk to people."

"What will I talk about?"

"Repeat a few wise sayings."

"I'll do it. I feel much better already. Thank you, Brother Kedrigern."

Kedrigern left him and returned to the tent in a hopeful mood. If Belsheer could hold out until they were back on Silent Thunder Mountain, the spell could be undone. If this mental stimulation could jog his memory, and help him recall Grizziscus's exact words, so much the better. Kedrigern would have him back in human shape there and then. He apprised Princess of the improved situation, and that night they slept soundly, their minds at ease.

The next day dawned so gray and chilly that it could scarcely be said to dawn at all, only to undergo a slight lessening of gloom. Scarcely had the travelers struck camp and started on their way, when a light drizzle began. Kedrigern asked Belsheer if he would like to ride inside his cloak, but received no response. He felt in Dudgeon's mane, and found no trace of the bee. Assuming that Belsheer had already flown off, unnoticed, to warmer, drier accommodations, he thought no further on the matter.

The drizzle soon settled to a steady soft rain. The forest air was misty and dank, but the heavy canopy of leaves intercepted most of the rain, and the travelers avoided a soaking. When they stopped at mid-morning in a grove of fine old old oaks, they were able to recline on dry ground. Tergus and Bledge collected wood for a fire to warm them and dry out their cloaks.

Kedrigern noticed Bledge trying, with covert gestures and nods, to draw him apart from the others. He rose from the fire and walked off a short way, and soon the dwarf joined him. The little man looked about self-consciously, and in a lowered voice said, "There is a bee traveling with you, Master Kedrigern. A very large bee."

"Yes. His name is Belsheer."

"This morning, as we rode, he spoke to me."

"Good. I told him to start talking to people."

"He hovered next to my left ear and said: *It is better to sit on silken cushions eating raisin bread and honey than to starve in a filthy dungeon.*"

"I certainly wouldn't argue with that."

"Nor did I, Master Kedrigern. But a little farther on, he hovered by my other ear and said: *One friend is pewter; two friends are wood; an enemy is a rusty nail; a wife is cotton; children are porridge; but a horse is always a horse.*"

Kedrigern scratched his chin and looked off into the mist. "He said that, did he?"

"He did indeed. And not long after, he said: *A wise man knows his shoe from his glove, and never confuses either of them with asparagus.* I did not wish to tell the bee that he was talking gibberish, for I feared to offend a great wizard like yourself by being ungracious to your familiar. But what am I to—"

"Wait a minute, now. Belsheer is not my familiar," Kedrigern broke in. He quickly recounted Belsheer's story and explained to the dwarf his last night's advice to the enchanted bee. Bledge was overcome with sympathy.

"How dreadful, Master Kedrigern! A mighty wizard reduced to a bee, and in danger of remaining one!" he cried, wringing his hands. "Can I do anything to help him?"

"Listen attentively, and don't tell him it's gibberish. We don't want to undermine his confidence."

"Perish the thought. Would it be helpful for me to respond

with wise sayings of my own? Mine make sense, and might stimulate his mental powers.''

''A splendid idea, Bledge. Belsheer spent some time among the Harkeners to the Unseen Enlightened Ones—a harmless but confusing sect—and appears to have learned too much from them.''

''The very next time I see him, I will say: *A stitch in time saves nine*, or *As well be hanged for a sheep as for a lamb*.''

''That's the idea. I'm glad we had this chance to talk. I think you'll do Belsheer a lot of good,'' said Kedrigern, clapping a hand on the dwarf's shoulder.

''I was much distressed. I believed he was your familiar.''

''I don't have one. Most wizards don't,'' Kedrigern said as they started back to the fireside. ''Witches keep familiars, and some warlocks do, but very few wizards.''

''Are they not helpful?''

Kedrigern shook his head. ''More trouble than they're worth, if you ask me. Unless you get something like a sloth. I knew a warlock whose familiar was a sloth. Laziest man I ever met.''

''Cats are said to be popular.''

''Yes, but it's easy to get attached to a cat, and then losing it can be a hard blow. I knew a witch some years back—she was a friend of my teacher—who had a cat. A nice big tiger cat he was, good-natured, always grinning. One day he ran down a rabbit hole, and she never saw him again. She was a long time getting over the loss.'' They went on a way, and the wizard added, ''The closest I came to having a familiar was in my bachelor days, when I kept Manny around.''

''Was Manny a cat?''

''No, he was a spider. Great big fellow. Manny could spin a web as tough as chain mail, but he had a great sense of humor. He was more a roommate than a familiar.'' Kedrigern heaved a deep nostalgic sigh and said no more.

That afternoon they came to a small clearing which held a huddle of sagging buildings leaning together in the center of neglected fields and broken fences. The buildings, gray and much weathered, reminded Kedrigern of a bunch of drunken

peasants supporting one another in helpless interdependency.
Unlike drunken peasants, the buildings were silent. Not a sound
was to be heard in the clearing, nor a sign of life seen.

"The farm of old Clurt and Vubb," the dwarf announced
with a flourish of his hand.

"I see no one," Formidable said.

"They're probably cringing in fear somewhere in the root
cellar. They do that whenever strangers show up."

"I don't even see animals."

"They have only one horse, and he's nearly as old as they
are. He spends most of his time in the stable. The pigs and
chickens have learned to hide when anyone approaches."

Kedrigern and Princess had joined them by this time. Princess said, "Clurt and Vubb don't have much of a life, do
they?"

"They don't complain, my lady," Bledge said. He reflected
for a moment, then went on, "At least, I don't think they do.
They're a bit difficult to understand at times."

"We have not come for conversation. They have a stable
and a place to store my prizes while we pursue our quest,"
Formidable said, starting forward.

"If I may make a suggestion, my Formidable Prince: Allow
me to go first and show them Sproggart's head. It will cheer
them up no end."

With a tight smile, Formidable tossed him the bundle con-
taining the grisly trophy. Bledge tucked it under one arm and
set off for the farmhouse at a gallop. They followed him at a
more leisurely pace.

By the time they reached the building, Bledge stood in the
doorway flanked by an aged man and woman. Exactly how
aged they were was difficult to determine. Work, weather,
want, and time had left their bodies scrawny and dry as stalks
in winter, their faces like elongated walnuts. But their small
rheumy eyes shone, and they greeted the travelers with broad
smiles that revealed a single worn-down stub of tooth in each.

"Arrg varrgle narrgen garg," said one, in a muffled growl.

"Dard narf farrgen bardle," the other added.

"They welcome you," Bledge said. "The one with the kerchief is Vubb.'' Since the two were dressed in identical shapeless sacklike garments, with rough-hewn clogs on their feet, this distinction was significant.

They made some more noises, which sounded to Kedrigern like good-humored death rattles, and Bledge took the role of interpreter. Clurt and Vubb were happy to welcome the slayer of Sproggart, to care for his trophies, preserve the bandit's head for travel, feed everyone, and house them for as long as they required. All they asked in return was a hank of Sproggart's hair to work into a charm against troublesome neighbors.

That piqued Formidable's interest. ''What neighbors? Recreant knights? Ogres?''

After a joint statement that sounded like the raking of gravel, Bledge revealed that the pair were occasionally troubled by three giants, sons of the Speckled Hag.

Formidable beamed happily at this news. ''Giants! Wonderful!'' Turning to Kedrigern, he said, ''Remember, I get to fight them by myself. We agreed.''

''As long as they don't use magic,'' said the wizard.

''Of course. Tergus, care for the horses, and see if you can find a good place to store our trophies.''

Tergus looked about dubiously. ''I think everything here is ready to collapse.''

''Walk softly and don't slam any doors.''

Formidable's admonition was sensible, and they all followed it. They tiptoed inside, and found the interior of the tiny farmhouse clean, though not excessively so. With much mumbling and unintelligible gargling, Clurt and Vubb spooned out portions of supper. It was a gummy greenish substance about the consistency of mud, but not quite as flavorful. Kedrigern was hungry, as were all the company; even so, it took determination to get the stuff down and keep it down. To take his mind off the taste, the wizard tried to decipher the ingredients. He met with no success. Whatever comprised the meal had been boiled so vigorously for so long that it had lost all individuality. It was foodstuff, probably of vegetable origin. One could hope to identify it no more precisely.

After supper, they gathered around the fireplace. The single joint-stool was given to Princess; the others spread their cloaks or blankets and sprawled on the surprisingly clean floor. There was little conversation; all minds were on digestion.

Belsheer joined them, settling on the toe of Kedrigern's boot and at once commencing to groom himself. The wizard reassured Clurt and Vubb, who rattled something indistinct and nodded their heads, and Belsheer remained undisturbed. After a time he rose and flew to where he could hover between Princess and Kedrigern.

"*The pen is mightier than the sword*. Fancy that," he hummed, then returned to Kedrigern's boot.

"That's very good, Belsheer," said Princess.

"Yes. You're remembering good stuff," Kedrigern said.

"Actually, that's not mine."

Bledge spoke up proudly. "I told him that, Master Kedrigern. We exchanged many wise sayings along the way."

"Levelheaded chap, that Bledge," Belsheer buzzed.

"It sounds to me as though his wise sayings are wiser than the ones you heard from the Harkeners," Kedrigern said.

Belsheer paused before saying, "Yes, I believe they are. To tell the truth, half the time I had no idea what the Harkeners were talking about."

"Only half?" Princess asked.

Pausing again, grooming himself more energetically than before, Belsheer finally confessed, "In all honesty, Sister Princess, I never really understood a word. I just didn't want to admit my ignorance. Mind you, I often had the feeling that I *almost* grasped what they were trying to say. Do you know what I mean?"

"I do indeed," she said, and Kedrigern nodded in solemn agreement.

"But when Bledge keeps coming up with things like *The barking dog never bites* and *Look before you leap* . . . well, those are wise sayings, no doubt about it. And so nice and clear."

"Wait a minute," said Formidable. His brow was furrowed with the effort of contemplation. "The pen isn't mightier than the sword. That's not a wise thing to tell anyone, unless you want to get him chopped to pieces.''

"You're not supposed to take it literally, Formidable. It's not about a real pen and a real sword," said Kedrigern.

"I should hope not. *The sword is mightier than the pen.* Now, there's a sensible statement. But saying it the other way around is just nonsense. You might as well say *The flea is bigger than the horse*!''

Kedrigern thought for a moment, then said, "Well, with the proper spell . . .''

"No spells. You didn't mention spells before. No one's talking about spells. We're talking about so-called wise sayings.''

"Gardle fargle zark rargen,'' Clurt murmured sententiously, his little eyes agleam.

"What did he say, Bledge?'' Formidable asked.

Crestfallen, the dwarf translated, "Clurt says that anyone who thinks that the pen is mightier than the sword should try sticking a pen into those three giants.''

"You need fear the giants no longer, old man,'' said Formidable. "With my sword Embrenor, I shall rid you of that menace forever.''

"Marmengargg,'' said the old couple, as one.

"They thank you very much,'' Bledge explained.

"That's my mission. Remember: *Might makes right*.''

"No, it's *Right makes might*,'' Belsheer buzzed.

Formidable regarded the bee with an expression in which disbelief mingled with pity and disgust in equal measure. "If right truly makes might, wizard, why are innocent, helpless princesses always being menaced by evil men or foul monsters? Why are honest people always looking to a strong man with a sword to rescue them from evil? No, *Might makes right*, just as *The sword is mightier than the pen*. I'm good because I'm strong.''

"It's the other way around. You're strong because you're good,'' said Kedrigern. "It's goodness that gives you strength.''

"Then why aren't all good people as strong as I am?''

Kedrigern shrugged. "I don't know. Ask a philosopher. Yes—ask your brother Philosophical next time he's home from school. He owes you a few answers."

Gloomily, Formidable said, "That won't do any good. Once he starts answering a question, he goes on and on, and pretty soon I'm more confused than when he started. When I say so, he gives me a ratty old black book to read."

"*Judge not a book by its cover*," Belsheer buzzed.

"I suppose that's another of your proverbs," Formidable said with loathing.

"It is. It just came back to me." Belsheer shot into the air and began dancing about in intricate aerial figures, exultantly buzzing, "I remembered it! It's been years since I heard that saying, and it popped right into my head, Brother Kedrigern!"

Kedrigern and Bledge exchanged a conspiratorial wink, and the wizard said, "Well done, Belsheer. You're on the way now."

Belsheer descended to his perch on Kedrigern's boot. "I still can't recall a word of Grizziscus's spell. Proverbs and wise sayings are all very well, but I don't want to spend the rest of my life repeating them."

"That's the first sensible thing he's said," Formidable muttered.

Ignoring the remark, Kedrigern said, "Don't give up, Belsheer. Keep at it." Turning to Princess, he asked, "And what about your memory, my dear? Has anything more come back?"

"Not a thing, so far. But I have an absolute conviction that The Great Crawling Loathliness is the key. If we can only speak with it, my entire past will be unlocked." She reached out to take his hand, and said, "But what about you? This must be terribly hard for you."

"Well, I don't like the traveling, but as long as—"

"No, no, no, I mean the emotional hardship."

"What emotional hardship?" Kedrigern asked, perplexed by her remark.

"You're a poor foundling. When neither of us knew our origins, we had something to share. But if I regain all my memories, and can remember my parents, and relatives, and the people around the castle, and my toys, and the bold handsome princes who sought my hand, and you still don't know whose child you are, won't you feel awful?''

He placed his hand over hers and pressed it fondly. He smiled. ''Not a bit. I love a good mystery,'' he said.

···✦ *Eleven* ✦···

gifted children

THEY DEPARTED EARLY next morning, with the old couple's cheery "Gnarfargledarg" of farewell to send them on their way. The trophies were safely stowed, Sproggart's head was pickling in a crock, and the travelers were refreshed by a good night's sleep under a roof, albeit one in dire need of repair. Formidable was particularly spirited, since he anticipated the opportunity of doing battle against wicked giants.

Bledge rode in the lead, with Belsheer perched now on his hat brim, now on his shoulder, sometimes hovering near the dwarf's ear to deliver a terse saying. Formidable was next, with Tergus close behind. After an interval rode Princess, with Kedrigern at the end of the little column.

It was a silent procession, except for Belsheer and Bledge, and their colloquy was private and muted. The others were preoccupied with their hunger (Clurt and Vubb had offered as breakfast last night's supper, reheated, and been roundly refused), their warmth (the air was dank and chilly), and their own early-morning thoughts.

When the sun had burnt off the mist, they stopped at a brook to eat and replenish their water supply. They had not proceeded much farther when Kedrigern sensed a change in the atmosphere. It was a very subtle alteration—too subtle, apparently, to be detected by any of the others, even Princess and Belsheer, who might be expected to notice such things—but something was unmistakably different. He sniffed the air, and learned nothing. He drew out his medallion and surreptitiously inspected the environs; still he found no explanation for his uneasiness. Certain that something was amiss, magically speaking, yet reluctant to alarm his companions without a definite cause, he kept close watch on Princess. At her first sign of disquiet, he would give the alarm, whether he could specify a cause or not.

So intent did he become on observing his wife that he was not aware of Belsheer's approach until the bee was close enough to touch. Belsheer described agitated zigzags in the air before his face, then thrummed, "Enchantment, Brother Kedrigern! I sense enchantment hereabouts! Don't you feel it?"

"I've been aware of it since just after we stopped, but I can't pin it down."

"Neither can I. But it's real, I know it."

Unnoticed by either of the wizards, Princess had dropped back to join them. Seeing Kedrigern's concerned expression and Belsheer's excited movements, she asked, "Have you felt it, too?"

"We have, Sister Princess. It's getting stronger all the time."

"But we can't find a source."

"Then I'll go up and have a look," Princess said, unfixing her cloak and letting it fall from her shoulders.

"Be careful, my dear. There may be danger."

"I'll be very careful."

"As soon as you see anything suspicious, come right back."

"I will. I promise."

"We'll wait here. Belsheer, tell Bledge to call a halt," said Kedrigern, as Princess rose to treetop height, then leveled off and flew straight ahead, following the trail.

The rest of the party dismounted to await her return, and as they waited, all reacted to the warning. Formidable, once advised of possible danger, was keen to charge into it headlong. Bledge and Tergus, more restrained, plied Kedrigern with questions, to which he could give no certain answers. Belsheer would only buzz solemnly: *A danger foreseen is half avoided. Forewarned is forearmed.*

It was a noisy group to which Princess returned, landing gracefully at Kedrigern's side. As he smoothed her wings and draped the cloak over her shoulders, she composed herself, ignoring the questions now directed to her.

"The magic is all emanating from a little building in a clearing up ahead. It's a tiny place, no bigger than a henhouse, but that's the source," she said.

"An enchanted henhouse? Extraordinary! Even if I had all my memories back, I'm sure I'd never remember hearing of such a thing," Belsheer hummed.

"I didn't say it was a henhouse. It's about the *size* of a henhouse. It could be a woodshed."

"An enchanted woodshed is also extraordinary."

"Shall we have a look?" Kedrigern asked.

"Of course. Perhaps a bold deed is to be done," said Formidable. "Does that seem likely, my lady?"

"I received no indication. I couldn't even sense good or evil intent, just a lot of magic centered in that little shack."

"It is evil, my lady, depend on it," said Bledge in a subdued voice. "We are in the very shadow of Grotcliff, where once dwelt a hag of abominable malevolence."

"We know about her," Tergus said.

"Perhaps this shack is the dwelling place of her three giant sons," Bledge said, glancing about uneasily.

"Impossible," Princess said. "It could barely hold a small flock of healthy chickens."

"You forget that it's enchanted, my dear."

"Enough talk. Let us go forth," said Formidable, springing into the saddle and starting down the road at a lively canter.

The others had no choice but to mount up and follow. In a very few minutes they came to a barren clearing where a bedraggled shack, its roof sagging, sides weathered silvery by long exposure, stood alone at the very center. They halted at the edge of the woods. "Is that where the magic you speak of is coming from?" Formidable asked. His disbelief was unmistakable.

"That's it," said Princess.

Kedrigern studied the ramshackle structure through the Aperture of True Vision. He lowered the medallion, rubbed his eye, and raised the medallion for a second look, as the others all studied him.

"It doesn't register at all," he said, tucking the medallion back into his tunic. "There's a very powerful spell on it, but I can't—"

Suddenly, with loud exclamations and fierce gestures, three giants burst from the tiny shack. Each of them was twice the size of the building and ten times bigger than the doorway from which they all had emerged. Together, the three of them would have crowded a good-sized barn. It was impossible. Yet here they were, and they had come out of something scarcely large enough to hold a dozen chickens or a single cold day's firewood.

The giants snarled, roared, and bared their long yellow teeth. They brandished knobby clubs the size of ridgepoles, and stamped their feet on the bare ground with earth-shaking impact.

"Intruders!" shouted one.

"Trespassers!" cried the second.

"Enemies! They must die!" howled the third.

Formidable steadied his horse. Drawing his sword, he said, "They are mine, wizards."

"Not if they use magic," Kedrigern reminded him.

"They will have no time for magic."

Formidable's horse dashed forward, straight for the menacing trio. They spread out to receive his attack, setting their feet and raising their clubs, emitting jubilant and ferocious sounds.

"Brave lad. He hasn't got a chance against those three," droned Belsheer.

"Can't we do something?" Princess asked.

"A few arrows in their hides will slow them down," Tergus said, dismounting and stringing his bow.

"Help him, Master Kedrigern! Save us!" pleaded the dwarf.

"We agreed, Bledge. As long as these giants don't try any magic, I'm bound not to interfere."

"*An honest man would sooner break his leg than his word,*" Belsheer buzzed.

"But those creatures will mash the Formidable Prince to a pulp," the dwarf objected. "What will become of the Fair Glynfynnyn if that happens?"

Kedrigern raised his hands in a calming gesture. "If these are indeed the sons of the Speckled Hag, there may be less cause for concern than you think. Let us observe the combat, and see for ourselves."

"You know something you're not telling us," Princess said, giving him a suspicious look. He smiled, but did not reply.

Formidable was closing fast on the three giants, riding straight for the one in the middle. At the last possible moment, his horse wheeled to the left and Formidable disemboweled the end giant with a slash of Embrenor. As he swept around to attack the remaining pair, the middle one brought his club back for a crushing blow. It landed squarely on the skull of his unfortunately positioned brother, splattering it like a dropped melon. At sight of what he had done, the third giant went into a tantrum. He threw down his club and began jumping up and down, waving his fists, tearing his hair, and screaming in a bone-jarring basso. Formidable finished him with a single stroke.

While the others looked on, stunned, Kedrigern said in a detached voice, as of someone pointing out a mildly interesting bit of scenery, "The Speckled Hag had three giant sons on whom she conferred the gifts of carelessness, clumsiness, and peevishness. I think these were the lads."

Princess looked pained. "What a dreadful person she must have been."

"Absolutely horrendous," Kedrigern said. He waved to Formidable, who had dismounted to inspect his handiwork. The prince brandished his sword in return. He was beaming, and his step was springy and energetic.

Belsheer landed on Kedrigern's shoulder and observed, "That lad certainly loves to do a bold deed."

Bledge, looking almost as pleased as the prince, said, "He will save my lady, and deliver us all from the menace of The Great Crawling Loathliness. He will slay the monster with a single mighty blow. I am certain of it now."

Kedrigern nodded. "I'm inclined to agree. That's not what he had in mind when we set out, but it looks to me as though he's working up to it."

"We must remind him to hold off until we've had a chance to speak with the thing," said Princess.

"If that's necessary. The sight of it may be sufficient to bring back your memories."

"Mine, too!" Belsheer buzzed.

"The sight of The Great Crawling Loathliness usually makes people sick to their stomachs," Bledge informed them. "I have no knowledge of its effect on the memory."

"We must hope for the best," said Kedrigern.

Belsheer was ready with a proverb. "*Hope is a good breakfast, but a poor supper.*"

"Don't you know any encouraging sayings?" Princess asked.

"Not at the moment. Perhaps some will come back to me once we've seen the monster."

With a cheerful smile, Bledge said, "How about *A good hope is better than a bad possession*?"

"Very good, Bledge. I like that one," said Princess.

Formidable had by this time satisfied himself that the giants would cause no more trouble, and he called out to the others to join him near the magical shack. They all offered congratulations on his triumph, which he waved off with becoming modesty. Bledge and Tergus, though, would not be silenced. They became positively fulsome in their tribute, and the prince at last silenced them with a severe look and a peremptory gesture.

"It was no great deed," he said. "True, there were three of them, and so tall that they would have had to stoop to pass through the great gate of Kallopane, but I had my enchanted blade Embrenor, which assures me that I will always be equal to my opponents."

"Does it guarantee that you'll always win?" Tergus asked.

Formidable glared at him. "Certainly not. That would be cheating. The enchantment on my sword promises me a fair fight. That is all I ask."

While the others were talking, Kedrigern and Princess dismounted and studied the tumbledown shanty from within touching distance. A dozen paces were all they required to walk around it; they did so, and stopped before the open doorway. Within was impenetrable darkness.

"There's a lot of magic invested in this place. Can you feel it?" Kedrigern asked.

"Distinctly. Even so, it's hard to believe that those three giants actually were inside, and squeezed out this doorway."

"This sort of thing is not all that rare among wizards. You want a lot of room inside, but you don't want to attract attention, so you make the place much smaller on the outside, and shabby. Arlebar's house was something like that, if you recall."

"Yes, but it was still a house. This isn't even a shed."

"The Speckled Hag must have put something very important in here, to protect it so well. I wonder . . ." Kedrigern said, scratching his chin and looking thoughtfully into the interior blackness.

"Now, wait a minute, Keddie."

"My dear, think of the opportunity."

Princess looked apprehensive. "Do you think we should? It might be terribly dangerous."

"Can we simply turn our backs and walk away?"

She reflected on that for a moment, then shook her head slowly. He reached out and took her hand.

"I'll put a protection over us, and my medallion will also help to shield us against enchantments. Just keep tight hold of my hand."

"I will," she said.

He worked the spell, and they stepped into the dark entrance. Behind them, they could hear Bledge and Belsheer saying, *"The bigger they are—"*

*   *   *

They stood in a corridor that stretched out endlessly before them. Princess glanced over her shoulder and gave a cry of astonishment to see the corridor extend behind them as well.

"Stay exactly where you are," Kedrigern said. "Before we take a step, I want to make sure we can get out of this place."

"Please do," said Princess, holding tightly to his hand.

He concentrated for a moment, eyes closed, then repeated a spell in a voice scarcely more than a whisper. At the last word, he pointed downward. The floor around their feet glowed brightly, then faded. They took a pace forward and looked back at their footprints, soft white lights on the dark stone floor.

"Now we can explore. When we want to leave, we need only set our feet in those prints and take one step back, and we'll be outside."

Except for the fact that it seemed to run on to infinity before and behind them, the corridor was fairly ordinary at first glance, like a gallery in some large and roomy castle. Doors and shuttered windows alternated, with a door on one wall opposite a window on the wall facing, and so on, for as far as they could see. There was nothing special about either the doors or the windows; or, for that matter, the floor or the ceiling. The passage was wide enough for two to walk abreast without constriction, the ceiling just too high overhead to touch with fully outstretched fingertips. The doors and windows were closely crowded together. After they had passed a dozen windows, Princess stopped. She was frowning, and seemed troubled.

"Something is wrong here," she said. "The light comes through the shutters on both sides at the same angle." Kedrigern merely nodded, and she went on, "And these doors—they must all lead into tiny closets, because if there were rooms behind them, they'd block the light to the windows."

"This is an enchanted place. It isn't located anywhere in particular, so none of the usual laws of light and shadow and perspective and space apply."

"If it isn't anywhere in particular, where is it?"

"Nowhere in particular. It's partly everywhere, but not exactly anywhere."

Princess looked even more troubled. "That's impressive,

even for an enchanted building. The Speckled Hag must have been awfully powerful.''

"She was, but this isn't her doing. It must have taken most of her magic to find the way in. This is The Great Passage.''

"What is it? Where does it go?''

"It doesn't go anywhere. It doesn't have to. It's already there. It has a door and a window opening into every moment of the life of every person who's ever lived, or will live.''

Princess tugged at his hand. "Let's get out of here, now!''

Kedrigern stood fast. "My dear, think of the opportunity! If you can find the proper window, you can see yourself as a child. You can see your parents, your family, your childhood playmates, kindly servants and loyal retainers, beloved pets—your memories would come flooding back!''

She wavered, then shook her head and tugged harder. "No. This passage is too long. Too many windows. How would we ever find the ones that open on *our* lives?''

"They all do. Don't ask me how, but every window you look out—or into—will show an incident in your life.''

"What about the doors?''

"If you want to step back into a particular moment and change something, you go through the door—though how you find your way out again, I can't say. And if your two selves should meet—''

"Don't tell me any more. I won't go near the doors. But maybe I'll look in a window. Just one.''

Still clinging fast to Kedrigern, Princess reached out to draw back a shutter slowly and cautiously with her free hand. She looked out—or in—the window thus revealed, and gave a little startled cry.

"What is it?'' Kedrigern asked.

"Can't you see?''

"I see nothing.''

"Well, I'm there . . . by the fireplace, at home . . . only I'm old. My hair is white and I'm sitting in a big chair with my feet on a stool and a blanket tucked around me. I'm *very* old.''

"Did you age well?''

She looked closely, considered for a moment, and then said

with unconcealed satisfaction, "Yes. I look rather distinguished. Very alert, too."

"That's encouraging."

She turned to him in concern. "But where are you?"

"Probably out risking my neck for a client. Or in my workroom. Or out gathering herbs."

"I'd feel better if I saw you there."

"The window is concerned with you, and you alone."

"Maybe I'll just try one more," Princess said, leading Kedrigern to the next window. She drew back the shutter, quite
confidently this time, looked in, and cried, "That's the grand
staircase! And there I am, a little girl! I must have been about
four at the time. Can you see me?"

"Alas, no."

"What a pity. I was an adorable child. And it was a lovely
castle. That's my sister, standing right behind me. A fairly
attractive child herself, if you like fat smug little faces. But
what is she . . . ?" Princess gasped, grew pale, and squeezed
Kedrigern's hand in a spasm of knuckle-crunching intensity,
crying, "She pushed me! She pushed me down the grand staircase! All these years, I believed that it was an accident, but
. . . *she pushed me!*"

"Your sister?"

"My own sister. Pushed me. Right down the staircase,"
Princess said in a hard, cold voice.

"Dreadful. Perhaps we've seen enough, my dear."

"One more," she said. "Just one more, then we'll go." As
she reached for the shutter of the next window, she hesitated
and turned to Kedrigern. "Why don't you look in one?"

"I really don't want—"

"Oh, go on. Just one. You'll be sorry all your life if you
don't."

"I don't want to dig into my past."

"Maybe you'll see your future. You're the one who insisted
we come in here. It wasn't my idea."

"Yes, but you're the one who wants memories back. I
don't."

"As a wizard, you owe it to yourself to see how this place

works. It's an opportunity for professional growth.''

Kedrigern looked trapped and unhappy. After an unsuccessful attempt to think up a counter-argument, he muttered, ''If you put it that way, I can't argue. Just one quick look,'' and drew back the shutter of the nearest window.

The scene within was dim, illuminated only by a candle, and it took him a moment to distinguish the details. A figure was lying on a plain low bed in a strange room. The candle was on a stool near the head of the bed, and by its light, Kedrigern could make out his own features. His lips were moving, and he shook his head restlessly from side to side, like a man in a fever, or a troubled sleep. A motion in the gloom at the foot of the bed caught Kedrigern's eye, and looking closely he saw a figure gazing down on him as he slept. It was a figure he had seen before: tall and thin, in a dark cloak with the hood pulled forward to conceal the features; in one pale hand, a heavy scythe. Kedrigern swung the shutter firmly back in place and stepped away from the window.

''What did you see? Is everything all right?'' Princess asked.

''Yes, yes—quite all right. I saw myself sleeping, that's all.''

''At home? In our bed? Was I there?''

''No, I was in a strange bed. A strange room. An inn somewhere, I suppose.''

''It must have been a disappointment. But at least you didn't see your own sister pushing you downstairs. Do you want to try another window?''

''No. I think we should leave.''

''Just one more, and then we'll go.'' Princess pulled open the nearest shutter and looked in. She turned to Kedrigern, and her expression showed concern. ''I can see both of us. We're looking this way and discussing something. Formidable and the others are in the background. It must be a few minutes ago, just before we entered the doorway.'' She returned her attention to the window. ''Yes, it is. We've joined hands, and you're working the protective spell. It looks as though you've finished it. Now we're stepping forward—''

He tugged at her hand so hard that she staggered into him.

With a cry of "Let's go!" he dragged her down the hall at a run to their glowing footprints. They jumped into them just as the door began to open, and with a backward step, they were outside, standing hand in hand before the shack, breathless from their hurried exit. Behind them, they heard the voices of Belsheer and Bledge saying, "—*harder they fall.*"

"Yes, but first you have to knock them down," Formidable said.

"I don't think we ought to mention this to the others," Kedrigern whispered. "I'll close up the doorway. It's too dangerous to leave open."

"What would have happened if we had met ourselves in there?"

"One set of us would have disappeared. Maybe both sets. Maybe *everything* would have been annihilated. There's very powerful magic at work in there."

"Close it tightly," said Princess.

···❧ Twelve ❧···

second thoughts all around

THEY CAMPED FOR the night in a pleasantly dry cave about two hundred paces from a small waterfall that provided a pleasing muted background to their rest. The general mood was cheerful. They had met and overcome fearful obstacles and adversaries, and their goal was near: Bledge had assured them that with moderate speed, and no interruptions in their journey, they could expect to reach the castle of Glynfynnyn by sundown the next day.

Everyone pitched in to make the evening meal a success. Tergus caught and prepared fish; Bledge located tasty roots and greens; Kedrigern found proper herbs for seasoning. Belsheer regaled the diners with uplifting proverbs on such topics as rest, food, industry, and cooperation; afterwards, Formidable and Kedrigern told stories. Princess ended the evening with a medley of sweet song accompanied by the humming of Belsheer.

They slept undisturbed, and were on the trail again before sunrise. The positive sentiments of the previous evening quickly dissipated in the morning's dimness and the chill mist. Cheerfulness seemed somehow light-minded and inappropriate. Conversation was monosyllabic and grudging, restricted to the essentials. As they rode, each of the travelers was concerned

with his—or, in the sole case of Princess, her—own troubled
thoughts.

Princess: My own sister. Impossible. Still, there it was.
Right before my eyes. Dreadful sight. Could have broken my
neck. Bruised from head to foot. Looked like a plum for weeks.
Scarcely able to move. Remember *that* all right. My own sister.
Still no names, though. Mother, father, sneaking villainess of
a sister, all nameless. Faceless, too, practically.

And what about that plunge into the moat? Pushed? Can't
say. Possible, though. Light of new evidence. Nearly drowned.
And the antlers. Another close one. Mustn't speculate, though.
Only prejudice myself against. Miserable little sneak. No. Wait
and see what Great Crawling Loathliness. Reveal all. Past an
open book. Names, faces, places. No more mysteries.

Think about that. Mysteries not always bad. Skeletons in
every closet. What if they were all like her? Family of fiends.
Better not knowing. Let sleeping dogs *et cetera*. Turning over
a rock. Keddie said that once. May have had right idea.

No. Impossible. Nice girl like me. Blood will tell. Could be
wrong about sister. Bad light. Quick glimpse. Might have been
anyone. Clumsy servant. Disgruntled courtier. Fooling myself.
Her, all right. Black sheep in every family. What family? Might
be extinct by now. Destroyed by Great Crawling Loathliness.
"Family Tragedy." Father's very words. Sister carried off?
Serve her right.

Mustn't think like that. Loyal to family. Thicker than water.
But who? Definitely royal blood. Like Kallopane. Why not?
Sariax, Jussibee, all those nasty children. Ugh. Still not all
bad. Formidable my cousin, kinsman, whatever. Handsome,
too. Pious, Philosophical, all of them. Decent lot.

Dropping back to Kedrigern's side, she broke into his med-
itation with an abrupt, "It just occurred to me that I may be
related to the house of Kallopane."

"Really? What makes you think so?"

"Well, you found me in the Dismal Bog. Remember?"

"Indeed I do. Happiest day of my life."

"Mine, too," she said. They smiled fondly upon one another, and then she went on, "The very next year, you found Handsome in the same place. And he was a toad, too."

"So he was."

"Doesn't that suggest some kind of connection between us? It's hardly accidental that a prince and a princess would both be turned into toads and set down in the same place."

Kedrigern shook his head. "No, it's not accidental. But it's no proof of a connection, either. I've looked into the matter. It seems that that part of the Dismal Bog is a sort of clearing house for bog-fairies' enchantees, in particular those that have been turned into toads. The idea is to whisk them far from familiar surroundings while they're still confused and disoriented by the transition, and before they can seek proper help. You may be related to Kallopane, but there's no special reason to think so."

Princess's face fell. "Oh."

"I'm sorry, my dear. But if you're right about The Great Crawling Loathliness, we should learn the truth very soon."

"Yes," she said, and in thoughtful mood returned to her place in the column.

Formidable: Sword, I think. And light armor. Helmet and breastplate will do it. Nothing more. Speed essential. Doesn't breathe fire, or exhale poison. Dash in close and find a vulnerable spot. One quick thrust. Another job well done. Get it over with quickly, before that wizard decides I need help. Glory all mine. What's glory to a wizard? Gold, that's all they want. Up to us heroes to slay evildoers. Liberate captives. Rescue maidens.

Then what? Marriage? Have to be careful. Too soon for that. Great feats still to perform. Maybe someday. Not now. End up like Handsome. No tournaments, no quests, no bold deeds, no interest in anything but his wife. Ruined man. Learn from his example.

The Fair Glynfynnyn. Sounds good. Fair in the sense of "pleasing to the eye"? "Lovely to behold"? What if fair in the sense of "adequate"? "So-so"? Better check that before

too late. Avoid entanglement. Slay monster, tip helmet, ride
into sunset as soon as possible. Sorry, only kill monsters, don't
stay around to get married. Far horizons beckon. Destiny calls.
Fate summons. Hordes of monsters and evildoers out there.
Waiting. Maybe a maiden fair in the sense of "pleasing to the
eye."

Honor and glory. Debt of honor. Could be local custom.
You rescued her, you marry her. Otherwise perjured false and
recreant knight. Honor and glory up in smoke. Disgraced,
homeless. Every man's hand against.

Must be rules about such things. Better ask wizard. Check
with dwarf, too. Detailed description, or he can kill monster
himself. Empty threat. Will he know? Won't hurt to try.

Kedrigern was summoned from a reverie for the second time
that morning by Formidable's sudden appearance and his abrupt
question, "What are the rules about marrying princesses one
rescues, Master Kedrigern?"

"I don't believe there are hard and fast rules, Formidable."

"How can I be sure what rules govern the Fair Glynfynnyn,
then? I have no wish to marry."

"Why not? You're old enough."

"A name like 'Formidable' imposes certain duties. I have
great feats of arms to achieve, a life of adventure to live.
Married men do not have adventures."

"That's nonsense. I'm married, and I have adventures. I
have a lot more adventures than I care for," said the wizard
irritably. "My wife has adventures, too. We're both on this
quest of yours, aren't we?"

Formidable allowed the fact a moment to settle in, then
admitted, "Yes. But you're a wizard. It's expected of you."

"You're a hero. It's expected of you, too."

"And that is exactly my point," said Formidable. "I must
be available for bold deeds and daring rescues when the need
arises. A mighty swordsman and warrior must look upon himself as a public resource. He cannot be selfish."

"It's selfish to leave a lot of beautiful princesses hanging
around their palaces unmarried," Kedrigern countered. "It's

also dangerous. If they don't marry and have heirs, you've got political unrest, dynasties collapsing, usurpations, wars—dreadful inconvenience for everyone.''

"Surely a beautiful princess has no difficulty in finding a husband.''

Kedrigern shook his head. "The problem is finding the proper husband. Just anyone won't do. Maybe it works out in fairy tales, but I'm talking about the real world. If a beautiful princess marries someone unsuitable . . . well, look at Mazooba and Daragil. There's a perfect instance.''

"I've heard of Daragil. A great barbarian swordsman, wasn't he?''

"That's the man. It seems that a wicked sorcerer had put a spell on Mazooba, and Daragil overcame him with the aid of an enchanted sword and broke the spell; a fairly typical situation. Mazooba insisted on marrying him. All her councilors were against it, but she was adamant. A very headstrong woman, Mazooba. And Daragil was a pretty impressive specimen in those days. Trouble is, he knew nothing about running a kingdom. If you wanted a monster slain or a giant sheared in two, he was your man, but when it came to drawing up a budget or putting together a festival, he couldn't do much more than stare at the floor and grunt. Things worked out for a time, because Mazooba made all the decisions and the speeches, and Daragil just rode out every once in a while and did battle with something or other. But then Mazooba died—aftereffects of the spell, her doctor said—and Daragil was left in charge. He hasn't the vaguest notion of what to do, and everyone's afraid to make a suggestion for fear of being minced fine or pounded into mush. His kingdom is falling apart, Daragil has lost all respect—his people call him 'Darry the Dim'—his children are such repellent brats that people are continually putting spells on them . . . it's chaos, absolute chaos. And if you don't marry the Fair Glynfynnyn, the same thing might happen to her kingdom. You can't permit that, can you?''

Formidable mulled the question over for a time, then said, "I suppose I can't. But would the Fair Glynfynnyn expect me to restrict my heroic activities to our kingdom?''

"I wouldn't know. I've never met the lady. Why don't you ask Bledge?"

Bledge: Stroke of luck. Good man, this Formidable. Saved my hide, that's certain. He'll deliver us. And if he can't, the wizard can.

Nice work with those giants. Sproggart, too. Still, Great Crawling Loathliness bigger than giants, nastier than Sproggart. Tricky, too. Could be match for both of them. Ghastly prospect. What then? Word gets around. Never find another hero. Or a wizard. Sorry. Business elsewhere. Must run. Hardly blame them. Should have gone to Kallopane. Kept on going. Always work for clever dwarf. Willing to travel, expert juggler. Good with poisons. Loyal. Up to a point.

And if he wins. Hand in marriage. Worldly goods. What kind of master?

Bledge came back at a fast trot when Formidable roared out his name. When he joined the wizard and the warrior, Formidable looked perturbed. It was the wizard who addressed him, though.

"Tell us, Bledge, is the Fair Glynfynnyn married?"

"No, Master Kedrigern, and it is a wonder that she is not. So lovely a lady—"

"Lovely? You're sure of that? Don't hedge, Bledge," Formidable broke in.

"My Formidable Prince, she is loveliness itself! Beauty unparalleled! Fair of face and feature, form and figure, is the gorgeous Glynfynnyn!" Bledge asserted in a burst of alliteration.

"If she's the gorgeous Glynfynnyn, why doesn't she call herself that?"

"She is also humble and unassuming, modest as a primrose, and twice as lovely. Any man would happily risk death for the favor of her smile. And to win her hand in marriage . . ." Bledge flung up his hands, speechless before the challenge of finding words to express such ecstasy.

"Ah, then her hand in marriage is the reward for the hero

who slays The Great Crawling Loathliness?'' Kedrigern asked, and Formidable blurted, "Must I?"

"It is required of you, my bold prince," said the dwarf.

"Are you sure?"

"I will read you the proclamation." Bledge reached into his jacket and pulled out a scroll. It was a very small scroll. He unrolled it and studied it closely, running a forefinger down the lines of crabbed script. "It says right here . . . no, here . . . I think . . . maybe this is . . . no . . ."

"May I see it?" Kedrigern asked. Bledge placed the scroll in his hand. The wizard held it at arm's length, then brought it close, and finally shook his head in disgust, saying, "I can read sixty-seven different scripts, some of them not even human, but this is absolutely illegible. Even the Aperture of True Vision can't help me decipher this kind of writing. This is worse than the worst of Osmor the Nude."

Belsheer: Worse and worse. Cold. Sluggish. Wings like dried leaves. Must keep alert. Think wise thoughts. *No gains without pains*. Not much consolation. Working, though. Remembering spells. Enchantments. Grizziscus's will come back, too. Just have to persevere. Keep spirits up. *Willing mind makes hard journey easier*. Don't bet on it. Think. *Cogito, ergo* not a bee. Not yet. Feel the pull, though. Wax. Honey. God save our gracious. No. Must resist. Keep mind focused. Mustn't think of clover. Rosemary. Raspberries. Stop. *All things come to bee who*—No. Keep it simple. Nursery rhymes. *The queen was in the parlor, eating bread and*—Rotten idea. Back to proverbs. Safest way.

"Osmor the Nude? A scribe?" Bledge asked.

"No, a king. A very unfortunate man, undone by his own calligraphy; or rather by his own cacography."

"How did this happen? It might be useful knowledge for a prince," said Formidable.

"No fault of his own, really. Osmor was afflicted with very sensitive skin, which grew steadily more and more sensitive until in his thirtieth year he could endure no garment. Poor fellow had to sleep in a tub of milk and go about in the nude all day long. Hence the name. He was also an extreme prude, so he admitted no one to the royal presence. He ruled by written orders. But his handwriting was so execrable that no one in the kingdom could make sense of it. The result, of course, was chaos in the palace, unrest among the court, and confusion among the people. Finally, in desperation, a group of nobles seized power."

"From an anointed king?" Formidable cried, his hand closing on his sword hilt with a knuckle-whitening grip.

"I'm afraid so. But there was no violence."

"Nevertheless, rebellion cannot be countenanced. Once the monster that troubles the Fair Glynfynnyn is slain—"

"The Gorgeous Glynfynnyn, my prince," Bledge reminded him.

"—I must ride to Osmor's assistance." Turning to the dwarf, Formidable explained, "As a champion of the right, I must keep myself available. Can't allow myself to be tied down, you understand."

"Before you get worked up about this, let me finish," Kedrigern said. "The rebellion was very quiet and tasteful. Osmor didn't even know it had occurred. What happened was that the nobles simply got together and decided what needed to be done, then had a scribe write out their instructions legibly and affix the royal seal."

"Usurpers!" Formidable hissed between clenched teeth.

"As a matter of fact, the kingdom prospered. The nobles worked themselves to exhaustion and Osmor got all the credit. The people adored him. They were almost inconsolable when he died."

"Foully murdered!"

"He died of a severe chill. It seems he issued a series of commands that no more firewood should be delivered to the royal apartments, and his nightly tub of milk should no longer be warmed before being brought to him. At least that's what the orders seemed to say. A few of the nobles were certain that Osmor had written to request a new chessboard, and several read the document as a call for a tax on wool. The Lord Cham-

berlain was convinced that it was a satirical poem about a
neighboring king. When they asked Osmor, he flew into a
temper and shouted, 'You have my orders, now obey them!'
So they did the best they could. They stopped his firewood,
cooled his tub of milk, sent in a chessboard, levied a wool tax,
and circulated witty lampoons about the neighboring king. Poor
Osmor was dead within a week.''

"Betrayed by his nobles," Formidable growled.

"Undone by his handwriting. But we need not be troubled
by the fact that this proclamation is illegible, if Bledge can
give us the gist of it. Can you, Bledge?"

"I can indeed, good wizard," said the dwarf. "When my
lady was born, her parents proclaimed that the slayer of The
Great Crawling Loathliness that plagued their kingdom would
be honored in three ways: He would receive the hand of their
daughter in marriage, be awarded five thousand golden crowns,
and be called Liberator of the Land and Master of Moodymount. Though the king and queen have gone to their reward,
the offer still stands."

"Five thousand crowns? I could outfit my own company of
warriors—travel the world doing bold deeds," Formidable said
with a dreamy smile.

"Five thousand crowns? Nobody ever offers a wizard five
thousand crowns," said Kedrigern. "All a wizard ever gets is
a ring or a purse with a few coins in it."

Formidable gave a little mocking laugh. "More than he's
worth, usually. All wizards do is mumble and wave their hands.
A hero has to sweat, and bleed, and risk his neck."

Kedrigern rounded on him, eyes narrowed. "Fat lot *you*
know, sonny. Try working a spell when you've got a hungry
demon slobbering over your boots, or a magic mist closing in
all around you, or Death waving a scythe in your face. You
think heroes have it tough, do you? Well, let me tell you," he
began.

Tergus: Impulsive. Always been my problem. Rash. Should
have thought it over. Wasn't all that bad. Work hard one day,
sleep thirteen years. Can't beat the hours. Independence too.

Nobody breathing down. Or chasing monsters. Fighting giants. Man could get hurt. Seriously.

Pleasant meeting new people, though. Only met animals before. Not much conversation. But legend in my own time. Longer. Haunted Huntsman. Dread figure. Striking fear into hearts. Blast on horn. Demonic laughter. Brave men tremble. Sense of accomplishment. Nice to be known.

What now? Serve the prince. Strenuous work. Not boring. Not safe, either. Should have thought about this before. One day Haunted Huntsman. Next day servant. No big improvement.

"Good masters, you must not quarrel!" Bledge cried.

"He said wizards are worthless!"

"I did not! I said they were overpaid."

"I should have let you take on that army of skeletons back at the bridge. You'd soon see who's overpaid," Kedrigern said, his face reddening.

"And I should have let you face the giants."

"Any time, sonny. Any time at all. Just say the word, and I'll take on The Great Crawling Loathliness with one hand tied behind me."

Formidable pointed at the wizard and exulted, "Ha! What did I tell you? As soon as he learns that there's five thousand crowns at stake, he can't wait to face the monster."

"I don't see *you* offering to turn down the crowns."

"Certainly not. Bold feats should be rewarded."

"Masters, please," said Bledge, riding between them, raising his hands in a plea for peace. "Good masters, hear me." When they were both silent, looking at him with surly, petulant expressions, he said to Kedrigern, "It would be best, mighty wizard, if you left the monster to the brave prince."

Drawing himself up, Kedrigern demanded, "Do you dare to voice doubt concerning my power?"

"Never, great wizard! My confidence in you is unbounded. But you would be unable to accept the promised reward."

"What makes you think so?"

"You are already married, and to a lady of surpassing

beauty. The reward to the slayer of The Great Crawling Loathliness is indivisible: titles, hand of Glynfynnyn, and golden crowns—all three, or none.''

Kedrigern began to chuckle, then he laughed aloud. With a sweeping wave of the hand, he said to Formidable, ''Well, there you are, my lad. Slay the monster, and you can outfit your band of swordsmen and travel about chopping up everything in sight—if your wife lets you.''

Formidable was irate. ''What kind of reward is that? A man should be free to choose. What if Glynfynnyn and I don't take to one another? What if—''

Princess's voice, though sweet as ever, had the ring of struck iron as she broke in. ''Will you please be quiet? It's impossible to think with you two ranting and shouting and acting like rowdies. Keddie, you should know better than to provoke headstrong young swordsmen. Formidable, you should show respect for age and wisdom. Bledge, you should—you should get us to your lady's palace as quickly as possible. Do you think we have nothing to do but ride about in this filthy wood? No wonder they're bickering like fishwives.''

''Yes, my lady! Most assuredly, my lady! We should sight the castle by midday,'' the dwarf assured her.

''About time, too. All right, get back to your places in line. Don't hold everything up.''

''A thousand apologies, my lady,'' Formidable muttered as he rode forward.

''Sorry, my dear. Lost my temper for a moment. That young hothead . . .'' Kedrigern smiled apologetically and shrugged his shoulders.

''*Young* hotheads have an excuse,'' said Princess, and rode off before he could respond.

Kedrigern: Own fault. Never learn. All heart. Don't do curses. Strictly counterspells. Undoing nastiness of others. Healing. Helping. Bringing relief. Deliverance. Don't seek riches. Don't seek power. Don't seek anything. They come seeking me. Wouldn't stir otherwise. Happy home. Princess. Books. Spot's apple pie.

Help me, wizard. Disenchant my daughter. Despell my son. Lift curse on wife. Husband. Cattle. Vineyards. Whatever. And I go. Rain, snow, sleet, gloom of night. Over hill, over dale. Leave home and hearth. Princess. Books. Spot's apple pie. Vosconu's best wines. Into the unknown. Dirt, heat, cold, rain, wind, snow, mud, insects, brigands, monsters. Innkeepers. Must be crazy.

And what reward? Insults. Ingratitude. Rings. Purses of gold. Small ones. Token payment. Hard earned. Unfair. Five thousand crowns for one monster. Outrageous. Heroes grossly overpaid. Word to Wizard's Guild. Protest in strongest terms. Concerted action. Solidarity forever. Raise fees at once. Sharply.

Thinks we're greedy. Dummy. Formidable, but thick. All muscle, no brains. He'll find out. Marry Glynfynnyn, settle down. Run a kingdom. Give him three years. Then "Help me, wizard!" Ha. Help yourself, sonny. Fair Glynfynnyn. Gorgeous Glynfynnyn? Maybe. Dwarf playing coy. Maybe just fair. To middling. Used to be king. Miggendoc the Mediocre. Somewhere hereabouts. Married very plain lady. Could be. Serve him right. Ha. Lovely family. The Homely Prince. The Gawky Princess. Ha. Make a philosopher out of him.

Just doesn't understand. Tough life, wizarding. No security. Work hard for centuries. Nice little nest egg. Gold pieces, silver bars, precious stones, plate, jewelry. One spell and *phht*. Pebbles. Ashes. Handful of sand. Wiped out. Start from zero.

Time to get out. Give it all up. No more clients. No more travel. Peace and quiet. Princess. Books. Spot's apple pie. Vosconu's best wines. Favorite chair. Smell the flowers. Wouldn't dare try. Besides, too young. Hundred and seventy. Boyhood of wizard. Look at Belsheer. Before spell. And me? Health excellent. No occupational diseases. Witch's cackle. Troll's petrifaction. Hag's wen. Fairy's twinkles. Sorcerer's stammer. Not a trace. Robust. Three good centuries left. At least. Ready for anything. Nearly.

Good to keep abreast. Shop talk always interesting. Who's enchanted, who's disenchanted. Latest curses. Could be worse.

* * *

Tergus's urgent cry broke into the wizard's musing, and with a peevish groan Kedrigern turned to learn what new problem, obstacle, puzzle, enigma, or ridiculous petty difficulty had arisen to interrupt the consolation of his woolgathering.

"A stranger, Master Kedrigern! A stranger on the trail!"

Kedrigern was alert at once. "Friend or enemy? Human? Monster?"

"A man, somewhat the worse for wear. The Formidable Prince is questioning him."

"Then I'd better go and make sure someone asks sensible questions."

The stranger was huddled against a tree. Formidable loomed over him, scowling and fingering the hilt of his dagger. Kedrigern dismounted and joined them.

"Claims he's a minstrel," said the prince.

"Looks ragged enough."

"If you're a minstrel, where's your lute?" Formidable demanded of the woebegone man.

"Stolen, my masters! Brigands took my lute and my flute, and beat me," the stranger replied, his voice quaking.

"Who were these brigands?"

"A band of ruffians, my masters, led by an ugly fellow with a black beard."

Bledge, who had been listening, reached up to tug at Formidable's elbow. "When I was Sproggart's prisoner, I noticed that one of the brigands had a lute and another a flute. They could not play them."

"My instruments! What became of them?"

"Alas, smashed to bits."

The stranger slumped. "Then I am ruined. A wandering mistrel without a lute is like a hero without a sword."

"Where are you heading?" Kedrigern asked.

"I hoped to find a small palace with an opening for a minstrel, troubadour, *improvisatore*, *Minnesinger*, bard, or *jongleur*. I have many talents to amuse and divert weary nobles."

"Do you juggle?" Bledge asked.

"I have never mastered that particular skill."

"It is an art, and I am very good at it. But since you don't juggle, I'm willing to present you to my lady, the Fair—the Gorgeous—Glynfynnyn," said the dwarf.

The stranger stooped and offered his hand. "You are indeed gracious."

Formidable pushed him back. "Wait a minute. How do we know you're really a minstrel?"

"I am Vollian. Surely you have heard of Vollian the minstrel."

They all shook their heads and looked at one another in uncertainty and slight embarrassment. Princess, who had joined them unnoticed, resolved the question. "If you're a minstrel, improvise a song," she said.

"I have no lute, my lady."

Belsheer, who had landed on Bledge's shoulder, said, "I'll hum, if that will help. Just give me an idea of the tune."

"The bee talks!" Vollian cried, shrinking back.

"Certainly I talk. And hum, too. *There's music in all things, if men had ears.*"

"He knows a lot of wise sayings, too," said Bledge.

Kedrigern stepped closer and laid a hand on Vollian's shoulder to reassure him. "It's all right. He wasn't always a bee, he's been enchanted. Now, you just go ahead and improvise something."

"Shall I hum?"

"No, thank you. I'll sing *a capella*."

Vollian covered his eyes with one hand and stood motionless in thought for a time, then cleared his throat and took a step forward. He began to sing in a high, clear voice:

> "I'd tootle brightly on the flute,
> Or strum upon my cheery lute—
> But now of both I am bereft;
> My voice is all that I have left.
> And so I sing,
> Hey! Ring-a-ding!
> With a hop! And a hip!

And a merry little skip!
And I—''

Kedrigern raised a hand for silence. "You can come with us. Just don't sing anymore. Save it for Glynfynnyn."

"You can ride with me," Bledge said.

As they walked to their horses, Kedrigern said to Princess, "That was quick thinking. At least we know the fellow's really a minstrel."

She nodded, and with a wry smile, said, "We know why he's wandering, too."

"Maybe he's better when he has a lute."

"For Glynfynnyn's sake, I hope so."

Later that afternoon, Bledge announced that they were close to their destination, and advised caution and silence from here on. There was no telling when, or where, they might encounter The Great Crawling Loathliness.

"Would it help if I went up and had a look around?" Princess asked.

"It would indeed, my brave and gracious lady. If you see something huge and repulsive, it will be the evil thing," Bledge said.

Kedrigern looked worried. "Be careful, my dear."

"I will. I'll stay low."

"Not too low, my lady. The monster has a long reach."

Vollian paled. "Monster?"

Ignoring him, Princess doffed her cloak and rose from the saddle, her little wings beating rapidly. Vollian grew even paler and cried in a cracked voice, "She flies! The lady flies!"

"We're aware of her talents. No need to make a fuss," Kedrigern said, and Bledge frowned at the minstrel, laying a finger to his lips for silence.

Princess went to just above treetop height and hovered, one hand shielding her eyes. Suddenly she pointed, cried out in a tone of alarm, then went limp and plunged halfway to the ground. Her wings began to flutter fitfully, slowing her fall and giving Kedrigern time to work a cushioning spell above the ground whereon she landed in a crumpled heap. He was at her side on the instant.

"My dear, what happened? What did you see?" he pleaded, chafing her wrist.

"A monster. She saw a monster," Vollian whimpered.

"Water, quickly."

"Give her air!"

"Stand back."

"Wrap her in the blanket."

"Where's the water?"

"Here's brandy."

"Quiet!"

Amid the confusion, Kedrigern took the flask offered by Formidable and raised it to Princess's lips. She swallowed a bit, coughed, then opened her eyes wide and looked at the ring of anxious faces. She clutched at Kedrigern's tunic and whispered, "Home! I'm home!" Then her eyes closed and she went limp in his arms.

"What did she say?" Tergus asked.

"She's raving. Thinks we're home. The poor woman's had a terrible shock."

"She saw the monster! It must be hideous!" Vollian said, wringing his hands.

"It is," said Formidable, "But I will speak with it, and try to help it mend its ways. Else I shall slay it."

Kedrigern looked up. "Don't forget, we want to speak with it, too."

"You may. Just don't try any magic."

"I will if it tries any on me. Or on you. That's what we agreed."

Formidable mumbled indistinctly but angrily, thought for a moment, then said, "Very well, but I'll talk to it first."

"Agreed. Now let's get going. Bledge, what's the fastest way to the castle? Princess needs proper help."

The dwarf pointed to their left. "There is a trail that will bring us there in less than two hours—"

"Good!"

"—But it is perilous."

With one voice, Kedrigern and Formidable commanded, "Lead on!"

···⚡ Thirteen ⚡···

a little touch of loathly in the afternoon

AFTER TRAVELING FOR a time through dense forest in wary silence, they emerged into the open. While crossing a high ridge, they had a glimpse of distant battlements. Bledge identified them as distinctive features of Ma Cachette, home of Glynfynnyn, and of her family for many generations.

"You've guided us well, Bledge," said Kedrigern.

"Thank you, kind master. Now, if only we can evade The Great Crawling Loathliness, and make it safely to the castle, all will be well."

"What can you tell us about the thing?" Formidable asked. "I've not been able to learn much."

"No wonder, my bold prince. Between the monster itself, and the robbers and giants that roam the woods, and the Speck-kled Hag's spells, few travelers dare to enter our domain, and even fewer to leave. Ours was once a mighty kingdom, it is said, but lately we have dropped out of history."

"Perhaps you can drop back in. Formidable's taken care of Sproggart and the giants, and I've cleaned up the hag's bridge. Once we attend to The Great Crawling Loathliness, people will be able to come and go as they please," said Kedrigern.

"I speak to it first, though. We agreed," Formidable said,

and Kedrigern nodded. He was willing to do whatever Formidable asked, within reason, as long as it gave Princess a chance to question the creature.

He turned to see how she was faring. She floated smoothly behind him, spelled to remain about five feet off the ground and follow him closely. She was wrapped snugly in a blanket, still unconscious. Her color was good and her breathing regular. He returned his attention to the prince, who had just repeated his request to Bledge for more information about the monster.

"I have never spoken to anyone who actually saw it, but I have gleaned information from ancient archives," the dwarf replied. "The thing is said to be unconquerable. It has the strength of twenty-six men, nineteen women, fourteen children, and eleven dogs."

"What kind of dogs?" the prince asked.

"Vicious ones."

"Has it any special powers?"

"Besides its strength, The Great Crawling Loathliness can move for short distances as swiftly as a bird in flight. It sees in the dark. It can hear an ant inhaling at twenty paces. Its appearance paralyzes most men with fear."

"What about women?" Kedrigern asked, adding, "Just in case we run into it and Princess wakes up."

"The delicate drop dead on the spot. Stronger ones only run mad with horror."

Kedrigern blinked and looked back. Princess showed no sign of awakening.

"Its roar has been known to snap human sinews and crack bones," Bledge resumed, with something suspiciously like local pride. "The smell of it brings on paroxysms of nausea, followed by blindness and tremors. The touch of its flesh causes painful suppurating ulcers of an incurable nature."

"Is it intelligent?"

"A chronicler calculated that The Great Crawling Loathliness is smarter than any three philosophers, nine scholars, or eighty-seven alchemists."

"Is it said to be smarter than a wizard?" Kedrigern asked.

"No one knows."

They were all silent for a time, pondering this information. When they had left the ridge and re-entered the forest, Formidable asked, "Has the thing any weakness?"

"None is known."

"Can't you tell us anything encouraging?" Kedrigern asked.

"The prince asked me for information about the creature. I thought it incumbent upon me to tell him the truth."

"It's not always necessary to tell quite so much of it."

"Perhaps poetic truth would be more suitable. I know a poem that deals in an indirect way with—"

"Poem? Did someone mention a poem?" Vollian burst in from Bledge's far side. "Poems are my specialty."

"I was about to recite some pertinent passages of *The Lament For Hildemars* for the good masters," Bledge said.

"That wouldn't be fair, would it? I don't juggle, so you shouldn't do poems. Besides, I know the whole thing by heart, in several variant versions," said the minstrel.

"One of you give us the part about The Great Crawling Loathliness. I don't care which one," Formidable said, with a hard look at each of them.

Vollian glanced expectantly at Bledge. The dwarf, with a gallant flourish, conceded the honors. Smiling broadly, Vollian said, "With pleasure, my prince. An honor to serve you." He cleared his throat, took a sip of water, cleared his throat once more, and began:

"Cold and raw the sea,
   Cool and calm the forest,
   Hot and dry the sands of the desert;
   But the marshlands are soft and mushy,
     Like my brave Hildemars
     Since he did battle with the Loathliness.
Strong and unyielding is the rock,
   Flexible the spreading willow,
   Ever-shifting the wind;
   Sticky is wax,
     But stickier is my brave Hildemars
     Since he did battle with the Loathliness.

Loud the crashing of the waves,
Louder the roaring waterfall,
Louder still the assertion of the thunder;
A low moan is the night wind in the pines,
  Like the moan of my brave Hildemars
  After doing battle with the Loathliness.
Painful is the sword's bite,
Painful the demons in the stomach after overeating,
More painful still—''

"Wait a minute, minstrel. Stop right there," said Formidable. "I don't know who Hildemars is, and I don't care about him. I want to learn about The Great Crawling Loathliness."

"You will, my prince. This is merely introductory material. It establishes the mood. Very soon I will come to the passage that describes the creature in all its loathliness."

"Skip the introduction and get to the monster. Now."

Vollian gave a little sigh of resignation, cleared his throat yet once more, and began to recite:

"For loathliest of the loathly is The Great Crawling
Loathliness,
  Malevolent monstrosity of Moodymount;
  Insulting to the ear as the squealing of rats, the
rending of wood, the grinding of stone upon stone or
metal against metal;
  Fetid in the nostrils as ghoul's breath, fen's reek,
beggar's hovel, moat in midsummer;
  Repulsive to the touch as the slime of dungeon
floors, the—''

"Now just stop right there," Formidable commanded, red in the face. "I don't want to know about Hildemars. I don't want a description of the monster. I want to know how The Great Crawling Loathliness fights, so I can be prepared for an attack. That's all. Can you tell me that? Preferably in prose?"

Vollian looked from face to face for sympathy. He found none. "The poem is vague on martial information, my prince."

Bledge added, "No one has ever fought with the creature and come back to give an account."

"All right, then, I'll find out for myself. Once we get to Ma Cachette, I'll go through the archives. I'll question everyone," said Formidable.

"I'll be glad to help. Princess, too, once she's back on her feet," said Kedrigern.

"You need only ask my lady. The Fair—the Gorgeous— Glynfynnyn, as sole survivor of her line, is custodian of the creature's history. She knows all that is to be known," said Bledge.

"Good, I'll just—"

A noise came from the wood nearby. It was the sound of a large body in motion. Silence followed; then a shrill jarring cry made the horses rear and whinny in fear. And then The Great Crawling Loathliness was upon them. It burst from the trees and loomed in their path, a quivering low mound of oozy glistening slime.

The travelers were upwind of the creature, with a soft breeze at their backs; even so, the rank reastiness of its presence brought a hand to every nose. Even Princess stirred, moaned softly, and buried her nose in a fold of the blanket.

Bledge gasped. Vollian emitted a soft cry, as of one abandoning himself to despair. Tergus, without a word, stoutly took up a position at Formidable's side. Belsheer, equally silent, alighted on Kedrigern's shoulder. Princess only hovered, resting quietly once again.

"The thing certainly lives up to its name," Kedrigern said.

"Yes. Quite repulsive. And with these eyes, I see hundreds of it," said Belsheer in a disgusted buzz.

"Still, it's not as horrible as that poem would make it. I'm not ready to run mad with fear. The horses haven't dropped dead."

"No. And that cry wasn't so terrible, either. I've heard worse voices on demons," Belsheer said.

"Oh, much worse. Poets always exaggerate. This thing is just your ordinary monster. A bit more disgusting than most, but aside from that, I don't see anything very special about it," Kedrigern said.

Formidable, meanwhile, had ridden boldly forward, one hand raised, palm open, in a gesture of pacific intent. "Have no fear, Loathliness. I have not come to do battle," he called out.

"I have no fear," the creature replied. Its voice was deep and soupy, with an unattractive gurgling quality; and yet it sounded somehow feminine to Kedrigern's ears.

Formidable drew closer to the Loathliness. He rested his hands on the pommel of his saddle. "I am happy to hear that. Though I am, as you see, a heroic swordsman, I am concerned about the plight of monsters in our society. It is clear to me that we must learn to work together, or monsters like yourself may be driven to extinction."

"Work together," the Loathliness repeated.

"That's the idea. We could make a difference. You and I can set an example for monsters and heroic swordsmen everywhere."

"You have a fresh way of looking at things," the monster said after a pause. "That is good. I like fresh food." A long tentacle extruded swiftly from its side and whipped around Formidable, pinning his arms before he could draw his sword. The Loathliness lifted him from his horse and brought him closer, for inspection. Then with a shrill scream, it dropped him and flailed the limb about in a frenzy. An arrow extended from the root of the tentacle. Tergus reached for a fresh arrow, nocked it, and took aim, but at Formidable's command he lowered the bow.

Formidable dusted himself off and turned once again to face the Loathliness, which had sprouted a pair of pincerlike appendages and was working to remove the arrow. "I told you I came in peace. I seek a constructive resolution of our conflicting interests."

"Why?"

"Because monsters are an endangered species. Anyone who wants to be a hero goes looking for a monster to slay, and all too often, succeeds. Things have already reached a point where there aren't enough monsters to go around. Another generation or two of this, and there won't be any of you left.''

"I will be left. I am indestructible."

Kedrigern studied the abominable creature through the Aperture of True Vision and said, "I think it's telling the truth."

"Then Formidable is doomed," Belsheer buzzed.

"Not exactly, though I don't envy him. The enchantment on his sword assures him of a fair fight. That means they could battle it out forever, if they once got started."

"It doesn't look as though Formidable has much choice."

"No. But I don't intend to stand here watching. I want Princess to get proper care." Kedrigern turned to check on his wife's condition. He was encouraged to see that she had turned on her side, and was resting her face on her folded hands. Her faint had apparently given way to a healing nap.

"What if you're the only monster left?" Formidable asked the creature. "You'll be lonesome."

"To be loathly is to be forever lonesome," it replied.

"But it doesn't have to be that way. Think of it—you could have friends."

"I hate friends and friendship. I hate all things good, decent, and beautiful."

"That's not the right attitude."

"It is if you're a monster."

"But someday you might be the only monster left in the world."

"Then I will get to do all the evil things myself. That is a thought that gives me pleasure," said the Loathliness in a thick, nasty voice.

"I came here in peace, to offer understanding. You're making it very difficult for me," said Formidable. He was beginning to sound impatient.

"Soon I will make it worse. We will fight, and I will overcome. I always overcome. Then I will devour you and all your companions and all your horses."

Formidable drew his sword. "No, you won't. I've slain four monsters, each more horrifying than the one before. Except the first, of course. You will become number five."

"I have told you: I am indestructible."

"Ha! I heard you squeal when that arrow went in."

The creature made a liquidy mumbling sound that might have been laughter. "Foolish man. You mistook a cry of rage for a shriek of pain."

"Just a minute, both of you!" Kedrigern shouted. He dismounted and went to Formidable's side, hands raised. To the Loathliness, he said, "I want to talk to you," and then, to the prince, "You promised."

"All right, but no magic. *You* promised."

"Magic? What is this talk of magic? Do you think to do battle with me by means of magic?" gurgled the monster.

"Not unless you use it first. Actually, we don't want to do battle at all. We'd just like to talk to you," Kedrigern said in his most amiable manner. He had an idea for dealing with the thing.

"Why?"

"You have a long and fascinating history, but very few people know of you or your accomplishments. It's a shame for all your outrages, crimes, and depredations to go unacknowledged. Now, we've got a poet with us. If you'd just tell us your whole story, from the very beginning, we could set it down and make you famous. Or infamous, if you prefer."

"Why?"

The thing was being difficult, but Kedrigern forced a cheery smile. "Well, you don't get around very much, do you? You haven't had a chance to build up the sort of reputation your work deserves."

The Loathliness made no response, nor did it move. After a time, it asked, "Who are you, that you take such an interest in my work?"

"I am Kedrigern of Silent Thunder Mountain, a wizard of great renown. This is the Formidable Prince of Kallopane."

"I know you not."

"My point exactly. You never leave this place, so you don't know about us, and the world doesn't know about you. We're here to change that."

For a time the creature was silent and unmoving, apparently

deep in thought. Its next question took Kedrigern completely off guard. He had been expecting it to ask "Why?" but instead it asked, "Who is the woman floating behind you?"

"Floating behind . . . ? Oh, dear me," Kedrigern said as he turned and saw Princess hovering at shoulder height just a few paces away. She was now resting comfortably on her side, knees drawn up, face tucked into the crook of one arm while the other dangled. "It's my wife. Had a bit of a shock. Insisted that we come and speak to you. So, if you'd just begin at the beginning, we can—"

The Loathliness swelled. Here and there, parts of its surface jiggled, glistening oozily and greasily. When it spoke, its voice was gummy and mucid, but the words were clear. "I will begin at the beginning, and go on until I have come to the end. The beginning is the appetizer, and the end is the dessert. The little man will be my appetizer."

At the last word, a tentacle sprang from the creature's back, hissed through the air like a drover's whip, and plucked Bledge from his saddle. It drew the howling dwarf back, and held him hovering, turning him this way and that, and shaking him cruelly.

Formidable went into action at once, springing forward and slashing the tentacle with a stroke. Before Bledge hit the ground, another tentacle burst from the Loathliness and wrapped around Formidable's leg. He struck it off, as he struck off the two that came after it.

"No magic. This is my fight," he said, keeping his eyes on the thing.

"If that's what you want," Kedrigern said. He took the momentary pause to send Princess gliding back to the company of the others; but he held his ground.

A tentacle ending in a cluster of sharp talons came at Formidable, and he hacked it to bits. They came at him even faster, in twos and threes and fours, and in a magnificent display of swordsmanship and agility, he evaded them all and left them writhing and squirming in pieces on the ground.

But then a club-like appendage struck him on the forearm and his enchanted sword flew free. At the very instant that it left his grip, two slim tentacles whipped forth to close one on each wrist. A low emulsive burble came from the monster, and Kedrigern realized, to his disgust and horror, that it was chuckling. Then it began to pull Formidable's arms in opposite directions.

Even without an enchanted sword, Formidable was worthy of his name. He set his feet firmly and pulled against the monster. His face reddened; veins stood out on his forehead and sinews on his neck; he groaned for breath through clenched teeth; and slowly he drew his wrists back toward his chest. With a piercing, whistling snort of rage, the creature sent out two more appendages, winding one around each ankle to tug Formidable off his feet so that it might then proceed to pluck him apart unhindered.

This was more than Kedrigern could bear to see. He snatched up the fallen sword.

It was nearly as tall as he, and massive, but enchantment made it ride lightly in his hands. With swift sure strokes he cut Formidable free. The severed tentacles dropped to the ground, where they thrashed for a moment like dying serpents and then were still.

"Your sword," said Kedrigern, extending the blade.

"Thanks. You'd better take this,"' said the prince, tossing him his dagger.

"Enchanted?"

"No, but very sharp."

They braced themselves for the next onslaught, but the Loathliness made no move. Bledge had gotten away during the excitement, and wizard and prince were about a dozen paces from the monster, poised in place, so Tergus took the opportunity to loose four arrows, which purred overhead and sank into the squilchy hide in a neat row. The Loathliness did not react to them in any way.

"Could it be dead?" Formidable asked in an undertone.

"It's indestructible."

"Maybe it lost the will to live."

"Monsters seldom do. I think it's up to something."

They waited, watching closely, as minutes passed. The Loathliness exhibited no sign of life.

"I don't like this," said Formidable.

"It's better than having tentacles all over the place."

"Why doesn't it do something?"

"I wish it would talk. That would be quite enough. If we've come all this way for nothing, Princess will be heartbroken."

Still the monster did not stir. Then, very faintly, it began to emit the sound of heavy breathing. Soon its back could be seen to rise and fall, and its sides to expand and contract. It sounded like a gigantic bellows.

As Kedrigern and Formidable watched, alert for the first hint of hostile movement, Belsheer zoomed by them, circled, and hovering before the wizard's face, loudly hummed, "I remember! Brother Kedrigern, I remember!"

"What do you remember?"

"Spells! All of them!"

"That's very good news, Belsheer. I'm happy for you. But I hope you don't expect me to stop here and now to despell you."

"No, not that spell. That one didn't come back. But I remember all the others. And now that I've recalled them, the bee spell is sure to follow."

"It's growing!" Formidable cried.

Already, the Loathliness had increased perceptibly in size, and was becoming steadily larger, as if it were inflating itself. What it planned to do was unclear, but it was certain to be unpleasant and dangerous.

Formidable pointed to the horses. "Get back, both of you. Save yourselves and the others. Leave the monster to me."

"I will not. What kind of wizard do you think I am?" Kedrigern said.

With a shrill hiss, the Great Crawling Loathliness, now swollen to nearly twice its size and deepened in color to a blackish purple, began to emit dark fumes from hundreds of vents in its hide. Thick, rolling, viscous coils of oily blackness rolled from its sides and tumbled toward them, foul and impenetrable.

"It's going to suffocate us," said Formidable.

Kedrigern raised a hand. "I'll take care of this."

"No! No magic! Remember your promise!"

"But surely—"

"You promised!" Formidable cried.

"Maybe he promised, but I didn't," buzzed Belsheer, launching himself at the Loathliness as the blackness swirled around his companions' feet.

"Poor brave Belsheer," Kedrigern murmured. He took a tighter grip on the dagger as the monstrous effluence closed around his ankles.

And then, on the instant, The Great Crawling Loathliness vanished utterly, and most of the black mist with it. The few remaining wisps faded rapidly and dissipated on the first gentle breeze. The air was once again sweet and fragrant.

Formidable blinked in astonishment. "That bee slew the monster!"

"Nothing could slay it. I only hope Belsheer didn't strain himself."

"What did he do?"

"A banishment. Very nice one, too. It's tough to do a banishment so quickly without leaving something behind."

"There's not a trace of the Loathliness. Not even a smell."

"Belsheer is a professional. Even as a bee, he's a great wizard." Fixing his eyes intently on the ground, Kedrigern stepped forward, placing his feet carefully. "If you'd like to help me look for him, watch where you walk."

They moved slowly forward, and soon Formidable called out and pointed to the ground. Kedrigern hurried to the spot. Belsheer lay on his back, legs rigid, unmoving.

"Poor brave bee. He gave his life to save us," said Formidable.

"No, he didn't. He's alive!"

"Are you sure? He looks . . . well, look at him."

"Just groggy. A spell like that takes a lot out of a wizard, and when the wizard is that small . . . but he's alive. If he weren't, the spell would be broken. He'd be a man."

Kedrigern returned Formidable's dagger and picked up the bee very gently. He raised him for a close inspection. One

little black leg twitched, then another. Kedrigern smiled, and
Formidable sighed with relief. Sheathing his sword, the prince
said, "Our quest appears to be over, Master Kedrigern."

"Yours is. Mine's not. That monster knows something that
may mean a great deal to my wife."

"But it's gone. Vanished."

"It didn't just vanish. Belsheer sent it somewhere. And
wherever it went, I may have to go there. Or else bring it back.
Or do something. Right now, I don't want to think about it.
Let's get to the castle. At least I'll be able to break the news
to Princess in comfortable surroundings," said Kedrigern with
a sigh.

···❧ *Fourteen* ❧···

skeleton at the feast

BLEDGE GALLOPED AHEAD to bring the good news to the residents of Ma Cachette and to prepare for his companions' arrival. The rest of the little band rode on in a state of euphoria tempered by concern.

There was much to celebrate: A noble lady and her subjects had been delivered from the bane on the land; Formidable had brought a perilous quest to a satisfactory conclusion and performed several impressive feats of arms along the way; everyone had shown courage in the moment of crisis (everyone but Vollian, and he was making amends by composing a poem to celebrate the exploit). On the other hand, Princess and Belsheer were still unconscious, the link between Princess's memories and The Great Crawling Loathliness was as yet unrevealed, and that creature's present whereabouts were unknown. Formidable's mission was accomplished, but Kedrigern's might scarcely have begun. That possibility troubled the wizard deeply.

A cheering, waving peasantry greeted them when they came in sight of the walls of Ma Cachette. People waved handkerchiefs, tossed flowers, and blew kisses from the battlements. Under the direction of various court officials, Princess and Belsheer received immediate attention. Princess was floated to a large and elegantly furnished bedchamber. There Kedrigern

lowered her to the bed and removed the levitation spell. She
nestled into the bedclothes and sighed deeply, and her features
softened into a dreamy half-smile, but she did not wake. Under
the eye of Glynfynnyn's personal physician, ladies of the court
tucked her in snugly. Six servants stood ready to minister to
her needs and wishes. While Princess was being seen to, Bledge
carried Belsheer to a crystal bowl heaped with fresh flower
petals, laid him gently within, and placed the bowl on a table
in the sun, guarded by four men with instructions to inform
them at once of any sign of the bee's recovery.

"And now, my masters and my friends, the Fair Glynfynnyn
would thank you in person," said the dwarf, indicating with
a flourish open doors at the end of the long hall.

"We're very dusty," said Kedrigern.

"I'm all dirty from the fight," Formidable added.
"Shouldn't we clean up first?"

Bledge waved aside their objections. "My lady is eager to
see you as you are, complete with the marks of travel and
battle. Dirt and dust, so bravely won, are marks of honor."

"It's not polite to keep a lady waiting," Kedrigern said,
stepping forward. "We can freshen up later."

As they paced down the hall behind the dwarf, Formidable
looked over their surroundings and said, "This is a pleasant
little palace."

"Very cozy, for a palace."

"Of course, it's much smaller than my father's."

"Oh my, yes. But this appears to be a much smaller kingdom
than Kallopane."

"I wonder what it's called. I wonder if it's even a kingdom.
It could be a principality, or a duchy. Even a great estate. Odd
that it should be so close to Kallopane and yet be unknown,"
said the prince.

"Not really, when you consider how difficult it must have
been getting in and out."

Their conversation ceased at the door to what was clearly a
state chamber. A young lady wearing a small, tasteful crown
sat on a raised throne by the far wall, surrounded by dignified-
looking men and women. She stood, extended her arms, and

stepped forward, saying in a sweet clear voice, ''Welcome, deliverers of Lurodel and rescuers of its people and their princess. I, Glynfynnyn, bid you enter and claim your reward.''

This was Glynfynnyn the Fair, and Kedrigern saw at once that she was fair indeed, and unequivocally fair in the sense of gorgeous. The sudden sharp intake of breath and the loud gulp he heard at his side informed him that Formidable had made the same observation.

Glynfynnyn was tall and slender of frame, elegant of bearing, with perfect features framed by thick waves of auburn hair. She was truly beautiful; and as Kedrigern approached her more closely, he found her appearance disturbingly familiar. He knew he had never met this woman before, never seen her likeness, never been to the land of Lurodel or the castle Ma Cachette, yet he recognized those features. Had he met a sister, or a cousin? Her mother? Surely not, for Glynfynnyn's name, and the name of her land and castle, were all unknown to him until this quest. A more distant relation, then? Perhaps . . . but where and when the meeting had occurred were beyond his power to recall.

''What a magnificent woman! What a beauty!'' Formidable said in a reverential whisper.

''Yes, lovely. Reminds me of someone.''

''A goddess! An Aphrodite . . . a Diana . . . a Juno!''

''No, someone I've met. Just can't place her.''

''What courage! Think of her, alone, unprotected, fending off the assault of that hideous monster!''

''Must have been exhausting.''

''She need never be alone again, never fearful, never in want of a champion. From this day forward, I will be ever at her side, to guard, to protect, to cherish, to love forever!'' Formidable's voice, though hushed, was perfervid with adoration.

It was clear to Kedrigern that the young prince's views on marriage had altered greatly in the brief interval since he first caught sight of Glynfynnyn. And that, the wizard reflected, was all to the good. It avoided a lot of embarrassment and brought Formidable's quest to a happy, and traditional, conclusion. It would be nice for Glynfynnyn, too. He was a decent-looking lad, brave as a lion, and with a sensible wife to teach him prudence and good manners and keep him from running off, sword in hand, at every rumor of evil in the land, he might become a decent consort. And the match was sure to delight Sariax, and propel him to new heights of gratitude and generosity.

Of course, he told himself, the wonder would have been to keep Formidable, or anyone else, from falling in love with such a woman. She was a rare beauty. Except for Princess, Kedrigern had never seen her match—and at the thought of Princess, and the sight of Glynfynnyn directly before him, he knew why he had recognized her. Glynfynnyn bore a definite resemblance to Princess. The hair was a different color, and the woman before him was taller than Princess by perhaps the breadth of three fingers, and Glynfynnyn, to be sure, had no wings; but they had the same blue eyes, the same heart-shaped face, even some of the same gestures. The likeness, while not identical, was nevertheless unmistakable.

Prince and wizard came to the dais whereon stood the throne and Glynfynnyn, and dropped respectfully to one knee before her. She raised them with a touch on the shoulder and favored them with a radiant smile.

"Welcome, rescuers. Say, which of you fought the loathly creature?"

Formidable stood paralyzed, looking down on her as a child looks on a plate of cookies warm from the oven. He was mute. Kedrigern took the role of spokesman.

"It was a joint effort, my lady. The Formidable Prince of Kallopane led us, and fought the fiercest. He is your rescuer. We merely assisted."

"I thank you for explaining. You are the wizard, are you not?"

"I'm one of them. I am Kedrigern of Silent Thunder Mountain. My wife and the bee are also wizards. They've both had a bit of a shock, but Bledge has seen to it that they're well cared for."

"Bledge is the truest of servants. I hope that you will tell me all that has befallen you. Your adventures seem to have

been quite astounding. I have arranged a small private supper—
only my rescuers, chief courtiers, and oldest servants. Tomorrow the festivities will begin. But first," said Glynfynnyn,
turning her blue eyes upon Formidable, "I desire an intimate
supper with my deliverers." She took Formidable's big scarred
hand tenderly in both of hers. "Do you know the reward for
the one who delivers us from the monster, my Formidable
Prince?"

Formidable did not respond. Kedrigern eased closer to him
and drove an elbow into his ribs. At once, in a voice that
reached to all corners of the chamber, the prince cried, "I do!
I will! Yes, all three, no question about it, I accept! Name the
day!"

When the cheers and happy shouts had died down, Glynfynnyn said, "We will attend to that pleasant duty, brave
prince. Meanwhile, you may wish to repair to your chambers,
to rest and refresh yourselves before we meet this evening."

Kedrigern had to tug hard at Formidable's arm to get him
moving. As they left the chamber, the prince softly babbled,
"I never thought . . . never expected . . . so beautiful! Now I
understand Handsome . . . time to settle down. . . . Yes, he certainly had the right idea . . . wonderful woman . . . a man could
ask nothing more."

"Five thousand crowns won't be so hard to take, either."

"Do you think I care for gold? Take the five thousand
crowns! I bestow them upon you, to divide as you see fit."

"Really? That's very generous of you. You've got the mak-
ings of a good ruler, my boy—the very best kind."

"And as for the titles," Formidable went on, "I shall retain
that of Liberator. 'Formidable Prince of Kallopane and Liberator of Lurodel' has a ring to it. I shall appoint Tergus Royal
Huntsman and confer upon him the title 'Master of Moodymount.' Though he has served me but briefly, he has served
me well."

"What about Bledge? He served you and Glynfynnyn."

"Bledge shall be knighted."

"Better and better, Formidable. Spoken like a true prince."

"I *am* a true prince. And with such a woman at my side, I

shall be a magnificent prince." Now that they had reached the doorway, Formidable sounded like his old self. He walked with head high, strutting like a conqueror. But every now and then he sighed dreamily.

A guard stepped forward. His manner suggested urgency. "My masters, the enchanted bee stirs and attempts to speak."

"I'll go to him," Kedrigern said. He turned to the prince. "You'd better get some rest. From here on, it's going to be ceremony, festival, and revelry, and you'll be the featured attraction. You owe it to your people to keep awake and look your best."

"And to the Fair Glynfynnyn," Formidable said, nodding. "To her above all."

Kedrigern followed the guard to the table where Belsheer rested. He was concerned for his colleague, knowing the strain involved in casting a powerful spell, and doing it so quickly and expertly. He was concerned, too, about the story he had told Glynfynnyn, for he knew that even though Formidable had done all the customary heroic hacking, hewing, slashing, and smiting, it was Belsheer who had actually rid the land of The Great Crawling Loathliness. On the other hand, Belsheer, when he was not a bee, was a bachelor wizard nearly five hundred years old—not the likeliest candidate for the hand of a beautiful young princess. Surely he would understand that, and agree with Kedrigern's decision.

The sight of Belsheer was not encouraging. He lay on his back, legs twitching and moving feebly. Kedrigern bent low over the bowl and heard his faint, gasping, "Clover... Clover..."

"Belsheer can you hear me? This is Kedrigern."

"Honey... Wax..." was the all but inaudible reply.

"Don't relapse, Belsheer! Concentrate on your humanity. Hang on to it—I'll have you back in my workroom in a few more days."

"Thyme... Sweet clover... Rosebud..."

"Think of wise sayings. Come on, Belsheer, give me one of your wise sayings. Just one."

Long live the queen.

Belsheer's condition was very serious indeed. It saddened Kedrigern to think that after such a brave struggle against bee-hood, Belsheer had brought about his own downfall by a courageous act of sacrifice. Something had to be done. Kedrigern beckoned the guards closer.

"Do you know any wise sayings?"

They exchanged an uncomfortable glance. "Do you mean like *It's a long road that has no turning*?" asked one.

"Or *Time and tide wait for no man*?" asked the other.

"They'll do. What I want is for all four of you to take turns repeating a few wise sayings, very slowly, to the bee in the bowl. Do it at short intervals. Not too loud. When he starts repeating them back to you, let me know."

"We'll do as you say, Master Kedrigern," said the captain.

Leaving Belsheer in the care of the guards, who appeared to be sound and trustworthy men, happily not given to asking silly questions, Kedrigern hurried to the chamber where Princess lay. Her condition was unchanged. She slumbered on, her expression tranquil. The ladies of the chamber told him that her sleep had been peaceful: no tossing about, no crying out, no signs of disturbed dreams. The physician assured him that he could hope for no clearer sign of a complete recovery. They need only be patient, and allow Princess to awaken of her own accord. To disturb her sleep would be dangerous.

Somewhat comforted, he went to his chambers to make ready for the evening's celebration. He was not in a celebratory mood, but duty, he told himself, is duty.

The supper Glynfynnyn provided for her rescuers was subdued, elegant, and tasteful. In days to come, there would be cheering crowds, music, and elaborate spectacle; this evening there was only superb food and excellent wine served to a background of soft music in a setting of warmth and intimacy.

Glynfynnyn and Formidable sat side by side at the high table, with Kedrigern and Tergus at Formidable's left, Bledge and Vollian to the right of Glynfynnyn. The other places were occupied by high dignitaries of Lurodel and members of the household who had distinguished themselves in the course of the siege by the Loathliness. The mood was festive, but restrained out of consideration for Princess and Belsheer.

Kedrigern, not the most convivial of men even under ideal circumstances, had to force himself to partake in cheerful conversation when his thoughts were elsewhere; but he made the effort, not wanting to spoil the occasion for everyone else. The only time he felt a serious strain on his good will was when he found himself in a labyrinthine dialogue with a very old man named Hoddie, who had once held a position of some distinction—exactly what it was, he seemed to have forgotten—in the royal household. Hoddie's memory was erratic. His speech was difficult to understand, for he spoke in a vague allusive manner, he had no teeth, and his voice was thin and faint. Such portions as Kedrigern could grasp were filled with references to unfamiliar people and events, and just when matters were becoming clear, Hoddie would either veer off into an unrelated story or fall silent, nodding dreamily over his reminiscences. He addressed Kedrigern sometimes as if he thought him to be Formidable's father, sometimes his squire, and sometimes as a man named Hervil.

Between Hoddie's maundering and his own concerns, Kedrigern paid little attention to his food, letting course after course pass scarcely tasted. In an interval of peace, while Formidable was tête-à-tête with Glynfynnyn and Hoddie was staring ahead, meditatively gumming a bit of bread soaked in wine, Kedrigern became aware of acute hunger. He bolted down most of a hot eel-and-raisin pie, ladling over it a generous portion of anchovy-onion sauce. He washed the whole thing down with a goblet of chilled wine, and helped himself to a second serving. This whetted his appetite, and he attacked the next course, a thick sweet pudding, with gusto.

No sooner had he cleaned his plate than he felt a threatening twinge in his stomach. His mouth began to water profusely, and though he shivered from chill, his forehead was moist. Formidable turned to exchange a pleasantry, started, and cried in alarm, "Kedrigern, you're as pale as milk! Are you well?"

"No. I think something—" and here the wizard paused to

swallow uncomfortably before going on to say, "disagreed with me. Emphatically."

"We'll get you someplace where you can lie down. That will have you feeling better in no time."

Formidable rose in his place and beckoned urgently for the servants. Glynfynnyn hastened to the wizard's side, took his hand in hers, and said, "I'll have them take you to old Hoddie's chamber. It's right nearby." As he raised a hand in feeble protest, she went on, "Hoddie won't mind. We'll find another place for him tonight. The poor dear old man probably won't even notice."

"Thank you . . . my lady," Kedrigern gasped.

With a servant supporting him on either side, and a volcano threatening to erupt momentarily in his belly, he made his way from the midst of revelry to the calm quiet of a small, dim chamber close by. The servants helped him to a low bed upon which he collapsed. They placed a candle on the stool near his head, a pitcher of water beside it, and a large basin on the opposite side. They covered him with a blanket, for he was shivering, and then left at his whispered words of dismissal, happy to be gone, for they feared—as did he—that a scene of truly spectacular intestinal tumult was imminent, and did not wish either to witness it or to clean up after it.

For about half an hour, Kedrigern lay supine, manfully struggling against the forces of revolution and disorder rampaging through his digestive tract. He felt as though a pack of mad weasels from Hell were trying to claw their way out of his insides. He refused to spell relief for himself; in his present state, it would be difficult to concentrate. He could only wait, and endure.

When the worst of the discomfort had abated, he raised himself very slowly on an elbow to take a sip from the pitcher. The clear fresh spring water brought momentary calm to his enteric furor, and he lay back, breathed a deep, cautious sigh, and tried to compose himself for sleep. Disquieting squeaks and rumbles from within gave him a moment of alarm, but they subsided. He soon drifted into a restless slumber.

He awoke feeling chilled, as though a cold wind had passed

through the chamber. He raised his head, puzzled for an instant by the unfamiliar surroundings, then noticed the candle and the pitcher, felt a twinge like a hot needle lodging in his stomach wall, and realized where he was. And then he saw the dark form at the foot of the bed, and his memory went back to the image he had seen in the Great Passage. "Oh, dear me," he whispered to himself.

Pointing a gaunt and bony finger at Kedrigern, the intruder said in a sepulchral voice, "I have come for you, wizard."

Starting up, Kedrigern said, "What do you mean? I'm perfectly healthy!"

"Nevertheless, your time has come." Death held up his hourglass. A scant thimbleful of sand lay in the bottom of the upper portion, and it was pouring down at headlong speed. He set the hourglass down and gripped his scythe with both pale hands.

"No! You're making a mistake! It's an upset stomach, that's all! I'm in splendid health!"

"That's what they all say. Oh, the stories I hear!" Death laughed a hollow laugh, then in a mocking voice said, "But it's only a scratch, my lord Death!' Ha! 'He missed me by a cloth yard, my lord Death!' Ho! 'I think the person you want is my neighbor down the road, my lord Death!' There is no mistake, wizard. Your name is on my list for this very night. Prepare yourself, Pobbodamum," Death said, dropping his voice to a barely audible mumble on the final word, and raising his scythe for the fatal stroke.

"Wait a minute! What did you call me?"

"Never mind that. Your time has come."

"I want to see your list. I *demand* to see it!"

Death stood with scythe poised to strike. "Oh, really now, don't be difficult. This won't hurt a bit."

"Show me that list!"

"All right, all right. I'm not going to stand here all night arguing over a name." Death leaned his scythe against the bed and drew a parchment from his belt. Handing it to Kedrigern, he said, "Hurry, please. I have a very tight schedule. As soon as I deliver you, I have an appointment in Samarra."

Kedrigern dragged himself from the bed, standing erect with an effort he did his best to conceal. His stomach felt as if it had gotten in the way of a stampede. He took the parchment, which was damp and smelt unpleasantly moldy, and inspected it closely by the light of the candle. "My name is not on this list," he said, thrusting it at Death. "Show me my name. Go ahead, I defy you to find my name here!"

"It's here somewhere, I know it is. I check these things very carefully. Do you mind . . . ?" Death asked, and Kedrigern moved aside to allow him access to the candle. Death ran a skeletal index finger down the list of names, and with a cry of triumph, said, "Here it is, Mister Know-It-All! Here, right after Inflagrante, the Count of deLicto, and just before the Duke of Goosedowne. See?" Death pointed to a scrawled name. "Now, if *that* doesn't satisfy you, it's just too bad."

Kedrigern snatched the parchment back, studied the name, and resolutely said, "That is not my name."

"Of course it is."

"It is not! My name is Kedrigern. That's Pozgvodbribnyi."

Death took back the list and studied it for a moment. He waved it impatiently. "Don't be such an old fuss. It's just the handwriting. That's your name."

Now that the initial shock was past, Kedrigern had regained a measure of composure. He was still uncomfortable, but he managed to put on a cool façade as he said, "My dear Death, there is no calligraphy known to man that can make *Kedrigern* into *Pozgvodbribnyi*. You've done it again, old boy."

"Again? What do you mean, again?"

"You've botched it. You've collared the wrong man again, just as you did at Arlebar's a few years back. Do you remember Arlebar?"

"Of course I do. I remember all my clients. Charming old alchemist with the tidiest little beard. Running a bit to fat, as I recall."

"Arlebar was a wizard, thin as a reed, and his beard reached to his knees," Kedrigern said, smiling.

"Well, whatever *you* say, I remember him perfectly. He was as bad as you—made a terrible fuss about coming along."

"Arlebar went quietly. He was six hundred years old. He had aches and pains even magic couldn't fix."

"Now just you stop all this, do you hear?" Death said, stamping his foot. His voice was strained. "I've come all this way, and I have to rush halfway around the world, and you're holding me up."

Kedrigern gestured toward the door. "Feel free to leave any time."

"You don't care one bit, do you?" Death kicked his scythe to the floor, where it landed without a sound. "I run myself ragged, back and forth, this way and that, and just because some silly clerk makes a mistake in the instructions for the day, *you* want me to go off empty-handed." He aimed a kick at his hourglass and sent it rolling silently across the flagstones. "Why should I be the one to suffer, I ask you? Is that fair?" His voice had risen steadily, and was now close to a scream.

"Don't get upset," Kedrigern said. "I'll write a letter explaining everything. I don't want you to get into trouble, but I'm not going with you before my proper time. In the long run, it would cause problems."

"You humans are all the same. You're terrible people to work with. You treat everything as if it were a matter of Life and Me!" Death wailed. He flung himself on the bed and buried his face in the pillow, sobbing. Kedrigern looked on in some embarrassment and said nothing. After a time Death sat up, sniffled, and said in a maudlin monotone, "You don't know what it's like. No one knows, and no one cares. Never a vacation or a holiday, no time to myself at all, and I'm expected to get everything right every single time. I never get any help. I don't even get decent clerical assistance. If I could at least depend on my lists, the work could be tolerable, but this is too much. They've made me a laughingstock."

Kedrigern sat beside him and laid a consoling hand on his gaunt shoulder. "There, there, old man. Buck up. You're doing a splendid job, considering the working conditions."

"I don't know why I bother. No one wants to see me. No one thanks me, or asks if I'd like to sit down for a few minutes, or offers me a little snack."

"Do you like little snacks? I never thought—"

"I don't, but it would make things so much more pleasant. People put out cookies and milk for Santa Claus, but if they think *I'm* coming, they bolt the doors. How would *you* feel if everyone turned pale and shrieked when they saw you coming?"

"Surely some people must welcome you."

"Well . . . now and then. But they're usually in such a state that I can hardly bear to look at *them*. You have no idea what it's like to be around dying people all the time. I never have any fun. No one respects me."

"Now, that just isn't true," Kedrigern said. Holding up both hands, he counted off on his fingers. "Knights and warriors are very fond of your company. Executioners and surgeons would be lost without you. Kings and emperors and princes, and warlords, and marshals are always sending men by the thousands to meet you—good strong healthy lads, too, not sickly old invalids. I call that real respect."

Death sniffed and sighed. "Once I turn up, they all behave the same. They whine and beg and blubber and do all they can think of to get away. The kings and emperors and that lot are worst of all. Don't they think I have feelings?"

Patting his back, Kedrigern said, "Cheer up, Death. You're appreciated."

"Ha! Do you know what one of those snotty incompetent young clerks said to me last winter, when I was worked off my feet from the cold spell and the famine and the plague along the coast and the war in the lowlands? He had the brazen effrontery to suggest that I ought to turn in my scythe and use a sickle instead. 'That scythe must be pretty heavy for an old geezer like you,' he said. Can you *imagine*?!"

"Maybe he was trying to be helpful. That scythe must weigh a lot."

"That's not the point!" Death shrieked, jumping to his feet and waving his fists.

"All right, all right. Calm down." Kedrigern patted the bed. "Sit. Relax. Compose yourself."

Death hesitated, but at last resumed his place at the wizard's side. They sat in silence for a time, then Death said, "I feel a little better now. It did me good to get this off my chest. Thank you for listening, Kedrigern."

"I'm glad I could help. Maybe all you need is someone to talk to. You've got a very lonely job."

Death stiffened at once. "Nonsense. I meet people every day."

"Yes, but they all scream and try to get away. You just said so. You need friends. Buddies. Colleagues."

"I can't have colleagues. I'm unique."

"Don't be proud, Death."

"Why not? Some have called me 'mighty' and 'dreadful,' you know."

"That may be true, but you've still got a lonely job. Have you thought of taking on assistants?"

"It wouldn't help. If people get upset when I show up alone, how do you think they'd react if I marched in with a dozen assistants?"

"I was thinking of two or three."

Death's cowled head shook in a decisive negative. "I'd still have all the responsibility."

"You should learn to delegate."

Death turned toward him, and Kedrigern glimpsed two points of cold faint light deep within the dark hood. "Once I start to delegate, I'm through. They'll take away my hourglass and scythe and give me an egg-timer and a penknife. I'll end up bringing in drowned rats. It's no good, Kedrigern. I have to maintain my uniqueness."

Kedrigern conceded the point with a little grunt of sympathy. After a moment's reflection, he said, "How about collaborating, then? If you could get some of the people who have you working so hard, and involve them in your duties . . ."

Death's eyes gleamed with fresh interest. "I like that. Go on. Let's hear more."

"Well . . . you said that last winter, cold and famine and pestilence and war ran you ragged. How about getting them to share the work? You could travel together, all five of you."

Death gave a dainty little shudder. "Not cold. I can't *stand* cold."

"All right, then, just the four of you. War, Famine, Pestilence, and Death. You could call yourselves The Four Horsemen."

"That's catchy." Death rose and took a few slow steps, then turned and said, "I like it. It's workable. I can just picture us. War all in red—he adores red, even though it makes him look flushed. Famine in a pale grayish white, and Pestilence in something spotty, with some kind of absolutely ghastly stain here and there. And I'd wear black, of course. Oh, yes, it's a *marvelous* concept. I'll suggest it as soon as I get back from Samarra."

"Good. Now you'd better get your things together and go. I don't want to throw you off schedule."

"I'll hurry. It was worth the time, Kedrigern. I do appreciate meeting someone who cares, and tries to help. You're a dear. Believe me, when your time comes, I'll make it just as nice as I can."

"All I ask, Death, is that when my time comes, you be absolutely sure it's my time. Double-check. Please."

···❧ *Fifteen* ❧···

a family reunion?

NEXT MORNING KEDRIGERN awoke feeling no ill effects from his eventful evening, aside from a blunted appetite and a battered sensation in his midsection. He took a few sips of water and went at once to check on Princess and Belsheer.

Princess slept on, and her expression bespoke sweet dreams: an encouraging sight, but less so than he had hoped. Belsheer was moving clumsily about his bowl, showing no reaction to the periodic incantations of conventional wisdom from his guards. Kedrigern attempted simple conversation, but received no response. Belsheer was sinking ever deeper into beehood. Even an immediate departure and a headlong ride back to Silent Thunder Mountain, and the full resources of Kedrigern's library, might not save him.

As Kedrigern paced gloomily toward the kitchen, to get a crust of bread, a familiar figure hailed him with a cheery, "Hello, young fellow. We had a pleasant chat last evening, didn't we?"

It was old Hoddie, but he seemed quite altered, and all for the better. His voice was strong, his eyes clear, his carriage erect, his gaze firm. He beamed at Kedrigern like a child on a holiday morning.

"Hello, Hoddie. You're looking very chipper."

"I feel wonderful! I'm as fit as a pudding. Haven't felt this good in more than a century. And my appetite is back, too.''

As they proceeded down the passages and halls that led to the kitchen of Ma Cachette, Hoddie burbled on about his new-found vigor, reviving memory, regained strength and health, and all-around rejuvenation. Kedrigern, concerned about his wife and friend, only half listened. But when Hoddie mentioned his ambition to return to the practice of wizardry, Kedrigern stopped short and seized him by the lappets of his robe.

''Were you a wizard?''

''I certainly was. Not many people around here remember, but I was pretty good in my day. Do you mind?''

Kedrigern released him. ''Sorry. Surprised, that's all. Last night, you seemed . . . well . . .''

''I know. Felt that way, too. I've been feeling poorly for a long time. Weak as a funnel. To tell the truth, when I lay down to sleep last night, I was convinced it was all up with me. But now I feel as though I've been given a new lease on life!''

''Maybe you have. Am I correct in assuming that 'Hoddie' is not your real name?''

The old man laughed. ''Quite correct. It's what little Princess Glyn called me. Everyone else around here called me 'Grod-die,' but our dear little princess could not pronounce that.''

Kedrigern experienced a moment of doubt. ''Is your real name 'Groddie,' then?''

''No. But nobody here could pronounce 'Pozgvodbribnyi,' so they—''

''My friend, my colleague, not another word. I have some-thing to tell you,'' said Kedrigern, guiding him to a long chest that stood by the wall. They seated themselves, and he told of his last night's visitor. The elder wizard listened in astonished silence, and when Kedrigern was done, he kissed him noisily on both cheeks, clasped his hands in a firm grip, and gazed at him with tearful eyes. ''My rescuer—my dear friend—you saved my life,'' he said in a voice husky with feeling.

''Sheer luck. I just happened to get sick in the right place at the right time.''

''All the same, you saved my life. Tell me, is there any way I can repay you?''

"I need a counterspell, and I need it quickly. Do you have a copy of Isbashoori's *Guide To Countering Complex Curses, Subtle Spells, and Multiple Maledictions?*"

The old wizard tugged at his scanty beard, worked his untenanted gums, and after an interval of concentration, said, "I remember that title. Big thick book, isn't it?"

"That's right."

"Yes, yes. I remember now. It's coming back. Look, young fellow—what was your name again?"

"Kedrigern of Silent Thunder Mountain."

"Well, Kedrigern, my boy, why don't we get ourselves some breakfast and then go up to my workroom? I expect my books will still be there. A little dusty, maybe, and nibbled around the edges, but useful as ever. We will find this book, sure as ashes."

On their way, old Hoddie—for so he preferred to be called—told his story, an inspiring narrative of heroism, dedication, and loyalty that touched Kedrigern to the heart and made him all the more grateful that he had played a part in the deliverance of this land and its people. It seemed that when Glynfynnyn was a tot, she was devoted to her wizard royal. Old Hoddie and Princess Glyn were inseparable. One day, while they were gathering herbs in the royal garden, Hoddie explaining the virtues of each leaf and root to the attentive child, The Great Crawling Loathliness made an audacious daylight attack on the castle and snatched up Princess Glyn. Without hesitation, the wizard engaged the indestructible monster, hurling a powerful spell against it. The Loathliness dropped the child, who fled to safety, and turned to deal with the wizard. Their battle lasted two furious days, and left Hoddie drained of all but a vestige of his magic. The monster took advantage of his weakness to thump him mercilessly and fling him, insensible and powerless, on a dungheap.

Hoddie's beating had been severe, and his vital powers were greatly reduced. He retained just enough magic to keep from crumbling into dust. (He was, after all, well into his fifth century.) His body recovered slowly; his mind seemed permanently afflicted: memory gone, attention fragmented, will

broken. But Princess Glyn never forgot his brave deed. Hoddie
was an honored resident of the castle, a guest at every festival;
a place was set aside for him at every council. And now, after
nearly twenty twilight years, he was his old self again.

When he had given his account, Hoddie asked about Kedrigern's adventures. He remembered having heard some talk
of them the night before, but his memory of everything between
his encounter with the Loathliness and this very morning was
still sketchy. The moment Kedrigern mentioned his companions, Hoddie exclaimed, "Belsheer? Belsheer is with you? That
old dog!"

"Right now, he's a bee."

Hoddie gave a wild yelp of laughter and slapped his knee
in high glee. "I knew he'd get himself in a fix one of these
days. Belsheer! What happened—spell backfire on him?"

Kedrigern explained their colleague's plight. By the time he
was finished, they had arrived at a small, dark door in the upper
reaches of a tower.

"Sounds bad for poor old Belsheer. We must get right in
and find my Isbashoori," said Hoddie.

"Let's get that door open."

Hoddie folded his arms and frowned. "I hope I can remember the spell. I never trusted locks. A key can be lost or stolen
or copied. I always spelled my door shut." He closed his eyes,
reflected for a time, then laid his palms against the door and
began to mutter softly. An ominous deep growl came from
behind the door, and he quickly withdrew his hands, exclaiming, "Wrong spell! Sorry." He paused for further thought,
then placed his palms on the door a second time and again
pronounced a spell. Metal squealed, wood creaked, and the
door slowly swung open. Twin flambeaux burst into flame—
a nice touch, Kedrigern thought, noting it for future use at
home—to illuminate a high chamber blanketed in dust and
festooned with cobwebs.

"Nice place you have here," Kedrigern said.

"I always liked this chamber. It's private, but convenient.
Let me see, now . . . Isbashoori is . . . yes, over there someplace," said Hoddie, sweeping aside loops of webbing, to the

dismay and irritation of several fist-sized spiders who retreated upward to glower on the intruders. Ignoring them, he went to a bookshelf, brushed away the dust, and with a flourish drew forth a thick black volume.

It was a matter of mere minutes to locate the relevant spell and find the appropriate counterspell, and they hurried at once to the table where Belsheer lay. The guards looked harried, and a cloak had been thrown over the bowl.

"He tried to fly away, Master Kedrigern," a guard explained. "I saw him moving around in the bowl, and threw my cloak over him. I was careful not to hurt him."

Kedrigern bent over the bowl to listen. After a tense moment he straightened and said, "He's still buzzing. You did well, guard. If he'd gotten out, we might never have found him. You may leave us now." When he and Hoddie were alone, he said, "This is going to be tricky. I don't want to bring him back while he's in that bowl. He could shatter it and cut himself. And if we let him fly out and then despell him, he could have a nasty fall."

They regarded the bowl for a time. Hoddie suggested that they place it on the floor to remove the risk of a fall. They did so. After further consideration, they decided to try a delicately timed despelling maneuver. They marked the prescribed figure around the covered bowl and took their places. Kedrigern began to intone the counterspell. As he came to the final phrase, he nodded. Hoddie whipped off the cloak; Belsheer popped up; Kedrigern snatched away the bowl; and suddenly Belsheer was sprawled, fully human, on the floor. Kedrigern and Hoddie exchanged a smile of mutual congratulation on a job well done, and turned their attention to Belsheer.

"I'm back," he said in a soft, wondering voice. "I'm a man again." He patted his body, head, and legs, and said more loudly, "I'm a man. No more bee! Brother Kedrigern, you've done it! I'm a—Pozgvodbribnyi, is that you?"

"It certainly is, and as merry as mutton! Your friend Kedrigern saved me, too. Snatched me back from the very brink. And now I feel better than I have for centuries!"

Springing to his feet, Belsheer said, "So do I. All that fresh air and exercise and bee food—I feel three hundred again!''

The two elder wizards stood beaming and chuckling at one another, at Kedrigern, and at things in general. Belsheer began to laugh, Hoddie joined in, and soon both were doubled over, pointing at one another, snorting and chortling, as Kedrigern looked on.

''You . . . you were . . . a bee!'' Hoddie spluttered.

''I was! But I got . . . my monster!''

''Grizziscus . . . that fraud . . . fooled you!''

''I fixed him good. Used his own spell . . .'' Belsheer found himself unable to continue for a moment. He turned to Kedrigern, tears running down his cheeks, and gasped out, ''I banished . . . the Loathliness . . . to the Valley of Aniar!'' and collapsed, helpless with laughter.

Kedrigern had to think, but it came back to him. ''That's where Grizziscus was headed.''

''Surprise, surprise!'' Belsheer wheezed, then pounded on the floor, guffawing.

A guard opened the door, stood transfixed with astonishment for an instant, then dashed off. Kedrigern helped Belsheer to his feet. Hoddie wiped away the tears with the sleeve of his robe, emitted one last cackle, and said, ''I just remembered—there's a small cask of plum brandy stashed up in my workroom, been aging for nearly twenty years. Why don't we go up for a little taste?''

''Sounds better than nectar and pollen,'' Belsheer said. ''Let's go.''

''You two go ahead. I'll try to join you later. I want to look in on Princess,'' Kedrigern said, starting for the doorway.

As he turned a corner in the hall, he very nearly ran into Vollian. The minstrel's frayed and dirty garments had been replaced by a dazzling costume: long hose of bright green, a scarlet doublet, and soft yellow boots. He carried a lute, upon which he plucked chords.

''Master Kedrigern! Am I not splendid?'' he asked, stepping back and turning slowly to display his finery.

''Quite colorful. And you have a lute, too.''

''I'm composing a ballad about the deeds of the Formidable

Prince. I shall sing it at the festival to celebrate the betrothal of the prince and the lovely Princess Glynfynnyn. Would you like to hear what I've got so far?"

"Well, I'm on my way to—"

"It won't take long. I'll just sing the first few verses."

"Perhaps if I just—"

A chord on the lute drowned out Kedrigern's attempt at polite evasion. He sighed and gave in. Having endured a sampling of Vollian's creative power, he had no desire for more, and was, besides, anxious to check on Princess's condition. But he opted to sacrifice a few minutes now, and get the ordeal over with. He leaned against a column and gestured for Vollian to proceed. The minstrel struck a pose, plucked a chord, and began to sing:

> "Oh, listen to
> My song for you,
> A thrilling tale
> Of derring-do!
>
> In woodland drear
> Not far from here,
> A creature lurked
> Whom all men fear:
>
> The Loathliness!
> A ghastly mess,
> It causes pain
> And great distress . . ."

This went on for far too long, and Kedrigern's mind wandered afield. Vollian pointedly paused to clear his throat, and the wizard smiled and raised his brows expectantly.

> "This valiant knight
> Began to fight;
> It was a most
> Impressive sight.

This knight so true,
Whose name was Lou,
Then thrust his dagger
Through and—''

''Lou?'' Kedrigern blurted. ''Who is Lou? I thought this was about Formidable.''

''It is, it is. But who can work with a name like 'Formidable'? It doesn't rhyme, and it doesn't scan. I'm calling the prince 'Lou' for purposes of this ballad. That's poetic license.''

''I see.''

Vollian's face fell. ''You don't like my ballad. Tell the truth, Master Kedrigern. You think it's awful.''

Kedrigern hesitated, struggling to keep back his honest appraisal and yet not wishing to contribute to deception. At last he clapped Vollian on the shoulder and said, ''My advice to you, lad, is either to find a rhyme for 'Formidable' or play the lute as loudly as you can.'' And leaving the minstrel to ponder this musical wisdom, he proceeded to the chamber where Princess slept.

He came upon a scene of great commotion. Grand ladies and red-cheeked servants were rushing about, waving their hands excitedly as they bumped into one another, moving pillows, blankets, robes, platters, vases, and pitchers from place to place, all the while exclaiming to one another, ''She stirs!'' ''She speaks!'' ''Summon Glynfynnyn!'' ''Call for the wizard!'' ''Excuse me!'' ''Mind her wings!'' ''Oops!'' ''Water!'' ''Open the door!'' ''Shut the door!'' ''Sorry, my lady!'' ''More blankets!'' ''Now look what you made me do!'' and a score of additional ejaculations expressive of confusion, solicitude, and remonstrance.

Kedrigern shouldered his way through the hubbub to Princess's bedside. Her eyelids were fluttering. She yawned, stretched luxuriously, opened her eyes, then shut them again and snuggled into her pillow. Kedrigern seized a servant by the arm, pointed to a spot at his side, and ordered her to stand on that spot and not move from it until he ordered her otherwise.

"Everyone else out! Come on, all of you, out, quickly now, out!" he commanded, shooing them out with sweeping gestures. The palace physician objected, but to no avail. Kedrigern bundled him out with the rest of them. Turning a severe eye on the servant, he said, "When she awakes, if she asks for anything, fetch it at once. I'll see to everything else. Understood?"

The girl nodded anxiously, wide-eyed with astonishment but accustomed to obeying orders. Kedrigern seated himself on the bed, took Princess's hand in both of his, and patted it gently. She stirred, murmured something soft and indistinct, and opened her eyes. She gazed at him blankly for a moment, then sat up and looked around the room. "Keddie, I think I may be home!" she said, and flung herself into his open arms.

When they had both composed themselves, Princess fluffed up her pillow, set it behind her, and leaned back to tell all. "I went up to look for the Loathliness. I was scarcely above the treetops when I saw the castle, and I *recognized* it! I used to go up to the meadow on the hill overlooking our castle when I was a girl, and look down to see if I could see Mama and Papa, and from there, the castle looked just like this."

"Are you absolutely certain, my dear? Castles do tend to resemble one another."

"All the turrets and towers are in the right places. That's what gave me such a shock. And this room—it's familiar."

Kedrigern nodded. He had his misgivings. The forest from which Princess had taken off was certainly no meadow, and had not been for over a century, judging by the girth of some of the trees. But he did not wish to disillusion—or worse yet, to upset—his wife, so he said nothing. She ran her fingers through her hair, smoothed it back, and took her circlet from the bedside table. Settling it in place, she went on.

"I think the best thing would be to take a leisurely tour of

the castle, all by myself, and see what comes back to me. Do
you think Glynfynnyn would object to that? You have met her,
haven't you?''

"I have indeed. A lovely lady. We had supper together last
night. She's very—''

"Last night? How long have I been asleep?''

"Just under a day, my dear. As I was saying, Glynfynnyn
is very grateful to all of us. She's quite taken with Formidable,
and he's absolutely smitten with her. They're working out a
date for the wedding now.''

"That's two princes of Kallopane we've found lovely wives
for.''

"So it is. I'll have to remind Sariax of that when we're back
at his castle. And Belsheer is himself again, feeling better than
ever.''

"I'm so relieved to hear that.''

"For a time there, I thought we'd lost him. He worked a—
a powerful spell, you see . . . and it took a lot out of him. But
I got hold of a copy of Isbashoori and found the counterspell.
Oh, yes, I helped out another wizard, too, here at the castle.''

"You've been very busy. After I freshen up, we'll have
something to eat, and you can fill me in on all that's happened.
I'm absolutely famished.''

Kedrigern breathed a sigh of relief. He had nearly let slip
the fact that the Loathliness was gone, and Princess would have
no chance to question it. The news would surely upset her, and
he wished to put it off for as long as he could. "Good idea,''
he said. "Odd, how things have worked out in twos. Two
princes finding brides, two wizards assisted—''

Princess stiffened. She stared at the doorway, raised a trembling hand to point to the figure framed therein, and cried,
"It's Abrasia! My sister Abrasia!''

Kedrigern started up from her side, turned, and saw Glynfynnyn and Formidable in the doorway. Glynfynnyn's hands
flew to her breast. She paled, cried, "Mother!'' and fell swoon-
ing into Formidable's arms.

"—And now two princesses fainting. She called you
'Mother,' my dear, did you notice?''

"No, no, she was calling for our mother. That's my sister Abrasia. The one who tried to—well, let that be. But it's my *sister*, Keddie. I really am home!"

With Glynfynnyn's limp form in his arms, Formidable approached the bed. "Dear lady, would you mind moving over just a bit, so I can put my poor darling down?" When Glynfynnyn was stretched out and covered with a light blanket, he asked, "You aren't really her mother, are you?"

"Do I look old enough to be her mother?" Princess snapped.

"Certainly not, my lady! You look to be both of an age. That is why I wondered at her outcry."

"This lady, Formidable, is my sister. At least, I think she is." Princess leaned over to scrutinize Glynfynnyn's features. "Abrasia's hair was just that color. She certainly looks like Abrasia," said Princess, but her intonation suggested a shadow of doubt.

"There's a resemblance between you. I noticed it as soon as I saw Glynfynnyn. You could be sisters," Kedrigern said, sounding no more positive than Princess.

Under Formidable's vigorous chafing of her wrists and patting of her cheek, Glynfynnyn revived and sat up. She looked intently at Princess, then smiled shyly and said with some embarrassment, "I'm so sorry. For just a moment . . . I mistook you for my mother. In her youth, of course."

"Of course. But don't you recognize me? Abrasia dear, I'm your sister!" said Princess, opening her arms.

"But my name is Glynfynnyn. And I'm an only child."

"Don't be ashamed of me, Abrasia! The spell is broken. Kedrigern has freed me, and I'll never be a toad again. Oh, don't reject me. You're the only one who can tell me who I am!" said Princess, her eyes brimming with tears.

Glynfynnyn embraced Princess, patting her on the head and rocking gently back and forth as she said, "I would rejoice to have such a beautiful brave lady as my sister. But alas, dear Princess, I have no sister. I never had a sister. And since both my parents are lost to me, I never will have a sister."

"Or a sister-in-law, either," said Formidable. "Sorry, my love."

"But you look so like my sister Abrasia. And this castle," said Princess, looking around her. "Why do I recognize it if it's not my home?"

Glynfynnyn shook her head. "That puzzles me greatly. This castle was begun by my grandfather, and completed during the reign of my father. I have lived here all my life, and never left, not even for a short visit. If you had lived here, too, I would surely have noticed."

"I *did* live here. I played in the outer ward. I had my disastrous eighteenth birthday party in the great hall. I nearly drowned in the moat!"

"But that is impossible, dear Princess! The moat has been dry for forty years, and you are scarcely half that age. You could not have fallen into the moat."

"I *did*, I *did*! If you pushed me, Abrasia, I forgive you, only tell me the truth!"

"I never lie. On the very day my grandfather filled the moat for the first time, The Great Crawling Loathliness appeared. It drank the moat dry, then sprouted a long hose-like appendage by means of which it flooded the royal bedchamber. Grandfather was saturated and greatly incensed. He ordered that henceforth the moat remain dry, and so it has."

Princess shook her head in bewilderment. "How can this be? I remember so clearly . . . and yet you say otherwise, and I must believe you. But why, then, do I recognize this as my childhood home?"

Glynfynnyn could offer no explanation. Formidable looked on helplessly. An unhappy silence descended on the little group. Suddenly Kedrigern's face lit up. He clapped his hands together and asked, "My lady Glynfynnyn, is there anywhere a branch of your family who live in a castle identical to Ma Cachette?"

Glynfynnyn looked up excitedly; then her face fell. "No, there is not," she said. "At least, not any more. I know that at one time there was such a castle, because my grandfather

once mentioned the fact that Ma Cachette was an exact dupli-
cate of the castle in which he grew up.''

"And where is that castle?''

"I can tell you nothing about it. My grandfather was very
secretive on the subject. It was, I believe, the scene of a family
tragedy.'' At these words, Princess gave a little cry of dismay.
Glynfynnyn paused, then added, "Old Hoddie might have
known something about it, but he . . . alas . . .''

"Old Hoddie may surprise you, my lady,'' Kedrigern said,
grinning. "He is quite himself again.''

"He is? Did you——?''

With a careless gesture, Kedrigern said, "Professional courtesy. One does what one can for a colleague in difficulty.''

"You have saved my dear devoted old wizard!'' cried Glynfynnyn. She took Princess's hand in a firm grip. "There is yet
hope—we must summon Hoddie.''

Kedrigern turned to the servant, who had stood mute, transfixed by astonishment and incomprehension throughout all
these proceedings. "You heard your mistress—fetch the wizard. He's in his workroom in the west tower.''

She sped off at once. The four looked at each other, relieved and hopeful. But scarcely had the door shut behind the
servant than it swung open once again, and a guard burst in
pale and gasping for breath, to cry in a broken voice, "The
Great Crawling Loathliness! It's back! It's attacking Ma
Cachette!''

···⊰ Sixteen ⊱···

a family reunion

VIEWED FROM THE parapet of Ma Cachette, The Great Crawling Loathliness was every bit as loathly as it was at ground level; perhaps loathlier, since its undulant polymorphism was more grotesquely apparent when seen from above. The creature glided oilily over the ground, now swelling and now shrinking, oozing between trees and over stones, flinging out a tentacle here, a trunk there, an eye or two—or three or more—on long stalks in unlikely places, withdrawing these and then flinging out other, more bizarre, excrescences and protuberances elsewhere. Its surface was now sleek and shiny, now dull; now spiny, now scaly; now dry, now clammy; but never the same for long, and always loathly.

"So that's the key to my past," said Princess with a shudder of revulsion.

Kedrigern gave a sympathetic sigh and took her hand. "I'm afraid so. Does the sight of it call back anything?"

"It only makes me want to be sick."

"Be glad we're not downwind on ground level, my dear." Kedrigern turned to Glynfynnyn. "My lady, do you know anything of the history of the monster?"

"Very little. I know it's connected with my family in some unhappy way. It followed my grandfather here, and harassed him from time to time, but he would never reveal the reason, nor would my father when the harassment passed on to him. Now I am its target, but I know not why.''

Princess darted to her side and embraced her. ''Dear Glynfynnyn, we *are* related in some way! The Great Crawling Loathliness is *my* family's tragedy—my parents said so, though they never explained it to me. It is a bond between us!''

''It certainly appears so. Oh, if only Hoddie were here! He knows more about our family than anyone else,'' said Glynfynnyn, clenching her fists in frustration.

A loud thud startled them, and the stones beneath their feet shivered perceptibly. They looked over the parapet and saw the Loathliness drawing back a pair of long tentacles that ended in a spacious cup. In the cup rested a boulder about the size of a well-fed ox. Back went the tentacles, stretching ever thinner and more taut, until they suddenly sprang forward with the force of an unleashed catapult and sent the boulder crashing into the castle wall. Again the stones shook beneath their feet, and the light sklittery patter of falling mortar came to their ears.

''It seems a lot angrier than usual,'' Glynfynnyn observed. ''It's never thrown stones before.''

Formidable turned from the parapet. His jaw was set. His look was grim. ''I must confront this creature once more.''

''No! Not before I speak with it,'' said Princess, and at the same time, Glynfynnyn stepped into Formidable's path, arms flung wide to block his way. ''You shall not. I forbid it.''

''You forbid me to fight a monster?''

''It's my family's monster. I decide when it's to be fought, and how, and by whom. That's only fair.''

Grudgingly, Formidable admitted, ''Yes, I suppose it's fair, but I've never heard anyone talk this way before. The normal thing is to beg me to fight a monster. Don't you even want me to drive it away before it batters your castle down?''

''If you drive it away, how will I speak to it?'' Princess said.

''And if she doesn't speak to it, how will we ever find the answers we seek?'' added Glynfynnyn.

''If I don't do something, how long do you think Ma Cachette will last?'' the prince asked. As if to underscore his question, the walls shook from another blow.

At this point, Hoddie and Belsheer emerged on the parapet, earnestly conferring. Hoddie glanced at the foursome awaiting, turned back to Belsheer, then stopped in his tracks, did a classic double take, pointed a trembling finger at Princess, and cried, ''My lady! Queen Tidyanna, alive and younger than last time I saw you! How can this be?''

Raising her hands in a gesture of reassurance, Glynfynnyn said, ''It's all right, Hoddie. This isn't Mama.''

''She's my wife,'' Kedrigern explained. ''Princess, this is old Hoddie, the wizard royal of Lurodel.''

''Charmed,'' said Princess, offering her hand.

Hoddie looked about, bewildered. ''But the likeness . . . I never saw such a likeness.''

Glynfynnyn led him to Princess's side, saying, ''I was deceived at first, too. I even fainted.''

''Amazing. Simply amazing,'' Hoddie murmured. He kissed Princess's hand, then shook his head and said, ''But if you are not our dear departed Queen Tidyanna recalled to life, my lady, who are you?''

''That's what I've come here to learn. I know only that The Great Crawling Loathliness of—'' Here the castle walls shook yet again. When the noise of falling rubble stopped, Princess continued, ''—Moodymount is connected somehow with a tragic event in my family's history. All memories of my family—even of my mother and father—are few and vague. I can't even recall their names.''

Hoddie was trembling again; but the intensity of his expression made it plain that he was in the grip of excitement and not fear. Taking Princess's hand in both of his, he asked, ''And is your memory loss the result of—of a—spell?''

Princess shut her eyes and nodded.

''A bog-fairy's spell?''

''Yes. She made me a toad.''

Hoddie flung up his arms and did a little shuffling dance of sheer joy. ''Then the lost princess is found! The line of Korelian lives! Oh, we are as fortunate as pebbles!''

"Korelian! My father!" Princess cried, embracing the old wizard, then Glynfynnyn, and at last Kedrigern, to whom she said, weeping for joy, "I remember! Korelian was my father, and my mother's name was . . . Namansa! Yes, that was her name. Namansa—what a lovely name!"

Hoddie's spirits seemed to droop at the very sound of the name. "Alas, the tragic queen. Oh, my dear child . . . my poor sad little—"

A great thud, followed by a crash and the rumble of falling stone, drowned out his words. Loud shouts and cries of alarm came from below. Formidable called for their attention, and they turned to him.

"Now that my lady Princess knows her family name, there is no need to tolerate this monster. Glynfynnyn, my angel, I beg your permission to attack it."

"You must promise to be very careful. I don't want you mangled before the wedding."

"I will be careful, my dearest. I've been observing the thing. It's slow in moving to the left, so I'll—"

Hoddie threw himself between them. "No! My lady, would you have him attack your great-great-great-great-great aunt?!"

"What? That thing—my great-great-great-great-great aunt?"

"I may be off by a great or two, but she is your relative, as sure as mittens. No doubt about it."

"Then, my dear Formidable, I cannot permit you to take up arms against it—her. She may be loathly, but she's family. Before long, she'll be a relative of yours."

Kedrigern glanced over the parapet. The Loathliness was in the process of extracting a huge boulder from the ground. The boulder looked to be roughly the size of a haystack. Alarmed, he said to Glynfynnyn, "Would you mind if I distract your great-great-great-great-great aunt for a while? If someone doesn't do something, this wall is coming down."

"You must promise not to hurt her."

"My dear lady, she's indestructible. And we are not, so I'd better hurry." Kedrigern looked out once again. The creature was stretching out its tentacles preparatory to sending the massive boulder into the already much battered wall. Kedrigern plucked a vial from his belt, placed a single drop of the contents on the tip of his forefinger, and spread the substance by rubbing his thumb and first two fingers rapidly together. He sighted down his arm at the Loathliness, silently reciting a spell, and just as the creature's tentacles reached their furthest extension, in the split second before release, he snapped his fingers. With a rapidly fading cry of rage and surprise, the Loathliness went flying back toward the boulder, slamming into it with a great wet splat and tumbling off into the distance, tentacles and other protuberances flailing wildly. Kedrigern smiled at his audience. "A little slipperiness spell. Lost her footing. She'll be more cautious now, I think. Hoddie should have time for some explanations."

"It's a complicated story. I'll need a lot of time," said the old wizard. "There's an account of the whole tragic tale on my shelves somewhere, but it will take a while to find. How long have I got?"

They looked to the Loathliness. Far off, it began to swell before their eyes. A thick tentacle darted forth, wrapped around an ancient oak, and plucked it up as one would pull a weed. Other limbs sheared off roots and branches and rounded the base into a clublike dome. Then, gripping the trunk in a score or so of limbs, the creature started forward. Kedrigern watched as it gathered speed, then answered Hoddie.

"I'd say about two minutes. Any suggestions?"

Formidable cried, "Banish her again! Only this time, make her stay banished."

"Can you do it?" Kedrigern asked Belsheer.

"I think so. Last time, I was a bee, and pretty confused. I may have left something out. And being the size of a bee, I couldn't work at full power. But now—"

"Can you send her someplace nice? Whatever she's done, the thing is still my great-great-great-great-great aunt," Glynfynnyn said, and Princess added, "Maybe if you send her to some plane of existence where everything is loathly and repulsive, she'll feel more at home. The poor thing might even find happiness."

Belsheer looked doubtful. "That's a tough request. I don't know if I'm up to it."

"We'll co-spell the thing!" Hoddie cried. "I'm itching to work a spell again. Come on, we have three wizards here."

"Four," said Princess, extending her hand to him.

They joined hands. Kedrigern took Hoddie's other hand, and he and Princess both clasped Belsheer's right hand. With his free hand, Belsheer gestured rapidly, then pointed at the Loathliness, now about a hundred paces off and coming straight for the wall below them at a speed just a bit faster than a horse at full gallop. The other three closed their eyes in concentration. Glynfynnyn and Formidable clung together. Belsheer waited until the Loathliness was about to launch herself across the dry moat, then he shouted a single word.

The air rippled, and for a moment all was still. Then, from below, came exclamations of astonishment and relief, followed at once by shouts of joy.

"Be happy, great-great-great-great-great auntie, wherever you are," said Glynfynnyn softly.

"And wherever you are, please stay there," Belsheer muttered under his breath.

"So . . . I am the daughter of your great-grandfather's brother. Or, to look at it another way, you are the great-granddaughter of my uncle," said Princess, giving Glynfynnyn a hug.

They were assembled in Hoddie's workroom, hurriedly cleared of dust and cobwebs by a simple tidying-up spell. As they sat in a loose semicircle before him, the old wizard smiled on them benignly.

"Precisely so, my lady. And The Great Crawling Loathliness is *your* great-great aunt Glurnia, turned into a monster because of her cruelty to her baby sister."

"Who retired to a convent, where she died of shame," added Glynfynnyn, wiping her eyes. "How sad."

"So went the curse on the first Mendeborg, when he spurned the affections of a bog-fairy and married a mortal. In any generation with two daughters, went the curse, the older would do terrible things to the younger, until outraged fairies turned her into something awful. Things would not be so good for the younger sister, either.''

"I know," said Princess. "But please go on, Hoddie. What became of my family?"

"As I interpret the cipher, for two generations after Mendeborg I, no daughters were born in the family. In your father's time, my lady Princess, there were only two sons, Korelian and a much younger brother, Mendeborg—fourth to bear that name. But Korelian and his beautiful queen Namansa had two daughters, and the curse—all but forgotten—fell upon the family once again. It is said that The Great Crawling Loathliness appeared on the hill overlooking the castle on the night the second daughter was born, and her wicked laughter kept everyone in the castle awake.''

"I believe it. Abrasia was nasty to me from the earliest time I can remember. Bugs in my food, hot pennies in my slippers, pebbles in the bottom of my bathtub, dead mice in my bed— and then she got violent. She began to make attempts on my life.''

"How dreadful!" said Glynfynnyn.

"Well, she didn't succeed. By the time I was ten, I was pretty wary.''

"Ah, but her malice knew no bounds," Hoddie said, tapping with a skinny forefinger the book of cryptic writings that lay open on his lap. "Started early, too. When your christening was proclaimed, she tampered with the invitations in such a way as to outrage Bertha, cruelest and most vindictive of the bog-fairies—''

"—Who turned me into a toad, and immediately whisked me off to the Dismal Bog—''

"—Where I found you and restored you," Kedrigern added. "Your ordeal was grim, my dear, but it's over. And now you know the truth.''

"I don't know much of it. I still don't know my real name, or how long I was in the bog, or what's become of Abrasia . . . or where it all happened.''

Hoddie looked at her sadly, rubbed his red-rimmed eyes,

and said, "Ah, my lady, the whole story is written in cipher; the cipher is a difficult one; the script is tiny and crabbed, and my eyes are as weak as spoons. And much is missing. In fact, everything else I know was told me by Indelia, wife of Mendeborg V, who in her extreme old age recalled a story told by her father-in-law concerning his tragic older brother, Korelian. Unfortunately, her father-in-law was very absent-minded and had a serious speech defect, so it is difficult—''

"Tell me whatever you can, Hoddie. Please.''

"Very well, my lady.'' Hoddie closed the book, paused for a time to gather his thoughts, and then began. "Korelian and Namansa were devastated by the loss of their younger daughter. The entire kingdom—except Abrasia—mourned for the little princess. Abrasia rejoiced. She wore bright gowns, played merry tunes on the recorder, and danced on the battlements at all hours of the night. There were bitter family quarrels, and in one of them, Abrasia revealed her role in the little princess's transformation. Korelian, torn between his obligation to punish the one who had harmed his younger daughter and yet preserve the life of the older, pined away and soon died. Namansa went mad as moss. For a time, she would wear only green, and speak in croaks, like a toad. Abrasia had her thrown in a dungeon, declared herself queen, and embarked on a life of extreme wickedness. Shall I go on?''

Princess had buried her face in her hands and was sobbing softly. Kedrigern sat at her side and put his arms around her, and she fell on his breast and gave way to weeping. All were silent out of respect and pity for her suffering. In time she sat erect, sniffed, wiped her eyes, and said, "Pray continue, Hoddie. I must know all.''

"There is little more to tell, my lady. Abrasia's excesses grew. She consorted with barbarians and alchemists. She trafficked with the vilest of sorcerers. And at last, the curse caught up with her. At the urging of united good and wicked fairies, the Queen of the Fairies, with support of her full council, turned Abrasia into a repulsive monster and banished her to an accursed wood.''

"Serves her right, the nasty thing,'' said Glynfynnyn.

"Ah, but we must remember, Abrasia was acting under a curse herself. She was a sweet and lovely child until the little princess was born. Only then did she become wicked."

Glynfynnyn's eyes rounded. She stared at him for a full minute and then, in a small voice, said, "Then . . . if my parents . . . if I had had a baby sister . . ."

Hoddie nodded his head solemnly. "You would now be a nasty wicked lady, or maybe a monster. You could not help yourself."

Glynfynnyn started up, gazed with tragic longing at Formidable, then turned away. With a throb in her voice, she said, "I can never marry you, my formidable prince. I can never marry anyone. What if we had two daughters?"

Hoddie shook his head. "No need to worry. I'm almost certain that the curse has run its course."

Princess turned to her and raised her forefinger. "And just in case it hasn't, Keddie and I will work a corrective spell for you. It won't be difficult now that we know what we're up against."

"Male children run in my family," Formidable said. With a sigh of relief, Glynfynnyn flew to his arms.

Princess smiled sweetly upon the lovers, then turned once again to the old wizard. "Now that that's settled, Hoddie, what became of my mother?"

"Hers is perhaps the saddest story. When Abrasia was turned into a monster and whisked away, Namansa was released from her dungeon. First thing she did was grab a torch and burn down the castle and everything in it, also herself. Young Mendeborg escaped, came here, built this castle, but never talked about the past. It was too painful."

"That Mendeborg was my great-grandfather," said Glynfynnyn.

"Correct, my lady. Brother of Korelian."

"But who am I?" Princess cried desperately.

Hoddie shrugged. "Impossible to say. All family records, accounts, diaries, journals, annals, chronicles, histories, memoirs, and genealogical charts were destroyed in the great fire. If Mendeborg IV had not written down the whole story after escaping from the burning castle, nothing would be known. And he wrote in a cipher to which he left no key."

"So I'm never to know my name . . . or where I grew up . . . never to see my sister. All I know is that I'm an old lady."

"That's not true, my dear. You're a wizard. Years mean nothing to you. You're as young as you look, as young as you feel."

"I must be eighty years old!"

"But you look scarcely eighteen—your age on the day you were spelled. And with all the magic you've experienced, you may not look a day older for centuries. Besides, older women are fascinating."

"That's true. We are," she said. "All the same, it takes some getting used to. And I still don't know much, even after all this."

Kedrigern enumerated on his fingers. "You know your parents' names. You know your sister's name. You've learned your family's history. You've met your . . ." He hesitated.

"Go ahead, say it. I've met my great-niece."

"Dear Princess, never think of yourself as my great-aunt! You look like my sister—my baby sister!" said Glynfynnyn.

"Considering the fate of baby sisters in our family, I'd prefer to be your great-aunt."

Kedrigern took each lady by the hand. "Why don't you call yourselves cousins, and let it go at that?"

They embraced each other, and Princess admitted, "I suppose I should be grateful. The only important thing I don't know is my name, really. There's no point in looking for the ruins of the family castle. They'd be overgrown by now."

Glynfynnyn said, "You are welcome here whenever you wish to come, dear cousin. Consider Ma Cachette your home. And if you should ever find your unfortunate sister, she is welcome, too, provided she—"

"Abrasia! Of course! I forgot all about Abrasia. She may still be in that enchanted wood, and if we can locate it—"

"My dear, I'll get to work on it as soon as we're home. If the wood exists, we'll find it. And if Abrasia's there, you will despell her yourself, with your bog-fairy's wand," Kedrigern said with a dramatic flourish.

"Poetic justice!" Princess said, clapping her hands.

"My lady, I also will help. I will look through my whole library to see if anywhere is mentioned a monster living in an accursed wood who used to be a wicked queen who was very cruel to her baby sister," Hoddie said.

And Belsheer added, "I'll help him. And if we don't find anything here, we'll pay a visit to Tristaver. He knows all the gossip."

"Oh, thank you! Thank you both!" Princess said, hugging them both in turn.

"What are friends for?" Belsheer asked. "If it weren't for my friends, I'd be a bee."

"And I would not be anything," Hoddie said. "It is a debt of honor, dear lady. Also a pleasure and a privilege."

Belsheer glanced around, smiled, and said, "So, you see, *All's well that ends well*." They all murmured politely, and he went on, "*It's a long lane that has no turning*. Yes, *The end crowns the work*."

"I think that will be enough," Kedrigern said in an undertone.

"Yes. Yes, of course. Couldn't help myself," Belsheer said, and busied himself returning books to the shelves as the others, except for Hoddie, departed.

Days of celebration and nights of feasting followed as all of Lurodel, from the lowliest peasant to the grandest noble, rejoiced in this sudden profusion of blessings: the Loathliness banished, the wizard royal restored to his wizardly powers, and their beloved Glynfynnyn about to marry a reasonably handsome and manifestly formidable young prince. Other, less parochial causes for joy were also proclaimed and duly honored: a wizard restored to human form, a lost cousin (or aunt, or grandmother, or fairy godmother—accounts differed regarding the precise relationship) returned at last to the bosom of the family. There were those who considered the sudden reappearance of a long-lost relative dubious grounds for celebration, but smiled, cheered and drank deeply nonetheless rather than spoil the festive mood, or attempt to understand the ways of the nobility.

Tergus and Bledge had good reason to celebrate. Tergus appeared at all public events wearing the colors of Master of Moodymount, with the royal huntsman's gleaming horn slung from his shoulder on a highly ornamented baldric. Bledge, now Sir Bledge the Faithful, walked at his side in full knightly regalia. Each was richer by a thousand crowns, thanks indirectly to Formidable and more directly to Kedrigern. For his key role in the battle against the Loathliness, Belsheer had also been the recipient of a thousand crowns.

The time came at last for Princess and Kedrigern to set out for Silent Thunder Mountain, by way of Kallopane. On the morning of their departure, Formidable and Glynfynnyn came to the gates to see them off. As the ladies embraced and discussed last-minute family concerns, Kedrigern took his farewell of the prince. "I'll deliver all your messages, and give out the wedding invitations. Is there anything else you'd like me to do?" he asked.

"Not a thing. Nothing at all. You've done so much for me and my family already," Formidable said with a bemused expression.

Kedrigern clapped him on the shoulder and said, "We had ourselves quite a quest, didn't we?"

"Amazing. Simply amazing," the prince said, shaking his head as one emerging from a trance.

"Not for a wizard, my lad. A wizard's life is always amazing. It can be dangerous, and downright uncomfortable at times—especially when one is traveling—but there's always something amazing right around the corner. Never boring, that's for certain."

"But it all worked out . . . so neatly."

"That happens sometimes."

Formidable did not seem to hear. As if to himself, he said, "I went on a quest to save a monster. Not only did I save it, but now I'm going to marry its great-great-great-great-great grandniece. Your friend was a bee, and now he's a wizard again.''

"Where is Belsheer, anyway? I thought he'd turn up to say goodbye.''

"He's come down with hives. Aftereffect of the spell, he thinks.''

Kedrigern nodded. "Of course. Should have anticipated that.''

Formidable went on, "Your wife is eighty years old, but she looks younger than her own great-niece. I've never experienced things like this. I never suspected that such things really happen. Even my brother Horatio—we call him Philosophical—never suggested such things, and he knows everything.''

"Maybe you can teach him a few things now.''

"Yes, I will. Next time we meet, I'll take him aside and say, 'There are more things in heaven and earth, Horatio, than are dreamt of in your philosophy.' ''

"Spoken like a true prince,'' said Kedrigern.

He and Princess said their last farewells and mounted their horses. With a final wave, they set out for Kallopane and home.

···❦ *Seventeen* ❦···

a family reunion!

THEIR STAY IN Kallopane was delightful. With Sariax away and Jussibee fully occupied in the family's nurseries, attendance upon the honored wizards fell to the Wise Prince, brother of Sariax and Lord High Chancellor of Kallopane. Like the other males in his family, he proved worthy of his title; his conversation was as profound as it was pleasurable, and in his company the days passed quickly.

On the morning of their twelfth day in Kallopane, Kedrigern awoke to the startled realization that he had not longed for home for quite some time, and Princess had not said a word about continuing their search for Abrasia. Clearly, it was time to end this holiday and get to business. He said as much to Princess as they breakfasted, and her response added another surprise.

"Oh, why bother?" she said. "Everything I've learned so far has been either disappointing or tragic or both."

"What about Abrasia?"

"She's a monster somewhere, unless she's been slain by a hero, in which case she might be better off."

"You seem very dispirited."

"Well, who wouldn't be, if they learned that their relatives were loathsome monsters, or mad, or accursed? I envy you, Keddie. I never thought I would, but now I really do. You have no idea who your parents were, and you don't let it bother you a bit. I only wish I had taken the same attitude.''

''Don't you even want to find out your real name?''

''I think it's best that we abandon the whole quest. The way things have been going, if I ever do find out my name, it will be something stupid and ugly, and I'll hate it.''

''You sound very despondent.''

''I'm reconciled to the inevitable. I just have to get used to being called 'Princess' and never speaking of my family.''

''Glynfynnyn is a nice girl. No need to be ashamed of having her as a relative.''

''And explaining to everyone that she's my grandniece? No, thank you.''

He nodded and said no more. It saddened him that this quest had turned out so badly for Princess, but there was little he could do about it. The only real help he could offer was an oblivion spell, and that was a drastic last resort.

As they sat silent and thoughtful over the remains of breakfast, a knock at the door of their chamber brought Kedrigern to his feet. A voice called, ''A message for the wizards! A message for the Efficacious Master Kedrigern and the Enchanting Princess!''

''Everybody gets a nickname in this place,'' said the wizard under his breath as he strode to the door and flung it wide.

The messenger bowed and handed him a thick packet, doubly sealed. Kedrigern took it, inspected it, and found that the seals were those of the Wizards' Guild and Lurodel. He dismissed the messenger and returned to Princess, who looked up at him with curiosity and concern.

''No one knows we're here but our friends in Lurodel,'' she said.

''And that's where this is from. Belsheer and someone else have sent it, judging by the seals.''

Kedrigern inspected the missive through the Aperture of True Vision, and found that the outer packet was unprotected. He cracked first one seal, then the other, and unfolded the heavy parchment. Out fell a second packet. He picked it up and studied it carefully.

"What is it?" Princess asked.

"I'm not sure. But it's obviously been spelled."

Princess jumped up and took two quick steps back. "Be careful."

"We're perfectly safe. It's only a spell of pulverescence. If the wrong person tampers with it, this packet will crumble into dust. No danger, unless one is asthmatic." Kedrigern laid the enclosure, its seals unbroken, on the table. He unfolded the letter to its full extent, and clearing his throat, began to read the contents aloud, passing over those items he deemed mere conventions of social correspondence:

> "Dear Brother Kedrigern:
>   Greetings and best wishes to you and Sister Princess . . . etc., etc., etc. Life at Ma Cachette has been . . . etc., etc., etc."

His voice subsided to a muttered monotone as he hurried over the contents. He frowned. The frown deepened, and his low recitative took on a peevish sibilant note. But then, abruptly, he brightened, and giving the letter a quick crackling flourish he cleared his throat for a second time and read aloud:

> "Brother Pozgvodbribnyi and I have now thoroughly studied all documents to be found in the castle Ma Cachette, as well as the contents of his library, in our search for a clue to the whereabouts of Abrasia, older sister to Sister Princess and great-aunt to the Lady Glynfynnyn—"

"We agreed to speak of each other as cousins. Doesn't Belsheer remember that?" Princess broke in, stepping from behind the chair.

"Apparently not. I'll remind him in my reply."

"Please do."

"I will." Kedrigern returned his attention to the missive, sought his place, found it, and resumed:

"—to the Lady Glynfynnyn. Concerning Abrasia, we know that she had been transformed, by a fairy curse, into a loathsome monster, and condemned to reside in an accursed wood. We therefore confined our search to references to princesses, the elder of two sisters, who had been transformed . . . etc., etc., etc."

"Belsheer does go on," Princess said, sighing impatiently.

"He always was a prodigal writer," said Kedrigern, lowering the letter. "Very direct in his speech, but let him get his fingers on a pen and he could fill three long sheets just inquiring after your health." He smiled a faint reminiscent smile. "I remember once, when I was studying with Fraigus O' the Murk, Belsheer sent . . . but this is hardly the time . . . ."

"Hardly."

Kedrigern lowered his eyes to the closely written script, skimming the circumstantial account of his colleagues' researches, muttering in a muted whisper until he cried "Aha!" and picked up the narrative in the middle of a sentence:

"—apparently a common occurrence in the past two centuries in this part of the world, and in the nearer regions of the East and Northeast, though almost unknown in the South. We found references to no fewer than thirty-one beautiful princesses transformed into loathsome monsters through the agency of fairy curses. Of these thirty-one, fourteen were condemned to dwell in accursed woods for the duration of their punishment; three were assigned to rocky islets, whence they preyed on shipwrecked mariners; three were stationed in marshlands; one was allowed to move freely within the bounds of a particularly inhospitable province; one, which we have encountered, was confined to Moodymount and its immediate environs. The placement of the remaining nine was unspecified.

Further investigation revealed that of the accursed-woods-based monsters, one had been slain

by a valiant knight, one had successfully completed the
requirements for release from its spell, and two had
disappeared without a trace. Information on the rocky
islet monsters was not to be found, nor could we learn
anything further about those unassigned. Two accounts
of the marshland monsters turned up in annals from the
last century, but they were vague and confused, and
contradicted each other on significant points. We
judge them to be folktales.

We could glean nothing more from extensive and
painstaking examination; therefore we plan—"

"Slain!" Princess paled and clasped her hands when the full
import of the message struck home. "What about the monster
who was slain? Did it give its original name before it died?"

"Let me see. There's more."

"What if Abrasia's been slain? My last chance of learning
about my early life is gone—and so is my sister! What if she's
the one who escaped the spell? She may have wandered off
somewhere to live out her life in obscurity and mortification,"
said Princess, wringing her hands.

"Now, my dear, calm yourself. Surely Belsheer addresses
that point further on."

He studied the remaining lines. With a relieved "Ah!" he
turned to Princess, smiling broadly, and said, "You need fear
no longer. Listen to this,"

"Closer study leaves us convinced that neither
the slain nor the despelled monster was Abrasia, sister
to Sister Princess. The Great Crawling Loathliness
of Moodymount is also out of consideration. Thus we
are able to account for three of the thirty-one, leaving
only twenty-eight. Of these, seven can be removed
from consideration, reducing the field of possibilities
to twenty-one. However, in view of the wide and
uncertain distribution of these monsters and the lack
of clear—and in many cases, of all—information, we

believe that our earlier suggestion is the wisest course,
and will proceed . . ."

"What suggestion?" Princess asked, as Kedrigern stood in
puzzled silence.

"I don't know. I must have skipped . . . let me see . . . yes,
here it is."

". . . therefore we plan to set out from Ma Cachette
in ten days' time to seek the counsel of Brother
Tristaver, who is a veritable living chronicle of
sorcerous history, and we urge you to meet us
there, so that together we may consider all the
available information and lay plans for further
action in pursuit of Sister Princess's quest."

Kedrigern lowered the letter. "Not a bad idea. Tris picks
up all sorts of information in his travels. He loves gossip."

"Is that all they say?"

He raised the letter, scanning it speedily but with close attention, nodding over familiar passages, and concluded:

"Hoping to enjoy the pleasure of your company
and that of Sister Princess in the very near future, I
remain, as always, your most humble, most obedient
devoted etc., etc., etc.

P.S. Map enclosed. Remove spell before opening."

Tossing the letter on the table, Kedrigern said, "Well, my
dear, what do you think?"

"I think we're talking about a long search. I never dreamed
that there were so many enchanted princesses around. And
Tristaver may come up with a dozen more. This could keep
us busy for a century."

Kedrigern shrugged. "I have no pressing cases at the moment."

"It seems awfully selfish of me to take up the time of so many wizards on a purely personal quest. When I think of all the distressed people out there who need your help . . ."

"You're distressed, aren't you?"

"Well . . . yes, I am."

"Then why shouldn't we use our abilities to assist you? Why must we do good only for total strangers, most of whom have brought their problems on themselves and begrudge us even a 'thank you, good wizard' after we've worn ourselves out for them? Are Belsheer and Hoddie forbidden to help a friend? Am I not allowed to use my magic on behalf of the woman I love?" Kedrigern asked with a dramatic flourish.

"That's very nice of you."

"For your sweet sake, I will pursue this quest to the ends of the earth."

"You may have to. Twenty-one separate monsters, minimum. We know that twelve are still in accursed woods, but the rest might be anywhere. It's a very daunting prospect."

With a firm gesture, Kedrigern said, "It will toughen us up. Get us into shape. Give us plenty of practice and all sorts of opportunities for doing good along the way. What say you, my dear?"

She hesitated for a moment, then said, "Let's look at the map. And don't forget to remove the spell."

Kedrigern despelled the map and spread it on the table for their scrutiny. It was a very large map, richly detailed and drawn in bright colors. The lettering was very attractive and quite legible.

"Blood Brook?" Princess murmured uneasily.

"Yes. It runs into Doom River," Kedrigern said, pointing to the junction.

"Abhorréd Isles? Woods of Hysteria? Meadow of The Shrieking Hellwraiths?" Princess read, her voice hushed. "Tristaver doesn't live in a very nice neighborhood."

"Actually, he's said to have a charming little house in a scenic part of the country. He's given the surrounding area off-putting names to protect his privacy. Doesn't want people hearing names like Fragrant Gardens or Sun-Drenched Hills and flocking in. Tris hates crowds. Sensible chap, in that respect.''

Princess looked at him thoughtfully for a moment, then shook her head. ''You're all alike.''

''I'm not a bit like Tris!''

''You both have the sociability of a phoenix.''

''That simply isn't true. We're both married, aren't we?'' Kedrigern brightened. ''My dear, apart from the quest for Abrasia, we ought to visit Tris and his bride. It's only polite.''

She looked at him in astonishment for a moment before asking, ''Since when does that concern you?''

''I'm changing my ways. It would do you the world of good. You have several things in common with her . . . and she may even have some helpful information.''

''She may at that. And in any event, the poor soul will benefit from some sisterly advice. All right, we'll go.''

The trip was a pleasure, even for Kedrigern. Dewy mornings, warm sleepy afternoons, cool evenings and starry nights; every meal a picnic, the weather ideal, the scenery idyllic. He was in the mellowest of moods on the afternoon he and Princess forded Blood Brook, crossed the flower-decked Meadow of Shrieking Hellwraiths, and saw Tristaver's cottage in the distance. People were visible in the dooryard.

''Belsheer and Hoddie must have arrived already,'' Kedrigern said.

As they drew closer, Kedrigern waved, and his wave was returned enthusiastically by all four figures. They were bustling about in what looked to be great excitement. One of them began to run to the two riders.

''It's a woman. Glynfynnyn, I think,'' Princess said. ''That's odd. I don't see Formidable anywhere.''

''It must be Tris's wife. Glynfynnyn would hardly . . . but it certainly does look like . . . yes, it's Glynfynnyn. I'd recognize that lovely auburn hair anywhere.''

''Yes . . . it must be . . .'' Princess said softly.

A voice came to them from the approaching figure. Indistinct at first, it became clearer, but was not yet distinguishable.

Kedrigern turned to Princess, smiled, and said, "She's glad to see us. I guess they don't get many visitors."

"What is she shouting?"

"A greeting, I imagine."

But when they heard, very clearly, "Sister! Oh, my dear little Princess! Sister, dear sister, at last!" Princess zoomed up from her saddle and flew to the lady now stumbling across the meadow. Kedrigern saw Princess hit the ground running, and watched the two embrace, and kiss, and then embrace once more. As he drew nearer, he could hear laughter and weeping, mingled with cries of "Abrasia!" and "Dear little sister!" He dismounted and walked slowly to their side, awed by the incredible event he was witnessing. He could see three figures hurrying to join them from the far side of the meadow, by Tristaver's cottage.

"It's Abrasia! She's disenchanted!" Princess called to him, reaching out her hand to draw him into their embrace.

"And so is my dear baby sister! A toad no more!" said the other lady, laughing and sniffling back tears as she flung an arm around Kedrigern's neck.

There was more hugging, and kissing, including each new arrival to the scene, and more laughter and weeping, both separate and conjoined, and finally both ladies, exhausted, seated themselves on the grass, out of breath and out of words. Kedrigern spread a blanket for them. Belsheer kindly volunteered to return to the house for refreshments, and Hoddie, having already witnessed one tearful family reunion, accompanied him.

"So, my dear, our quest is ended," said Kedrigern, seating himself by his wife's side.

"Not quite," she said. "Dear Abrasia, do tell me my name. You're the only one who knows."

Abrasia's hands flew to her mouth in a gesture of dismay, and her lovely features clouded with concern. "Oh, my dear baby sister, I have done you a terrible wrong."

"You were under a curse, Abrasia. You could not help yourself. But tell me my name, loving sister, do!"

Weeping piteously, Abrasia threw herself into Princess's

arms. "How can I ask forgiveness when I have deprived you of a name, my unfortunate darling baby sister?"

"Deprived . . . ?"

Sniffling and wiping her eyes, Abrasia said, "In the confusion caused by the appearance of Bertha the Bog-Fairy at your christening, no one ever actually got around to christening you. Mama and Papa discussed the matter often, but were reluctant to proceed for fear of what Bertha might do. They always called you 'Dear little Princess' or 'Our darling little Princess,' and that eventually became the name by which you were known throughout the kingdom. It only made me nastier. I felt that being the elder by a full year, I should be the one called 'Princess.' "

"And so you should, dear sister. It must have been terrible for you."

"Not really. At the time, I quite enjoyed being nasty," Abrasia said, wiping her eyes. "I was terribly wicked. The family tragedy, you know."

"Yes, I know. We've met Great-great-aunt Glurnia. She was the Great Crawling Loathliness of Moodymount."

"You must tell me all you know, Princess dear."

"And you must do likewise, dear Abrasia."

As the reunited sisters exchanged family tidbits with great joy and gusto, Kedrigern and Tristaver diplomatically betook themselves for a stroll about the meadow. When they were out of earshot, Kedrigern said, "You're looking good, Tris. Married life agrees with you."

Indeed, Tristaver was looking more relaxed than he had for many a decade. His silver hair and beard were neatly groomed, and instead of the gaudy regalia he customarily affected, he wore an unadorned black cloak over a plain gray tunic and trousers, and well-polished black boots. He was the very picture of the wizard at home and happy to be there.

"She's a wonderful woman, your sister-in-law."

"How did you happen to meet her, Tris?"

"I was doing a quest. A young warrior maid was seeking the Grove of Desperation. Brave child she was, too, but of course, courage would avail her nothing against the forces of evil magic, so I had to lend my protection. The guardian of the grove turned out to be this lovely lady, under an extremely powerful fairy curse.''

''A loathsome and repellent monster?''

''That scarcely does her justice. I have never seen anything so hideous in my life, and certainly do not wish to see such a creature ever again.''

Kedrigern nodded. ''I know what you mean. I've had to deal with their great-great-aunt. She's under the same curse. Horrible.''

''It's all part of that low fairy cunning. They had to leave an escape clause in the curse, so they worked it that she'd be free if she could make someone fall in love with her just as she was. And she was ghastly. Quite a disincentive to affection.''

''Fairies are a shifty lot. Even the good ones are tricky.''

''And to make it worse, they let her know that once she was despelled, she'd become as sweet and gentle as an angel. So, being a monster, she had no desire to be freed from her spell and turned into something nice.''

''Ingenious. Diabolical, but ingenious,'' said Kedrigern. They walked on for a time in silence, then he turned to Tristaver and said, ''So what did you do?''

Tristaver grinned. ''Love charm.''

''You used a love charm on a monster?''

''No, on myself. It was the only way to break the curse.''

Kedrigern stopped. He laid a hand on Tristaver's shoulder, looked him in the eye, and said, ''Very resourceful. Bravely done, old man.''

Lowering his eyes, Tristaver said, ''Thank you, Kedrigern. The praise of one's peers is really the only praise that counts.''

''Not just my praise, Tris—my gratitude. I was prepared for a long hard search, and not much chance of succeeding.''

''Glad I could help a brother wizard.''

They walked in comfortable silence to the edge of the meadow. When they looked back, their wives were waving, and they retraced their path to join them. As they walked,

Tristaver said, "I imagine we'll be seeing more of each other in future."

"I shouldn't be surprised. And our wives will probably be wanting to visit Glynfynnyn, too. She's one of the family." Kedrigern paused for a time, then said, "It feels odd, having relatives all of a sudden."

"Yes. I know what you mean. Unfamiliar feeling. You're my brother-in-law now."

Kedrigern nodded. "And you're mine."

They said no more until they greeted their wives, who were sitting hand in hand on the blanket, smiling eagerly and expectantly, as if bursting with some happy message. The sisters looked at each other, laughed, nodded, laughed once again, and then Princess said, "We had a wonderful idea."

"An inspiration," Abrasia added.

"We were talking about Great-great-aunt Glurnia—"

"Poor old thing, she's still a monster—"

"And we thought with Hoddie and Belsheer here—"

"And the two of you, and my talented sister—"

"All that magical power—"

"Surely we can do something for the old dear—"

"Bring her back—"

"Bosom of the family—"

"Wouldn't that be lovely?" they concluded, in unison.

Kedrigern and Tristaver looked at one another. Tristaver shrugged. Kedrigern said, "I imagine we might be able to do something. We seem to have disenchanted everyone else in the family. Why not old Glurnia?"

"We'll work out the details over lunch," Tristaver said.

"I knew we could do something," Princess said. "I'll help, of course. Once Glurnia's freed, the family will be together again. We'll be one big disenchanted family."

Kedrigern sat down by her side. "That reminds me of something in a chronicle I once read. Let me see, now . . . 'Enchanted families are all alike; every disenchanted family is disenchanted in its own way.'"

A thoughtful and appreciative silence ensued. At last Abrasia said, "That sounds like the sort of thing that would come at

either the very beginning or the very end. Do you recall which
it was, Kedrigern dear?"

"It was the end," said Kedrigern. "Definitely."

—THE END—

Tristaver smoothed his beard slowly, with a thoughtful gesture. He frowned. "That doesn't sound like an ending to me."

"Now, now, my dearest husband, we must not question our
loving brother-in-law's memory," said Abrasia with a sweet
smile bestowed in turn on each of the wizards.

"It was the end," Kedrigern repeated. "No doubt about it."

"Don't be dogmatic," said Princess.

"I'm not being dogmatic. I'm right."

"You're being dogmatic."

"All right, it wasn't the end," Kedrigern said, throwing up
his hands. "It was the middle. It was the third paragraph of
Chapter CCCCLXIII. It was a footnote to page 91. It was
anything you like. But not the end. Absolutely not."

—THE END—

"Don't be huffy, either. That's worse than being dogmatic."

Kedrigern sighed and shook his head. "Sorry, my dear,"
he said. He reached out to take his wife's hand.

"Why are we talking of endings, anyway? This is really a
beginning for all of us," she said.

"And for Great-great-aunt Glurnia, too," said Abrasia.

Amid the general good humor sparked by these observations,
Kedrigern alone was reserved and silent. Beginnings were all
well and good; fresh starts and clean slates were very fine
things; but they all involved change, and Kedrigern did not see
much in his life that wanted changing. He thought of his comfortable chair by the fireside, of his books and his workroom,
of Spot's cooking, and of the sunny dooryard where he could
take afternoon naps even in the depths of winter. He thought
of Gylorel and Anlorel, of Dudgeon, and of his growing stable
of curious creatures. He sighed at the cozy memory of all the

comforts, joys, and consolations of the little cottage on Silent Thunder Mountain. And then he thought of what the future held: In-laws, some of them formerly enchanted; in time, nieces and nephews; visiting, entertaining, family gatherings and celebrations and get-togethers for the holidays. Traveling. Lots of traveling. Before long, children of their own. Oh, yes, definitely. And given the rate at which he and Princess would age, they might have scores of them. He pondered that.

"You're very quiet," Princess said.

"Just thinking. My dear, do you realize that our lives are going to be normal?"

She appeared startled. "Normal?"

"We have relatives now. A family. In-laws. We're just like regular people."

Princess fixed him with an analytic look for a time before saying, "Do you really believe that?"

"Yes. Aren't we?"

"Regular people do not, as a rule, live under a curse for seven generations."

"Well, no. No, as a rule, they don't."

"Nor have they spent a portion of their lives as toads."

"No."

"Or loathsome monsters."

"I suppose not."

"Nor are they generally wizards."

"Oh, no, certainly not."

"So what, exactly, do you mean by suggesting that our lives are going to be 'normal'?"

He reflected for a time, then turned to her, smiling broadly, and said, "I can't imagine what I was thinking. You've put my mind at ease."

"On the other hand, our lives will certainly be different in future."

His face fell, but only for a moment. *Different* was endurable. *Different* could mean less traveling. Less traveling meant time at home with Princess, lots of it. *Different* could even mean no more intrusions and interruptions and importunate strangers, enchanted bees and disenchanted huntsmen and who knows what else, bursting in on them whenever they wanted to be alone. *Different* could mean little Princesses and Kedrigerns, and time to watch them grow.

He smiled and held out his hand. "Yes, I imagine they will be. But let's talk about that when we're home, all by ourselves. At last."

-THE END-